I0523107

DANIEL PATTERSON

ANOTHER CHANCE

A **PENELOPE CHANCE** MYSTERY

Print edition published—May 2017
ISBN-13: 978-0990824275
ISBN-10: 0990824276

10 9 8 7 6 5 4 3 2 1

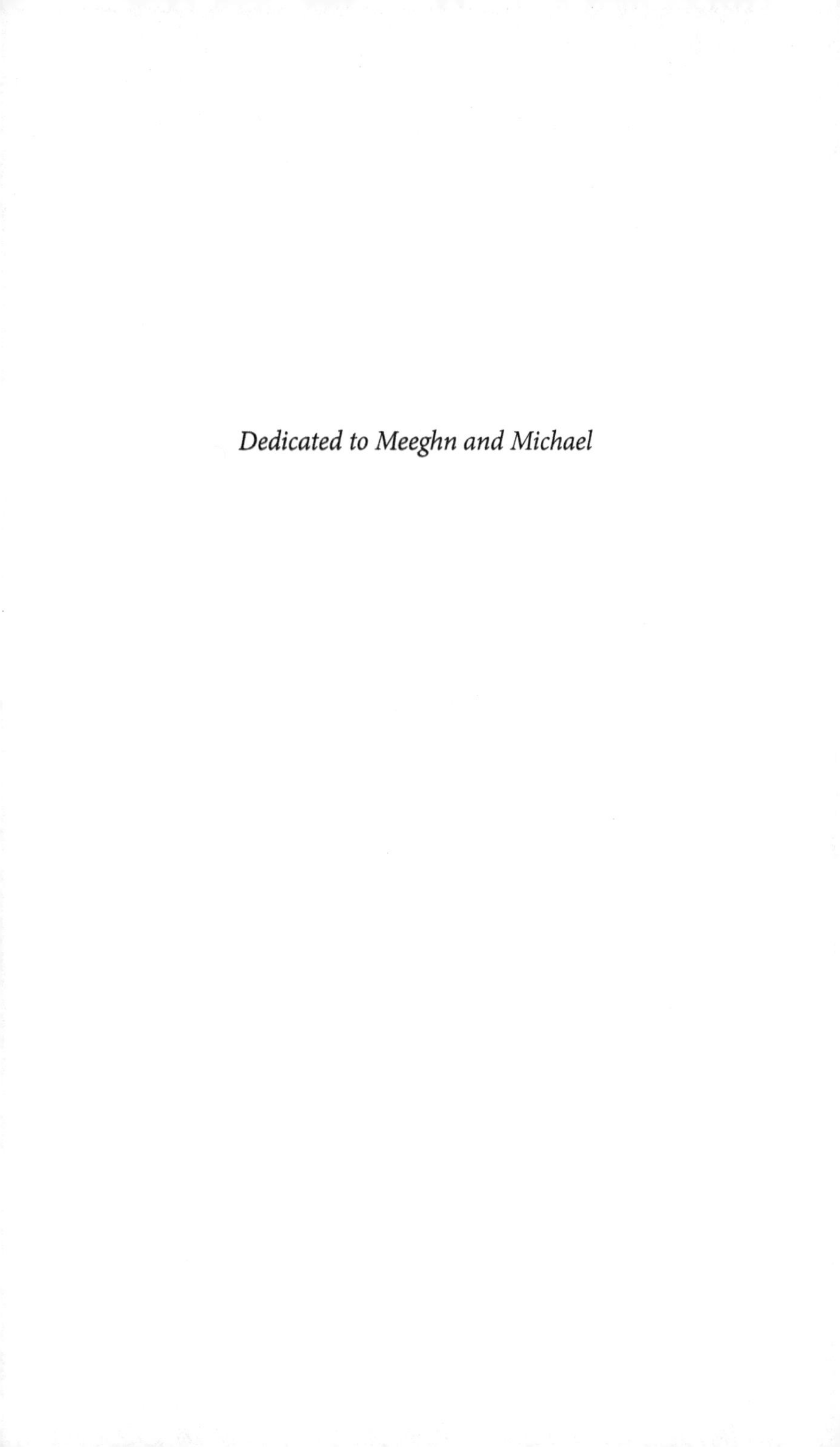

Dedicated to Meeghn and Michael

Also by Daniel Patterson

ANOTHER CHANCE

PART 1

CHAPTER 1

HE RAN A GLOVED finger over the pistol grip handle of the Remington tactical shotgun tucked under his jacket. The thick black leather coat hid the weapon well.

With his partner by his side, they walked through the automatic doors and into the lobby of Grace Memorial Hospital. They had less than three minutes to get in and get out.

Kevin Scott started his count.

One.

Two.

Three.

No sign of security.

Four.

Five.

Six.

He kept his head down. The brim of his baseball cap

would hide his face from the security cameras. He wouldn't pull up the bandana he wore around his neck until right before they entered the clinic. They had to look natural—as natural as one could look wearing all black on a hot, March, Florida afternoon.

Seven.

Eight.

Kevin and his partner walked through the main lobby and made a quick right toward the glass double doors that led to the free clinic and pharmacy.

Nine.

Ten.

He pulled his bandana up over his face.

No turning back now!

He looked to his partner. Piercing, light blue eyes were the only things visible underneath the bandana and hooded sweatshirt.

Twelve.

They pushed through the doors and entered the clinic. Kevin's partner stayed behind, just inside the entry, while he walked on to the pharmacy. He glanced at the young medical receptionist as he passed. An older nurse stood by her side. She looked calm and able. The receptionist seemed less so. She would be the first to squeal.

Fourteen.

His partner pulled out a Kimber semi-automatic handgun and pointed it at the queue of people waiting at the counter.

Everyone froze. It was a moment of silence before the storm.

It took only a fraction of a second for a person's eyes to grasp the danger. It took even less time for that person to snap out of the freeze that their body went into while the brain processed which was more important: fight or flight. After that, there was almost no time before the body took over and the mind was only along for the ride.

Kevin saw the events as if they happened in slow motion. Time stood still. Faces contorted with shock. Brains whirred. Terror replaced the shock, and then came the screaming. It was always the screaming that snapped him back to reality.

He needed to control the room.

Nineteen.

Kevin took a deep breath, pulled the shotgun from his jacket and shouted, "Everybody down on the ground!"

Twenty.

His partner jumped into action. "I want wallets, jewelry, and phones."

Twenty-two.

Kevin stepped inside the pharmacy and pointed the shotgun at the pharmacist behind the counter.

"You! Oxycodone and diamorphine in the bag, now!" He slid a duffle bag across the counter. "Now!"

He lost count. Twenty-something? He picked up at twenty-five.

Twenty-six.

"We're all out," the woman said.

A hospital out of medication?

Kevin rushed up to the pharmacist and waved the barrel of the shotgun in her face. She turned an ashen color, and he could almost see her knees collapse under her. "Oxy and morphine in the bag . . . now!"

She disappeared behind a shelf with the bag. Somewhere around thirty seconds now. They had to get out of there.

"No funny business back there," Kevin yelled at the pharmacist, as he glanced back into the waiting area. His partner collected everyone's valuables in a leather satchel. Time was money. Literally.

Thirty-three.

Thirty-four.

Everyone seemed to be cooperating, and the bag was bursting.

Thirty-five.

Thirty-six.

As he turned his attention back to the pharmacist, a scream reverberated in the waiting room. The receptionist . . . it had to be her. The older, more experienced nurses could deal with a stressful situation. It was in their blood. But receptionists were there to answer phones and greet people.

"Dr. Gordon!" the receptionist screamed as a doctor appeared from one of the exam rooms.

His partner pointed a pistol at the doctor.

A shot fired.

CHAPTER 2

THE DOCTOR WENT DOWN, and a red flower of blood blossomed from his right shoulder.

It looked like the bullet went clean through and lodged in the wall.

Counting, where was he? He kept losing track. Couldn't have been more than a couple of seconds.

Forty-five?

The pharmacist dropped the duffle bag on the counter and screamed when she saw the doctor bleeding on the floor.

Kevin stopped counting. They had to get out of there!

He snatched the bag and turned to see a patient come out of the exam room the doctor had left. Kevin looked over at his partner who was panicking—rigid body, finger on the trigger.

From the ground, the doctor saw it too.

It happened almost at the same instant; the trigger pulled back, and the doctor reached up, face twisted in a snarl as he pulled the patient to the ground.

The bullet splintered the wall above them.

Kevin's heart beat in his throat, making it impossible to breathe under the bandana.

"You won't get away with this," the pharmacist said.

"Fine," Kevin answered, grabbing the woman by the arm. He'd had enough of her bravado. "You want to play hero? Let's see how you feel with a bullet in your skull."

She began to sob, her arrogant mask cracking and showing the fear underneath. Kevin knew that would happen. That was the plan. He couldn't have anyone thinking they could stand up and fight. Fear had to do the bullying for him. He wouldn't shoot the pharmacist; he only needed her as a shield if they had to shoot their way out.

Using a chokehold, Kevin pulled the pharmacist into the clinic lobby. She gurgled, and her hands clawed at his arm. He relaxed his grip.

"We have to get out of here," Kevin said to his partner, who waved the gun around, ready to shoot at anything that moved.

The doctor was on his feet and shuffling closer. If anyone had a hero complex, it would be him. He saved lives, so he couldn't let it rest now, could he?

"Come on now, son," he said in a tone that was both calm and reassuring.

The doctor came closer still, and Kevin could see his eyes now. Warm eyes. Caring eyes.

"You don't have to do this," the doctor continued. "You have what you wanted. Let her go."

Kevin blinked hard for a moment. He wasn't going to fall for this man's words. He wasn't going to let the doctor talk him out of this.

"You don't want to hurt her, do you? Come now. I'm sure there's got to be another way," the doctor said.

"What do you know about it, Doc? What do any of you know about this life?"

The doctor was so close he could feel the kindness radiating off him like a poison—a mind-altering poison. Kevin hated this man. He hated him because it was impossible not to like him.

The room was silent.

No police were coming.

No security guard was coming.

Kevin threw the pharmacist to the ground, and the doctor took a step closer. He swung the barrel of his shotgun like a baseball bat in the doctor's direction and connected with the side of the man's head.

A shot fired at the same instant.

Kevin looked at his shotgun and then at his partner.

The smoking gun his partner held pointed at the doctor.

Kevin looked into the doctor's eyes one last time as the man's limp body crumpled to the floor, life fading from his face. Those eyes would haunt him forever. He hadn't wanted the doctor dead. He hadn't wanted anyone dead.

His partner ran to the lifeless body and went through his pockets for valuables.

Blood pooled beneath the doctor.

Kevin grabbed his partner by the sweatshirt and ran.

In the hospital lobby, an older man in a security uniform saw them and went for his service revolver. They knocked the guard to the ground, ran past a couple of nurses, and headed for the parking lot.

The burgundy, 1979 Cutlass Supreme was waiting for them in the handicap space.

They dumped the guns and the haul in the backseat. Kevin got behind the wheel as his partner jumped into the passenger side. The engine roared to life, and the tires squealed as he stepped on the accelerator and pulled out of the parking lot. The hospital shrank into the distance in the rearview mirror.

"That was close," his partner said. "Still, we made it in less time than I thought. Just over two minutes? Were you counting?"

The air around Kevin did nothing for his body, no matter how deeply he breathed. *Two minutes? It felt like an eternity.* "We said we wouldn't shoot anyone!"

"You were letting that doctor get to you. I could see it in your eyes. You got all soft on me. I had to do it."

Kevin's blood-splattered hands gripped the steering wheel. If that doctor was dead, it made him a murderer. He may not have been the one who'd pulled the trigger, but he'd killed him all the same.

Life was difficult before. Now it's going to be unbearable!

CHAPTER 3

SEATED NEAR THE BACK of the Alachua County Criminal Justice Center, Franklin, Florida, Police Officer Penelope Chance waited anxiously for the jury to emerge. Five long months the thirty-two-year old officer had waited for this moment. Would justice finally be served?

Gainesville and Franklin residents filled the courtroom to capacity, and reporters from the major news outlets squeezed in along the back wall.

A large wooden door opened near the jury box, and the murmuring of the crowd reached a critical mass as twelve ordinary citizens filed into the court and resumed their seats. The vaulted ceilings magnified the buzz of the spectators, and a barrage of camera flashes lit up the dreary room like lightning during the day.

Penelope scanned the faces of the jurors for some indication of what to expect, but she couldn't read them—

they looked resigned and a bit weary. Their job had not been easy.

The bailiff called the court to order and the room fell silent.

Everyone stood as the Honorable Pam Gonsalves entered the room through the tall, heavy door from her chambers. She wore a traditional, black robe with a white lace collar. Her silver-blue eyes and blonde hair with a few gray streaks gave her a look of wisdom and authority. She called the court to order and waited until the whispers and flashes stopped completely.

Judge Gonsalves nodded to the bailiff and addressed the crowd. "It's been brought to my attention that the jury has reached a verdict. Is the State ready to proceed?"

"The State is ready to proceed, Your Honor."

"Defense?"

"Defense is ready, Your Honor."

"Madam Foreperson, has the jury reached a verdict?"

A distinguished-looking woman stood and addressed the court. "Yes, we have, Your Honor."

"Please present the verdict to the bailiff."

She looked grim as she handed the bailiff a large, manila envelope.

Penelope's mind raced. It had been a lengthy trial, and the public defender was good at his job. A conviction wasn't certain, but Penelope had faith—faith in the investigative work that had led to this moment, faith that the truth was on her side. And most of all, she had faith that God would not let this man's crimes go unpunished.

She glanced at the empty seat beside her, and a longing

tugged at her heart. Her fiancé, Dr. Jacob Gordon, should have been sitting in that seat. With him by her side, she would have been strong enough to handle whatever happened in the courtroom that day. But Dr. G., as his patients knew him, was on call and wasn't able to be in court to support her.

A hand squeezed her knee. She turned to Doug Foster, her best friend, and adoptive brother. Penelope's mother and father had died in a house fire when she was eight. Doug's parents had been her godparents, and they'd adopted and raised her as their own. Doug was the closest thing she had to any real family.

"Things aren't always the way they seem," Doug said in a whisper.

"What do you mean?" she whispered back.

Doug pointed to the empty seat. "Jacob . . . he would've been here if he could. You know that, right?"

Penelope tucked a strand of honey-blonde hair that had fallen out of her ponytail behind her ear and managed a weak smile. Sure, she was being selfish, but why did Jacob have to be on call *today*, the one day she needed him most?

CHAPTER 4

THE BAILIFF TOOK FOREVER to cross the courtroom with the envelope containing the verdict. Penelope glanced at Doug, and try as he might to spare her feelings, he couldn't hide his uncertainty. Not from her. She knew him too well. She quickly looked away. She was grateful for his support, but she wanted to search the crowd for her fellow Franklin Police Department officers to gauge their reactions to the tense atmosphere.

Chief Curtis Jackson, seated closer to the front, directly behind the State's Attorney, looked tired and worn. His large frame sagged somewhat, and Penelope tried to write this off to his age and his thirty plus years of service. If Chief Jackson had doubts about the verdict, she didn't want to know it.

Seated next to Jackson was Officer Jim Saunders. Saunders was a transplant from Georgia, across the state's panhandle, where apparently it was customary to wear handlebar mustaches. He looked well rested, which was unusual, considering his wife, Anna, had given birth to their second child two weeks ago. Perhaps it was that "proud parent feeling" he radiated.

Judge Gonsalves cleared her throat as the bailiff handed the envelope across the bench. As she accepted it, she cleared her throat again. She reached for a pitcher of water and poured some into a glass. Penelope shifted in her seat as the judge took a few sips, cleared her throat once more, and continued to drink.

"Seriously?" Doug whispered.

The judge was a mite theatrical. But being impatient wasn't going to hasten anything. Penelope jabbed him in the ribs with her elbow. "Shhh!"

Doug sighed, closed his eyes, and clasped his hands in his lap. If she didn't know better, she would have thought he was praying for patience. Doug respected Penelope's faith but didn't always share it.

Judge Gonsalves slit open the envelope and pulled out a slip of paper. She then set the envelope down and reached for her reading glasses. Penelope shot Doug a glance of warning, but he only rolled his eyes and did not speak. The judge perched the lightweight reading glasses on the tip of her nose and inspected the verdict.

It was impossible to tell what it said from her expression.

Across the room, Penelope spotted Dr. Gabriel Pike, her college psychology professor and advisor. She had originally studied to become a child psychologist, but it was Pike who had suggested she apply her behavioral and social sciences skills to law enforcement.

Dr. Pike's expert testimony had been convincing, and she took heart from the fact that he was on their side. She always thought he looked a little like George Clooney, and she still wasn't quite ready to admit that she may have had a small crush on him. Now in his late fifties, with his straight dark hair sprinkled with gray, he looked even closer to the part—still the picture of confidence. He reached out to her when the arrest first made national news, but so far, she had been too busy to contact him.

As if he could sense her eyes on the back of his head, Pike turned and flashed an encouraging smile.

A rush of warmth washed over her, and she quickly averted her gaze.

Judge Gonsalves leaned in toward the microphone. "Will the defendant please rise along with counsel?"

The defendant stood, head bowed. He looked more contrite than he had at any point in the investigation; during that time he had taunted Penelope and shown no remorse for his actions.

"Madam Clerk, you may publish the verdicts." The judge handed the verdicts to the Clerk of Court and looked straight ahead as did the jury.

"In the Eighth Circuit Court of Alachua County, Florida, the State of Florida versus Michael Anthony Findley, case number 09102013GF001065Z. As to the charge of first-degree attempted murder count one, we the jury, find the defendant guilty, so say us all." Penelope looked at Doug and saw that his eyes were brimming with tears. She quickly looked away. "As to the charge of first-degree murder count one, we the jury, find the defendant guilty, so say us all."

Penelope gasped as the emotions she had kept bottled up throughout the trial poured forth. As the clerk continued to read the remaining verdicts, she turned to Doug and hugged him tightly. His tears fell on her neck as he wept openly. Findley's actions had cost Doug greatly. Doug had been a prime suspect in the murder case in the minds of everyone but Penelope. Her hard work had vindicated him. She brought the right man to justice, and this was likely to be the only closure Doug would receive for the death of his ex-wife Camille, the mother of his son, Trevor.

"Thank you Madam Clerk," Judge Gonsalves said when the clerk had finished. "In light of the tragic circumstances surrounding this case, I want to express my deepest condolences to the victims of this horrendous crime. Evil is apparently real, and it was present in Alachua County on the fifth of October, 2012. On that day, its name was Michael Findley. Many lives were affected, and a child lost his mother due to the actions of one man, and that is a terrible shame."

Findley showed no visible emotion.

"Michael Anthony Findley, you will be sent to the Florida State Prison where you will await sentencing," the judge continued.

"You did it, Penelope!" Doug said, his voice husky with emotion.

She gathered him in her arms and held him snuggly. "*We* did it," she whispered.

Alongside a rush of relief, she unexpectedly felt pity.

How could she feel anything but disgust for Findley after what he did to her best friend, her family? Findley would be going away for a long time. Hopefully, he would have access to spiritual growth and healing while serving his sentence. He would, after all, have plenty of time for reading and thinking.

CHAPTER 5

MICHAEL FINDLEY WAS ESCORTED from the courtroom, and as people left their seats, Chief Jackson approached Penelope with his characteristic warm smile and one of his giant hands extended to her. His perfect white teeth flashed like sunshine against his deep brown skin.

"Congratulations, Chance," he said. As he shook her hand, he covered it with his other hand and gave it a comforting squeeze. "You did us proud."

"Thanks, Chief. That means a lot to me."

It did mean the world to hear Chief Jackson's words. He had been her mentor and a second father to her, as she worked her way through the ranks of the Franklin Police Department. There was a hidden tension now between them because nobody else knew that Jackson was contemplating retirement. He had championed her to become his successor, only to have her decline the offer.

"I'm ready to head back to work," she told Jackson with a smile.

A deep laugh rumbled in Jackson's chest. At six foot two inches tall and well over two hundred twenty pounds, that was a lot of rumble. "I'm sure it can wait until you're back from vacation, Chance. Take the rest of the day off. I'd say you've earned a little R and R."

The idea of taking some time off sounded great right about now. The tension of the past five months, the sweet victory of the verdict, and the unexpected sympathy and compassion that laced through it all—it was a lot. She looked forward to taking the next week to start planning her wedding. She'd been back and forth between Franklin and Gainesville most days during the trial, and it had left her little time for anything else.

"Penelope Chance," called a familiar voice. "You must be feeling pretty good about this verdict right now, isn't that right?"

Penelope turned to face Dr. Gabriel Pike. She was torn between exasperation at his corny catchphrase "isn't that right" that she had heard so often in college and pure joy at seeing an old friend after a long separation.

Dr. Pike, or Professor Pike as he preferred his students to call him, matched Jackson's height. His bright blue eyes sparkled underneath his neatly groomed salt and pepper hair, and his lean, toned physique filled out his rumpled gray suit nicely.

"Professor Pike. Great to see you." Penelope turned to Jackson. "Chief, this is Dr. Gabriel Pike. He was my psychology professor and advisor back in college. Professor Pike, meet Curtis Jackson, the Chief of Police back in Franklin."

The warmth left Jackson's eyes as he put up the wall that was his public persona. He did not show his human side to strangers. Not until they had earned it.

"Dr. Pike," Jackson said as he held out his hand.

Pike took the offered hand and shook it. If Jackson squeezed, the professor didn't let on.

"Chief Jackson, so very nice to meet you," Pike said with a smile, his face smooth and friendly. "So you showed Miss Penelope here the ropes, isn't that right?"

"I wouldn't go so far as to say that. I've done some fine-tuning, perhaps, but Officer Chance has nine years of experience, a sound mind, and she goes with her gut."

Penelope glowed under this praise, which Jackson did not bestow often. Not an ordinary day, not at all.

"Well, that she does. Any police department would be lucky to have her," Pike said. "I told her that when she graduated. It's nice to see her thriving in her working environment."

"Professor, I'm sorry for not returning your calls. My life has been a circus since the trial started."

"I haven't been your professor for ten years or more, Penelope. Please call me Gabriel. And I understand. The high profile case and all."

"Care to catch up over a cup of coffee?" Penelope offered.

Gabriel's eyes twinkled. "I'd like that."

Chief Jackson nodded at Penelope and tapped Doug

on the shoulder.

Doug turned and gave Penelope a hug. "Celebration dinner at my place tonight?"

"You're on," she answered, giving him a squeeze.

Gabriel turned to navigate his way through the crush of spectators and reporters. Penelope followed.

"I'll see you *after* your vacation, Chance," Jackson called out. "Not a day sooner."

"Yes, Chief," she said over her shoulder.

CHAPTER 6

THE COFFEY SHOP WAS an odd but comfortable combination of mom and pop shop and sleek urban style, located in a square, one block east of the courthouse, owned by Travis and LeeAnna Coffey. Penelope and Gabriel found an empty table on the patio.

"Still take it black with two sugars?" Gabriel asked the question with a perpetual smile on his lips.

"Yep," she answered and smiled back.

While she waited for Gabriel to return, Penelope turned her cell phone on for the first time that afternoon. She had six missed calls, four voice mails, and three text messages, all from the Franklin Police Station. Didn't they know she was in court today? And didn't they know she was on vacation? Those messages could wait. Jacob's was the only voice she wanted to hear.

She dialed his number and waited for the call to

connect. "Please pick up. Please pick up." The call went straight to voice mail. "Jacob, we did it! Guilty on all counts. I miss you. Call me when you get a break." She paused, and then added, "I love you . . . Oh, and Doug wants us over for dinner tonight." She took a shaky breath and ended the call. She slipped her phone into her purse and surveyed the shop.

A hand-lettered blackboard menu hung against the back wall, and homemade pastries lined the curved glass display cases while jazz music played softly in the background. Flyers and business cards covered a notice board advertising everything from free kittens to poetry readings to investment seminars. In the evenings, the shop was probably full of hipsters and club-goers, but right now a sea of suits surrounded them. There were a few women in pantsuits, but mostly men who looked to be forty years or older.

She spotted Gabriel standing at the service counter, behind an elderly woman wearing bright teal pants and an oversized white shirt with hand-painted flowers. The tattooed barista handed the woman a tray with two cups of coffee and two pastries, but the woman's handbag was so large she had trouble balancing the tray and she nearly dropped it. Gabriel swooped in, catching the tray from beneath with one hand and a gallant smile. He gestured for her to move along and followed her to the table where her husband was waiting. Gabriel placed the tray in front of them.

Penelope smiled as a few people who had witnessed this act applauded, and Gabriel gave a small, embarrassed bow and then returned to the service counter to complete his transaction.

Penelope continued her assessment of the surroundings. She was able to pick out some fellow law enforcement officers from the crowd. It was the way they stood or even sat, with their shoulders straight and tall. She let her eyes examine further and noticed the telltale coat bulges that almost certainly concealed service weapons.

Her people-watching was interrupted when Gabriel popped back into view holding two steaming cups of coffee. He set Penelope's down in front of her, and she wrapped her hands around it gratefully.

Gabriel sat down and faced her. "So how does it feel to investigate a big murder case?"

He looked like a proud father.

"I was just trying to prove Doug's innocence," Penelope replied. It was now starting to seem real. Her testimony and investigative work had led to Findley's conviction. "I'm thankful that Findley is off the streets, but I'm still rattled. That case was too close to home." She looked down at her coffee, trying to hide the nervous energy she was sure he could see in her eyes.

Camille Foster's murder had rocked the city of Gainesville, the town of Franklin, and it turned her world upside down. It had nearly destroyed her adoptive brother's life—not to mention his young son Trevor's, and it had caused several other people to be injured. Some severely. She liked her quiet little town when it was just that—quiet. Michael Findley had disrupted that peace and changed things, maybe permanently, in ways she wasn't sure she even yet understood. Doug was certainly different now, and Trevor seemed withdrawn, although visits with a counselor appeared to be helping him adjust.

Jacob, her Jacob, who had not once checked in with her all day, had seemed distant lately, and he was distant geographically. Penelope had been driving to Gainesville a couple of times a week for the last several months helping the prosecution with the case against Findley. Jacob said he understood, and she believed him, but things were a little . . . strained.

This line of thinking was sure to show on her face, especially in the presence of a forensic psychologist, and she tried to change the subject to take her mind off of it. "I can't believe they called you in as an expert witness. It is a small world!" she said.

Maybe this misdirection would work, and Gabriel would start talking about himself, instead of her involvement in the Findley case. She took a sip of her coffee. Too hot to drink. She blew on it and took another sip.

"It is quite a coincidence that I got involved in this case. I do mostly consulting on high-profile police cases these days, but I do get called in on court cases from time to time. If they need someone to create a profile of a psychopath or reconstruct a murder scene, they call me or one of my colleagues. But for this one they had asked for a colleague, Dr. Teresa Behrmann. She was all prepped and ready to go when she had a family emergency and was called away at the last minute. I was next in line, I guess. You know, Penelope," Gabriel said, suddenly intense, "I admire the way you threw yourself into this case. That's the Penelope

I remember. No nonsense on the job, and sweet as pie the rest of the time. I have no doubt you've found your calling, your true calling in life. You feel it, too, isn't that right?"

Penelope smiled and nodded. She took another sip of coffee and tried to take heart from what he was saying. She had a God-given gift that she used to help others and to protect them from harm.

"So Penelope, recent court victories aside, how's life been treating you?" Gabriel leaned back in his chair with his characteristic relaxed grace and looked her in the eye.

"Well, Professor—"

"Gabriel, please," he interrupted.

"Well, Gabriel," she continued, the familiarity feeling a bit odd, "life has been pretty good."

"So things are good with work? Still enjoy being a cop?"

"Oh, yes! Chief Jackson is thinking of retiring and recommending me as his successor."

"Congratulations!" Gabriel said, looking impressed.

"Thank you, but I declined."

"Declined? Why? That would have been a great opportunity."

"Well, I still have a lot to learn and after this Findley business, I realize that solving crimes and helping people is where I want to be. The chief understood and suggested I qualify for detective."

"Detective Chance. It has a nice ring to it."

Penelope smiled. Even though she didn't need that kind of reassurance, it was nice to hear praise from someone who had helped her get on her feet so long ago.

"It is exciting. I haven't had much time to think about

it, but the chief decided to postpone his retirement and train me after I pass the exam."

"That's wonderful!"

"It's through God's will and grace, of course. I couldn't have done any of this without His strength. Oh, and I'm engaged now."

Gabriel raised a questioning eyebrow.

"His name is Jacob Gordon. He's a doctor. A medical doctor. He works at Grace Memorial a couple of days a week and he runs the clinic back in Franklin the rest of the time." She couldn't put her finger on why she sounded so flustered, but Gabriel seemed amused.

"Well, congratulations! Engaged. That's wonderful. You all set a date yet?"

"October first."

"This year?"

"Next year." She tried to hide her uncertainty. They had set the date just after she wrapped up the Findley case. But between her responsibilities at the police department and Jacob splitting his time between Gainesville and running the only medical clinic in Franklin, they hardly had time to see each other, let alone discuss wedding plans. "I am using vacation time next week to do some initial planning," she added.

"That date sounds familiar. Why October first?"

"Jacob thought we'd have an easier time booking a venue for a mid-week wedding, plus the milder October temperatures should be ideal."

That was part of the reason. The date was her idea. Next year would be the twenty-fifth anniversary of her biological mother and father's deaths, and she wanted to replace that tragic memory with a happy one. But the professor didn't need to know all that. She took a few sips of coffee to have something to do with her hands and to mask the trembling she was certain had started around her mouth.

Gabriel set his cup down and leaned in toward her. With concern in his eyes, he looked at her for a moment.

She met him with an even gaze.

"You really okay, Penelope?"

"Are you analyzing me, Professor?"

Gabriel smiled. "Just concerned."

"Oh, I'm fine. Just got a case of the nerves after that trial. It's usually not so personal, you know? And the way the judge took her sweet time to read the verdict . . . I thought I was going to jump out of my skin. I'm glad it's over."

"Absolutely! You must be exhausted. I don't want to keep you from—"

"Oh no, I'm good. I have to be at Doug's place for dinner a little later, but I'm still good on time."

"Are you sure?"

Penelope smiled. "I'm sure. Thank you."

Gabriel leaned back in his chair, and they drank their coffee in companionable silence.

CHAPTER 7

IT WASN'T LONG BEFORE Penelope's thoughts wandered back to the Michael Findley case.

She shook her head.

"What is it?" Gabriel asked. "What's on your mind?"

"It's just that . . . after everything I've done, everything I've seen, I still wonder about the senseless actions of men like Findley." Penelope's eyes looked past Gabriel into the distance. It was well past five o'clock and people were starting to make their way home for the weekend. Soon the crowd would transition from weary workers to relaxed revelers. "I mean, I know that this world is full of so much beauty and that humans have an endless capacity to love one another, yet we can't seem to . . . do right by each other. It's this line of work, I guess." She refocused her eyes and saw that Gabriel was still looking at her intently.

"You questioning your faith?"

"Oh, no. Not one bit." The thought had not even occurred to her. She looked him straight in the eye and said, "I have no doubt that God's plan for me is to serve the people in my community, and someday have children of my own and raise them to be strong and good."

Gabriel smiled. Despite his age, he always managed to look like a mischievous kid.

"You think that's funny?" Penelope asked when she saw his eyes twinkling at her across the table. "It may seem simple to some."

"Not one bit," he said. "I think it's admirable that you have connected with something many people are missing in their lives."

And she could see that he meant it.

The bustle of the busy coffee shop seemed to fade away, as the two friends remained suspended in a bubble of memory, connection, and faith for the rest of the hour.

The peal of bells from a nearby church shook her back to the moment. *Six o'clock already?* Jacob should be off work by now. Would it be rude if she checked her phone?

Almost on cue, a cell phone went off at another table nearby. And then another. Four phones at three separate tables, and each of the persons answering their phones was a person Penelope had suspected was in law enforcement. Her hand automatically went to her phone in her purse. No new calls or messages.

"Something is happening in Gainesville," said Gabriel as four quiet conversations went on around them.

"It certainly looks like it," Penelope agreed, head swiveling to watch two of the suspected detectives at one table signal to a third at another.

"You feeling left out?"

Embarrassed that he could read her that well, she gave a little smile and said, "Not my jurisdiction. I'm sure they'll be fine without me."

"And I'd say you're entitled to a break from excitement."

"Yes, but if I were to be truthful, I do enjoy the rush. We don't get a lot of action in Franklin, and Lord knows I'm grateful for that, but—"

"It's nice to get the chance to play the superhero once in a while," Gabriel finished for her.

Penelope nodded and reached for her purse. "Professor . . . sorry, I mean Gabriel, it's been great catching up, but I better get going."

"Of course, Penelope."

Gabriel stood, and she noticed a slight stiffness as he stretched his legs and stood to his full height. *So he's not Superman after all.*

"We'll have to—" Mid-sentence, Penelope's cell phone rang. She glanced at the caller ID. *Franklin Police Station.* "Excuse me, I should take this."

Gabriel nodded.

"This is Chance," she answered.

"Chance! Where have you been? I've been trying to reach you all afternoon." It was Officer Alex DeBose who was a second year rookie with the Franklin Police Department, and Penelope was his training officer. "Did you get any of my messages?"

"I've been in court all day. I haven't checked messages. What's up?" Penelope's stomach growled at the sudden realization that she hadn't eaten all day.

"There was an incident at Grace Memorial Hospital earlier this afternoon."

"Incident? What type of incident?"

"Don't worry Penelope," DeBose sounded like he was choosing his words carefully. "I'm sure Jacob's gonna be fine . . ."

Penelope's heart dropped to her stomach. "What about Jacob? Is everything okay?" She glanced at Gabriel, sure he could hear the panic in her voice.

"There was a robbery at the pharmacy," DeBose continued, his voice shaky. "The perps started snatching bottles of pills . . . then Jacob intervened."

"He did what?"

"He . . . intervened."

Penelope's body went numb. "DeBose? What happened to Jacob?"

"He's been shot."

CHAPTER 8

"PENELOPE, WHAT IS IT?" Gabriel asked. "What's wrong?"

She heard him speaking, but he seemed miles away.

He placed a hand on her shoulder. "Penelope?"

"A robbery . . . Jacob . . . my fiancé . . . he was shot."

"When? Just now?"

"No, earlier today, while we were in court. I never should have turned my phone off. I should have checked my messages. I've got to get to the hospital," Penelope fumbled in her purse for her keys, spilling the contents in the process. She went down to her knees to gather her belongings, willing her hands to stop shaking.

Gabriel bent down to assist. "Give me your keys, I'm driving you."

"No, I'm good."

"You're not good, Penelope. Hand them over."

She complied.

"Where is your car?" he asked.

"It's at the courthouse."

It was a short walk back to the courthouse parking lot and Penelope and Gabriel covered it at a quick trot. Penelope forced herself to stay calm, and remember her law enforcement training. But right now, she didn't feel like a cop—she felt like a terrified member of a victim's family.

What was Jacob thinking? Why would he intervene? And how was she going to live without him if he was gone?

Gabriel shoehorned his six-foot-two-inch frame into the driver's seat of Penelope's 1975 MGB and moved the seat all the way back. "Breathe, Penelope. Say a prayer if it helps. I'll have you there in ten minutes."

She was way ahead of him in the prayer department. God was so much a part of her life that her thoughts went to Him for comfort and guidance sometimes without her being conscious of it.

She grabbed her phone, angry with herself for hanging up on DeBose before she could get the full story. She called back, but there was no answer. She called Doug, but he hadn't heard anything. She promised to keep him updated. Next, she tried Chief Jackson, but got no answer.

Gabriel turned left onto University Avenue and headed west to Grace Memorial Hospital. Traffic was particularly bad that night, and the drive seemed to take forever. Gabriel did his best Frank Bullitt impression, weaving the little green sports car in and out of traffic like a pro. But the ten-minute drive quickly turned to twenty.

Penelope called the Franklin Police Department's main

line, but Judy, the dispatcher, knew no more about the situation than Penelope did.

She dialed the hospital's information line next.

It connected to an infuriatingly polite electronic answering system. "Thank you for calling Grace Memorial Hospital. If you know your party's extension, please dial it at any time. For patient information, please press twenty-two. For—" Penelope pressed 22. "Please enter the first three letters of the patient's last name using the corresponding numbers on the dial pad . . ."

Penelope hung up with a growl.

"Try 555-4639, that's the nurse's station in the ER," Gabriel suggested.

She did and was promptly put on hold. She hung up again.

"OK, try 555-6478. That's the number for the doctor's lounge."

That number rang eight times and then the call reverted to the answering system.

Tears of frustration came to her eyes and Penelope tried her best to stay positive.

"We're here," Gabriel said, parking the car near the ER entrance and handing Penelope the keys. "I'll check on you later," he added as Penelope ran from the car.

CHAPTER 9

THE AUTOMATIC GLASS DOORS to the Grace Memorial Hospital emergency room slid open, and Penelope headed for the counter.

"Jacob Gordon?" she said.

The ER duty nurse, Sandy Scott, recognized her and pressed the button that unlocked the door to the emergency room. Without thanking her or looking back, Penelope wrenched the handle open as soon as she heard the buzzer.

Just inside the entrance, someone called her name. She turned and saw Dave Sayre, one of the hospital security guards, talking to a uniformed Gainesville police officer. His face fell when her eyes caught his. He brushed off the officer and hurried over to Penelope.

"Penelope! Follow me. I'll take you up to ICU. He's in room three-oh-two."

ICU? That's not good. Penelope couldn't bear to ask

Dave about Jacob's condition and mumbled, "Thanks," as she followed him down the brightly lit hallway.

When they got to the elevator, Dave pressed the up button. The silence grew thick while they stood and waited for the next elevator. Penelope turned toward the stairs but paused when Dave turned to face her.

"It all happened so fast," he said. "Those guys knew what they were doing."

"I'm sure you did your best, Dave."

"It's usually so quiet around here."

"Things are bound to get shaken up from time to time," she told him, barely hearing the clichéd words coming from her mouth. "This kind of stuff happens to the best of us."

A *ding* sounded, and the doors of the elevator parted. Penelope paused and glanced toward the stairs.

"You coming?" he asked.

Penelope took a deep breath and stepped into the empty elevator without a word. Dave pushed the number three, the doors closed, and she got that sinking feeling she always got in tight spaces. She took another deep breath and held onto the rail. They rode together in silence and as soon as the doors opened onto the third-floor, Penelope burst through them and raced down the hall. Dave shuffled after her.

Penelope stopped in her tracks when she saw her friend, Detective Donny Greene of the Gainesville Police Department, standing in front of Jacob's room. He was wearing one of his customary dark tailored suits, and several uniformed officers surrounded him. They stopped talking as she approached.

Donny turned to Penelope and held both his hands up, but that wasn't going to stop her. She stepped passed the officers and placed her hand on the doorknob as she took a calm breath.

Please, Lord, let him be okay.

She opened the door, but she wasn't prepared for what she saw next.

CHAPTER 10

ROOM 302 WAS EMPTY.

"He's going to be okay, Chance," Detective Greene said from the open doorway. Donny usually had a wisecrack for everything, but he was serious as he said, "They're bringing him back from x-ray now. You want me to wait with you?"

A surge of relief flooded her body. "That's all right, Donny. I'll wait here and collect my thoughts. Thank you."

The detective nodded and closed the door.

Penelope sank into the first empty chair she saw. She took a few calming breaths, bowed her head and closed her eyes. "Thank you, God."

A few moments later, she walked into the tiny bathroom and saw a person she hardly recognized in the mirror.

A few wisps of flyaway hair had escaped from the tie that had held them back. Her usually vibrant face seemed drawn out, her skin pale and gaunt. Dark rings had taken shape under her green eyes, making her skin look even more lifeless. She pulled her hair out of its ponytail and watched the blonde strands fall around her face.

She splashed cold water on her cheeks and patted them dry with the rough brown paper from the dispenser. She took a deep breath and turned just as a female nurse wheeled Jacob into the room.

The nurse wore light pink scrubs that complimented her suntan. Her platinum blonde hair was cut in a neat bob that bounced playfully over her shoulders. The two of them laughed at some private joke.

"I'll take your word for it, Nurse Bunny," Jacob said.

"Jacob!" Penelope called out.

"Oh! Hiya, Penny," Jacob slurred when he noticed her standing in the bathroom doorway.

"I heard you were shot!"

"I was shot. Nicked actually—twelve whole stitches. It was the barrel of the shotgun that caught me by surprise and did the real damage." He pointed to the second bandage on his temple and grinned. "But the medication is making it almost worthwhile." He turned to face the female nurse and was met with the V-neck of her shirt. Jacob dissolved into a fit of giggles, and the nurse wheeled him to the bedside.

"Dr. Gordon is on some strong pain medication," the nurse said, struggling to keep a straight face. "Along with those stitches, he has a concussion. He gave us quite a scare."

"Penny, this is Nurse Bunny."

"*Bonnie*," she corrected him.

"She's been taking real good care of me."

"I can see that." Penelope's voice was frosty.

"This whole getting shot thing sounds way scarier than it is," Jacob added, trying his best to downplay the situation.

Nurse Bonnie moved away from the bed and spoke to Penelope. "Keep a close eye on him and if you see him experiencing any nausea or dizziness, call a nurse right away."

"Or what? He'll drop dead?" Penelope said in a sarcastic tone.

The nurse frowned. "It could indicate brain bleed, which could lead to seizures or even stroke."

"Can you excuse us Bunny?" Penelope said.

"Bonnie," the nurse said, matching Penelope's frosty tone. "Take good care of him. We don't know what we would do around here if anything ever happened to Dr. G."

"I'll be sure and do just that," Penelope said.

Nurse Bonnie turned to Jacob. "I see that you are in good hands now, Dr. Gordon." She nodded at him and moved toward the door. Penelope stood her ground, making the nurse walk around her.

Jacob leaned to one side to look past Penelope and flashed Bonnie a big smile and waved good-bye.

CHAPTER 11

PENELOPE GLARED AT JACOB, barely able to speak. "I thought you were shot!"

"I was shot."

She stepped toward him. "I thought you were nearly dead . . . shot!"

"You seem angry that I'm not."

Tears of anger, frustration, and relief finally began to fall. "You scared the life out of me! Please don't you dare ever get shot again."

She closed the short distance between them, hugged him gently and laid her head against his chest, trying not to hurt him. At that moment, she felt whole. She held on to that feeling.

"I'm sorry," Jacob said after a few minutes.

Penelope released her embrace. "You should be," she teased, but with an undertone of concern. "What did I tell you about playing the superhero?"

"It all happened so fast. I didn't want to see anyone get hurt. One minute, I was with a patient, and the next thing I knew I was shot. Even now it's just a blur." Jacob tried to sit up in the bed and Penelope saw him wince.

"I'm glad you're okay." There was something about Jacob's story that didn't sit right. She didn't give it another thought. Right now she was just glad to see his face.

"Oh!" Jacob said, taking Penelope by the hand. "I almost forgot to ask . . . how did it go in court today?"

"Guilty on all counts."

Jacob gave her hand a squeeze. "I'm so proud of you, Penny. I want to hear all about it."

Penelope told Jacob all about her day, and twenty minutes later there was a knock on the door.

"Come in," Jacob called.

Dr. JR Bray, the attending physician, entered the room wearing surgical greens and a white lab coat with a stethoscope tucked into his pocket.

The doctor adjusted his round wire-rimmed glasses and leafed through a chart. "Evening, Penelope. Mind if I interrupt? I'd like to see how our patient is doing."

Most of the hospital staff knew Penelope, not just as law enforcement, but also as Jacob's fiancée.

Penelope nodded. "He's still a little loopy. It's not serious, is it?" Panic and fear still lurked in the recesses of her mind. Jacob's injuries had reminded her how much she had to lose.

"Not at all," Dr. Bray said. "But I would like to keep him overnight for observation." He looked at Jacob. "I'm sure Dr. Gordon will feel right at home. He practically lives here, anyway."

The small joke about Jacob's long hours would have gone over better in a different light. Five months ago Penelope would have responded to the joke with a quip of her own, something about Jacob being in love with his work. But tonight she couldn't appreciate the humor.

"Will you give us a minute?" Dr. Bray asked, snapping her back to the present.

She blinked and looked at Jacob. He looked as if he were trying to read her thoughts. She flushed under his steady gaze. They were both in high-pressure lines of work, and they had what it took to be calm in a difficult situation. But tonight, Jacob was the only one taking this in stride.

"Of course. I'll be outside with Donny."

"Always on the job," Jacob said with soft, smiling eyes. He meant it as a compliment, a personal joke. He pulled her in for another hug.

She smelled his familiar cologne and tried not to hug him too hard. "Look who is talking."

He released his embrace and as she pulled away, he brushed a lock of hair from her face. He kissed her on the cheek and then said, "Everything's going to be okay."

Penelope smiled and made her way to the door. She pulled her hair into a tight ponytail, and switched to cop mode.

CHAPTER 12

OUTSIDE OF JACOB'S ROOM, Detective Donny Greene sipped a cup of vending machine coffee from a paper cup. His warm brown eyes studied Penelope. The thirty-five-year-old detective kept himself in great shape and never seemed to age. Donny credited his Italian genes for his perpetual tan, wrinkle-free face, full head of dark wavy hair, and ruggedly handsome good looks.

"How's the doc?" he asked.

"A little banged up, but I think he'll survive," she said, closing the door behind her. "His doctor wants to keep him overnight. Seeing you here nearly scared the life out of me, Donny."

Donny flashed a playful smile. "Well, we wouldn't want that, would we?"

"Don't you typically work homicide?" she asked.

"Not just homicide. Robbery, assault, arson, and

missing persons, too—our division investigates most major crimes."

"So you caught this case?"

"No, it's not my case."

"Then what are you doing here?"

"I heard the call . . . and when I found out who was involved . . . I asked if I could assist. I wasn't sure if you had heard, so I called your boy DeBose over in Franklin. I thought you would have been here hours ago."

"I was in court all day and had my phone off."

"Ah, the Findley trial. Had I known where you were, I would have come and got you myself."

"Thanks, Donny. I appreciate that. So who's the lead on the case?"

"Detective Edward Ballard, I don't think you know him. Thirty-five years with the Gainesville PD. A good cop, and a real by-the-book kind of guy, if you know what I mean."

"Did they take Jacob's statement already?"

"One of the uniformed officers got his preliminary statement, but I'm sure Ballard will want to talk to him in depth when he's feeling better."

"Got any leads?"

"Whoa, there, Chance. Slow down . . . I know what you're thinking. You need to sit this one out. Ballard isn't going to want you meddling in his case."

"Meddling? Jacob was shot and could have died today. I just want to be kept in the loop."

"Just in the loop, huh?"

"Yes. Just in the loop," Penelope reassured him. "What do you know so far?"

The detective shrugged, took another sip of his coffee, and flipped through his notes. "Not much. There were two armed white or Hispanic males. One about six feet tall with dark hair and eyes. The other about five feet eight inches with light blue or gray eyes. They gained entry to the pharmacy and grabbed a bunch of pills. They knew what they were looking for and where to find it. A few dozen bottles of—" Donny paused and squinted at his notepad. "Oxycodone and diamorphine. Drugs like that have a high street value. Ballard's been working three other robberies in the Gainesville area in the past three months, all with the same MO. But this is the first time anyone has been injured."

"Was anyone else injured or just Jacob?"

Donny paused as a female orderly in her mid-twenties pushed an empty wheelchair into Jacob's room. After the attendant had disappeared into the room, Donny turned his attention back to Penelope.

"You better watch out. Looks like the doc has a date."

Penelope rolled her eyes.

She and Donny had first met while attending the police academy ten years ago. He had come to her defense when several recruits accused her of cheating on the obstacle course. With a few well-chosen words, Donny put the recruits in their place. She didn't need the help—she had set the course record fair and square—but she appreciated Donny's gesture. They'd been great friends ever since.

He later joked that he only spoke up so she would go on a date with him, but she put a stop to that before it started. He was always cracking jokes to try and lighten the mood, but today wasn't the day for jokes.

Donny took her gesture of annoyance in stride and continued, "They assaulted the pharmacist and the security guard during their getaway."

"What about security cameras? They've got one pointed right at the pharmacy, don't they?"

"Yeah, I watched the footage with Ballard this afternoon. The perps were dressed in dark clothes, and they never looked at the cameras head on." Donny took another sip of coffee and sighed. "We have this under control, Chance. Why don't you head on home and take care of the doc?

"Yeah, I'll do that. But take my number in case anything comes up." The minute the words left her lips, she knew he'd have a smart remark.

"I've been waiting a long time to hear you say that," he said with a coy smile.

CHAPTER 13

AS PENELOPE AND DONNY exchanged numbers, the door to Jacob's room swung open, and the orderly wheeled Jacob out. He looked strangely vulnerable in the wheelchair. It was such a great contrast to the able man he usually was, dealing with emergency situations without ever losing his cool. He flashed Penelope an unbalanced smile.

"He's all yours, Penelope," Dr. Bray said.

At those words, Jacob winked at Penelope. Under any other circumstance, she would have been amused, but tonight his playful attitude outlined the fact that she'd nearly lost him. She tried to conjure up a sense of humor and failed.

"All mine? Are you sure he's ready to come home? Wouldn't it be safer to keep him here overnight?" she asked.

"That would be best, but your fiancé is a stubborn one," Dr. Bray said.

"I want to go home and sleep in my own bed," Jacob said. His medically induced good mood had faded.

"What he needs is good old fashioned rest and TLC. He sustained a serious head trauma, so keep an eye on him. Wake him every two hours or so to make sure he's coherent."

"Every two hours?" Penelope and Jacob asked in unison.

The doctor smiled at Jacob. "If you won't spend the night here, I'm going to have to insist that someone check on you." The doctor turned to Penelope. "Just for the next twenty-four hours and just to make sure he's still coherent. And I'd suggest recruiting a few friends or family members to help. That way you can take turns checking on him. I've given him some paperwork that explains what you need to do. And if anything seems out of place, then send him straight back here."

Penelope glanced at the stapled pages on Jacob's lap and gave the doctor a nod.

"Call if you need anything," the doctor said, walking away and motioning for the orderly to follow.

Penelope was careful to keep her face blank as her mind sorted through the events of the evening. She didn't want to leave now. She wanted to view that surveillance footage. She wanted to find the criminals responsible for doing this to Jacob. But she also wanted to take care of the man she loved.

"Donny, are you going to be around for a while?" she finally asked. "I'm going to call Doug and see if he can help watch Jacob."

Donny drew up his eyebrows and Jacob's medically induced good mood disappeared completely.

"You're dumping me off with Doug?" Jacob said before Donny could answer Penelope. It was an accusation, not a question.

"I'm not *dumping* you off. If you're not going to spend the night here, under proper medical supervision, and if someone needs to check on you every two hours, I'm going to need some help. We can go to Doug's house or your Aunt Jessica's. The choice is yours. But you're not staying home alone."

A playful smile returned to Jacob's lips. "But I won't be alone. I'll be with you." Apparently, the pain medication hadn't worn off completely.

"You heard what the doctor said about getting family help. If I fall asleep, I need to know you're taken care of."

"Then why did you ask Donny if he was going to be around?"

"Yeah," Donny chimed in. "I love you guys, but I'm not playing nurse." He placed a hand on Jacob's shoulder and added, "No offense, Doc."

"None taken," Jacob said.

"I want to come back and review a few things related to the robbery," Penelope said.

Jacob pursed his lips into a thin line before he spoke again. "Isn't this supposed to be the part where we celebrate your court victory and thank God my injuries weren't life-threatening?"

"It is . . . and we will. But I need to do something while you're resting."

"This isn't even your case. Why can't you let Donny and the other detectives do their jobs?"

She didn't look him in the eyes. She couldn't. This wasn't just about Jacob and finding the people who did this. It was about doing something to keep her mind busy—so she didn't lose it emotionally and shatter into a million tiny pieces. If that happened, she might not be able to put herself back together. Jacob was the first person she had trusted not to leave her since she was a little girl when everything she loved was ripped away from her. He was the only person she had believed when he said he would stay forever. And the thought of losing him had cut close to the bone.

After five grueling months of the Michael Findley trial, and being strong for Doug, she didn't know how much longer she could keep it together. Work was the one place she could escape. And if it meant finding the suspects, it would be a bonus. Two birds with one stone. That kind of thing.

"I'm sorry, Jacob. I need to do this."

"What are you trying to prove?"

A bubble of emotion pushed up into her throat, and she attempted to breathe around it. "I'm not trying to prove anything."

Jacob wanted to argue. She could see it in the tick in his jaw. But she didn't need to be convinced. There wasn't much more that she could do that Donny wasn't already doing, but she had to do something. She pulled herself together and slipped her mask in place. "Donny, you think you can okay it with Detective Ballard for me to watch the surveillance footage?"

Donny rubbed his chin.

She leveled him with a hard stare, telling him as much with her eyes. He looked unsure for a moment like he was going to try to dissuade her. But then he seemed to change his mind.

"You still studying for your detective exam?" he asked.

Penelope nodded. She'd been bugging him on occasion to take her on a ride-along so she could get a feel for how he operated. She wanted to be prepared when she became a detective. Even though she had Chief Jackson to show her the ropes, her life so far had taught her that she was often thrown into the deep end.

"I am. What are you thinking?"

Jacob's eyes burned into her back. She ignored him.

"I'll ask Ballard if you can view the tapes in an unofficial capacity. If you bring me dinner, I'll stick around until you get back."

And with that Penelope called Doug and wheeled Jacob off.

CHAPTER 14

"THIS ISN'T NECESSARY," JACOB said, looking out of the passenger window of Penelope's MGB. "I don't need someone watching over me."

"Jacob . . . you heard what the doctor said. I don't want to take any chances and Doug insisted on helping."

"That's not the point. We haven't spent much time together since . . . I can't even remember when. And now you want to barrel headfirst into the next case?"

"This one is personal," Penelope said stiffly.

"They're all personal to you, Penny," Jacob said in a gentle tone. "The last one was about Doug. This one is about me."

He was right. The one way she knew how to deal with life when it threw her a curve ball was to immerse herself in work.

"This isn't even in your jurisdiction," he said, bringing

in another angle. Being a doctor made him persistent and talented at stopping people from bringing more harm on themselves.

"I want to keep busy while you're resting, okay?" Emotions rose up into her throat, and she swallowed them. Jacob was her everything. It was difficult not to be selfish and to want to lock up everyone she loved so that nothing could happen to them.

"I'm okay, Penny. Just take me home. I don't want to be a bother," he pleaded, giving it one last shot as they turned onto Paradise Road—the road that led to Doug's house.

"Nope. Doctor's orders," she said, with a hint of sarcasm. "I need to know you'll be okay. Plus you'll get to spend some quality time with Trevor."

She pulled into the driveway at Doug's place, and Trevor bounded through the front door followed by a scruffy looking spotted tabby cat the boy affectionately called Fruit Noops. Trevor was already in his pajamas, with little Batman logos scattered across the flannel pants. His blond hair was still damp from a recent bath.

"Uncle Jay-Jay!" Trevor cried out.

"Remember he's hurt, Trevor," Doug called from the house, and Trevor slowed to a walk. He stopped in front of Jacob and tipped his head to the side, studying him.

"He doesn't look so bad," the six-year-old said.

Jacob laughed. "If only doctors were so optimistic," he said, ruffling the boy's blond hair.

"Not exactly the celebration I had in mind, but come on in," Doug said, joining them in the driveway. "Dinner is ready if you're hungry."

"We made sloppy joes," Trevor said.

"I don't have much of an appetite. You don't have to go to all this trouble," Jacob said to Doug, and then he looked pointedly at Penelope.

"No trouble at all. We were expecting you. Happy to help," Doug said. If he noticed the tension between Penelope and Jacob, he didn't show it. The easy-going smile that he wore so often lingered on his face, always ready to make her laugh and lighten the mood.

"Come on. I'll show you your bed," Trevor said, running ahead of them as they walked into the house.

"He's excited," Penelope said.

"I don't know how I'm going to get him to sleep tonight," Doug admitted.

Penelope watched with concern as Jacob shuffled slowly along behind Trevor toward his room.

Doug studied her the same way she was studying Jacob. "He's going to be fine, Pen," he said. His blue eyes intensified, the concern he felt for her appearing in his glance. He swept his messy brown hair to the side and his brow creased.

"I'm nervous," she admitted. "It was a close call. You hear about these things every day, you know? Especially in my line of work. Then something like this grazes past you, so close you can feel the shivers of death on your skin."

"I know how that feels."

She'd been so caught up in her world that she hadn't been considerate of Doug's feelings. He'd been through an immense ordeal and had to deal with some intense emotions.

"I'm sorry," Penelope said.

"Don't be. I'm saying I understand what you're going through, and I'm here for you."

Jacob and Trevor met Doug and Penelope in the living room, and Jacob sank into an armchair. He was pale, and he breathed in shallow gasps. He still had very little energy, and Trevor was enough to wear anyone out with his vibrant personality.

"So, what do I need to know?" Doug asked.

Penelope handed Doug a paper bag containing prescription pain medication and explained how and when Jacob had to take them.

"I'm still alive, guys," Jacob said irritably. "I can remember my own medication."

The bite in his voice was very uncharacteristic, and Penelope shook it off.

"He also has to be woken up every two hours, to make sure he's still coherent."

"That's only for children. I'm fine," Jacob groaned.

It was going to be a long night for him. All he wanted to do was sleep.

"You have to perform a cognitive assessment."

"What's that?" Trevor asked.

"It's a test to see if Uncle Jay-Jay's brain is still working right," Penelope said, and Trevor giggled. It didn't sound too flattering, putting it that way, but how else was she supposed to explain it to a child? "When we wake him, we have to ask him questions," she continued. "He has to remember five words. If he can, it means he's okay."

"Any words?" the boy asked.

"Any words, just different ones every time."

Trevor bounced up and down.

"I can do that! Dad, can I do that? I can test him to make sure his brain doesn't need to be fixed!"

Penelope couldn't help but laugh. Jacob rolled his eyes, but a smile played on his lips as well. He couldn't be irritated with Trevor's enthusiasm and his childlike way of interpreting things. It was nice to see the old Jacob surfacing. The one she loved with every fiber of her being.

"If you need to go back to the hospital, Trevor and I can take the first shift."

"That would be great. Thank you. I shouldn't be long. I want to review the surveillance footage with Donny."

Doug held up a hand and smiled. "No need to explain. I understand. You still have your spare key?"

"I do. I'll check on Jacob at midnight, if you and Trevor can check on him at ten o'clock."

Doug smiled at his son. "We can do that. Can't we, Trev?"

"We can do that, Aunty Penny."

"Doug, do you mind if I grab a sloppy joe to go? I promised Donny I'd bring him dinner."

"Donny Greene? You better bring two."

Penelope made Donny a sandwich, and when she returned Jacob was asleep in the chair. She walked over to Trevor and bent down. "You be good and watch Uncle Jay-Jay for me while I'm gone. I want a full report. Okay?"

"I'll give Uncle Jay-Jay a gold star every time he gets the right answer," Trevor said with excitement and gave Penelope a hug.

Penelope walked over to Jacob, gave him a quick kiss on the cheek, and then whispered, "I'll check on you in a couple of hours."

It was going to be a long night for Jacob.

CHAPTER 15

PENELOPE HIT TRAFFIC AS soon as she turned onto State Road 20. Her fingers tapped on the steering wheel, vaguely following the tune of an old Roy Orbison song on the radio. The station had been cutting in and out and she turned the dial when the song ended, trying to find a station with less static. She flipped through a top forty pop station, a mariachi station, and another pop station. She switched over to the AM stations and tried to find a talk show. She heard someone droning on about the weather and stopped. There was a forecast of rain.

Penelope glanced at the looming darkness in the evening sky. Unfriendly clouds covered the half moon. The next instant a crackle and roll of thunder lit up the sky with an eerie glow.

Storms in Florida could be violent and sudden. She turned the radio off. She would need all her wits about her to drive in a thunderstorm. Another flash and she started counting. "One-one thousand. Two-one thousand. Three-one thou—"

Another whip-crack sounded and the first drops of rain pelted the canvas convertible top.

"No, no, no! Not now!" Penelope grumbled, watching the drops on her windshield grow fatter and fatter.

Soon her windshield wipers were on full speed, and visibility was still poor. She craned her neck trying to see past the curtain of water and the endless line of cars. She wasn't going to get back to Grace Memorial Hospital any time soon. If only she had her police cruiser. Normally she didn't like to draw attention to herself, but on this day she wouldn't have minded trading her anonymity for a faster trip.

Moments later, two Florida Highway Patrol cars sped past her on the right-hand side of the one-lane road. Their lights were flashing, but there were no sirens. The gaps between the lines of cars were small, but the travelers were in a hurry and used to navigating both this traffic and this weather.

She heard the *blurp* and *whoop* of the sirens kicking on. Whatever they were rushing toward had happened very recently.

She could hear nothing but the sirens and the loud patter of the rain. Traffic slowed even more. The sirens stopped, but she could still see the lights flashing through her murky windshield.

"Dear God, please keep us safe on this road as we head to our destinations. Please watch over the people involved in whatever is happening ahead and let the ambulances find their way to them in this awful traffic jam. Amen."

A dark figure with a road flare waved cars out of the single westbound lane and onto the right-hand side of the road. The cars inched forward at the pace they had been moving before the storm hit.

Probably just a fender-bender.

State Road 20 was a primary commuter route for much of the Franklin and Gainesville area to the Atlantic coast. The Department of Transportation had been talking for years about widening the dangerous, hilly and curvy stretch between Gainesville and Franklin. In the past three months alone, Penelope had been called to assist the Highway Patrol in a half dozen accidents on the stretch.

Just last week a University of Florida student tried to pass another vehicle in a no-passing zone. Her 2004 Toyota Corolla collided head-on with another vehicle, killing both drivers instantly.

Penelope tapped the gas pedal as the cars in front of her moved past the accident. As she pulled alongside the scene of the wreck, she could see two cars had collided. It looked like the westbound blue Chevy Tahoe truck crossed the center divide and sideswiped the eastbound silver Honda Accord. She sent a silent prayer of thanks upward when she saw that everyone seemed okay.

Then she saw the little girl.

She was small, probably five or six years old, and appeared to be unconscious. Her long, black hair streamed behind her onto the wet pavement. Though visibility was low, Penelope could see a woman crouched beside the girl.

She recognized the agony of a helpless parent. One of the officers held an umbrella over the child's immobile body while another was on the radio, probably to the ambulance.

Penelope knew the drill well—stabilize the victim, administer first aid if necessary, and update the paramedics upon arrival.

The Highway Patrol seemed to have a handle on the situation. She would not be able to help by stopping and offering her services. Ahead more lights flashed as an ambulance barreled down the right-hand side of the eastbound lane.

That was all she saw before driving past the scene and continuing to Gainesville.

CHAPTER 16

THIRTY-FIVE MINUTES LATER PENELOPE arrived at Grace Memorial Hospital. She grabbed the bag with Donny's dinner, and headed straight for the pharmacy, hoping to get a glimpse of the crime scene.

Donny stood inside the clinic speaking to an older man in plain clothes. The man was a couple of inches taller than Donny, about six-one, with a face that suggested he'd seen it all. A neat gray beard covered the bottom half of his face and offset his hairline, which had receded. Penelope pegged him to be in his late fifties. As she got closer, she could see his gunmetal gray eyes and the bit of black that leaked into the gray hair above his ears. He wore a beige overcoat like one would see in an old *Colombo* TV episode.

As she approached the clinic's glass double doors, a uniformed officer with a clipboard took a step toward her. Without breaking stride, she gave a nod toward Detective

Greene. The officer knocked on the glass door, and Donny gave the officer the "she's okay" nod. The officer opened the door, and Penelope entered the clinic.

It looked like a bomb had gone off.

Papers littered the floor next to the nurse's station. A chipped cup lay in a puddle of coffee. It had cream caked around the edges and along the bottom, muddling the muted green color of the tile floor into beige. A few chairs were knocked over, scattered like toys in the messy room, and magazines decorated the floor.

From where Penelope stood, she couldn't see into the pharmacy where a forensics team hovered over the floors searching for evidence. Behind the bit of counter that was visible, two nurses appeared to be taking inventory.

It was controlled chaos.

Penelope's gaze slid over to the far wall where a smear of blood started at a bullet hole and dragged to the floor in a skewed arch.

"Detective Ballard, this is Penelope Chance, the officer I was telling you about," Donny said, snapping her back to reality.

Detective Edward Ballard held out his hand, and Penelope shook it. "I've heard a lot about you," he said. "Detective Greene tells me you work out of Franklin, and you're studying for the detective exam?"

"I am," she said.

"And you worked with Detective John Riley on the Foster murder case?"

"That's right."

"Well, it's about time Franklin had its own detective.

So, you're going to be shadowing Detective Greene for a couple of days?"

Penelope looked at Donny. He looked back, meeting her gaze with eyes that she knew were telling her to play along. So she nodded affirmatively. "I guess I am."

If that was how Donny had gotten approval for her to take a look at the surveillance videos, she wasn't going to make it difficult for him.

"Well, you'll be learning from the best. Tell your Chief Jackson I said *hello*." He nodded curtly and walked into the pharmacy. He wasted little time with words. Not the fun and games type.

When Ballard was out of earshot, Penelope turned to Donny and handed him the bag she had been holding. "Dinner as promised."

"What did you bring me?"

"Homemade sloppy joes."

Donny peeked in the bag. "Two of them? Yum!" He unwrapped one of the sandwiches and took a bite.

"So . . ." Penelope said. "I'm shadowing you for a few days?"

Donny swallowed and wiped his mouth with the back of his hand. "You want to learn from the best, don't you?" he said, giving her a wink. "Besides, I had to give him a reason why you're here. Ballard doesn't like people trampling through his crime scene. Like I said before, he's serious about doing things by the book."

"Being a fellow law enforcement officer and engaged to a victim isn't enough?"

"In a small town like Franklin, maybe. But in Gainesville,

things work a little different. You can't start investigating someone else's case. There are procedures to follow."

Penelope wasn't used to those types of restrictions. She'd been working in a small town for a long time, and the small town ways meant that she often got to do what she wanted, when she wanted. There was a lot of space for her to stick her nose in any business her gut told her to, and a lot of the officers, including Chief Curtis Jackson, trusted her gut.

CHAPTER 17

PENELOPE FOLLOWED DONNY DOWN a tile-floored hallway to an unmarked door. He held it open and waved his hand toward a little desk with a computer screen.

She sat carefully in the rickety office chair, doubtful of its sturdiness. Donny pulled up a seat beside her and used the mouse to cue the video.

The video was taken from the surveillance camera above the glass double doors that led into the clinic. It had a wide-angle view of the main reception area, and portions of the waiting room and pharmacy were visible. The video was grainy, black and white, and difficult to make out. She recognized Sylvia Brown, the floor nurse, Tina Shifflett, the medical receptionist, and Deborah Thompson, the pharmacist. She knew the staff well enough to recognize whom she was seeing. Her familiarity with the hospital was an advantage here.

She saw Sylvia leaning over Tina, who was pointing at something on a clipboard. Sylvia was listening and nodding as her younger colleague went over a checklist of some sort. From the bottom of the screen where the glass double doors led into the clinic, two dark shapes came into view.

The perpetrators matched the descriptions she had heard from Donny. There wasn't much about them that was identifiable except for the long, dark coat one of them wore. Penelope jotted a note on her notepad. The perp in the long, dark coat made his way to the pharmacy. As he passed, Sylvia and Tina froze. Some of the people in the waiting area panicked and threw their hands in the air.

The perp in the waiting area collected valuables and was rough with the people that did not cooperate.

The perp in the pharmacy pulled out a black bag and shoved it across the counter. There was a brief back and forth before the perp brandished his shotgun, and Deborah disappeared inside the pharmacy.

About ten seconds later, Tina leaned on the reception desk, knocking over a stack of paper and a cup of coffee. The second perp waved his gun in her direction and shouted something. There was no audio, but Penelope could see their mouths moving as they yelled. He was probably ordering her to shut up.

The door from an examination room swung open at the top left of the screen, and Jacob appeared in the doorway. He'd probably heard Tina's scream. He spotted the second perp and a look of confusion spread over his face. Before he could fully assess the situation, the perp lifted his gun.

Penelope flinched, and her chair creaked.

She saw the first shot fired. Jacob flew backward as he took the hit. A gray patch grew on his shoulder, and he sank to the ground, leaving a streak of blood on the wall. Above his head was a hole where the bullet had come to rest.

Seconds later a patient emerged from the examination room. The perp took aim and Jacob pulled his patient to the ground. The second bullet bit another hole into the wall, and the patient dropped unharmed to the floor.

Penelope breathed out a shudder.

The first perp came out of the pharmacy. The black bag, now bulging, hung from his arm. He had Deborah in a chokehold with one arm, and he held a shotgun in the other. Deborah's face was contorted with fear.

Just then, Jacob slowly got up and moved toward the perp with his hands stretched in front of him. He was doing his best to talk the robber down.

Penelope silently scolded him for placing himself in harm's way, and at the same time she admired his strength in a stressful situation. He inched his way closer and both perps seemed to be frozen. Whatever Jacob was saying appeared to be working.

The first perp released his hold on the pharmacist and tossed her to the ground. In the same motion, he swung his shotgun and hit Jacob in the head. The second perp fired a third shot, and Penelope tried to keep her composure as Jacob crumpled to the floor.

She had to remain professional. *It's just a video.* Jacob was safe. She reached for the cell phone in her purse and switched it from vibrate to ring—a reminder to check on Jacob.

The perp that had clubbed Jacob stared at his gun and then at his partner. He looked down at Jacob's lifeless body as if he felt sorry for what he had done. Penelope made a note of it.

A dark pool of blood turned the floor black around Jacob. The second perp rushed toward Jacob and pulled off his watch and rifled through his pockets. The first perp grabbed his partner by the sweatshirt and yanked him toward the door, and they disappeared out of camera range.

Penelope glanced at the video timestamp—all of this happened in less than two minutes. She paused the video and took a shaky breath.

"You okay?" Donny asked.

Despite Jacob's claims to the contrary, he had been injured pretty bad. Seeing her fiancé get shot like that filled her with fear. "I'm fine." More determined than ever, Penelope asked, "Are there any other angles? I noticed two other cameras in the clinic. Do we have that footage?"

"We do." Donny took the mouse and opened two additional video files. "The clinic has three cameras, one in the pharmacy, one in the waiting area, and the third in the main clinic—the one we just watched. We can watch all three in sync."

Donny's fingers ran over the keyboard and then the three videos were split across the screen so they could be viewed simultaneously. Some of the other videos showed what they hadn't seen before, but there was nothing noteworthy.

Penelope carefully watched the second perp. "Donny, look at the way this guy is moving."

"Yeah?"

"Something about it is off. Can you see it?" The perp moved around the clinic, collecting valuables. "Anything?" she asked.

He shook his head. "I don't see it."

She replayed the waiting area video to get a better look at the second perp. "I don't know Donny . . . my gut is telling me something is off about this guy." It was like an itch she couldn't scratch.

Penelope clicked the replay button and watched the entire scenario play out for a third time. She flinched at the violence of the attacks on the pharmacist and on Jacob, but it was a little easier to watch this time. As soon as the perps ran out the door, she replayed it a fourth time.

She was about to play it a fifth time when her phone rang.

CHAPTER 18

WHEN PENELOPE WALKED INTO the hospital lobby to take the call, she saw the forensics team in the clinic packing up for the night. The veteran detective was nowhere to be seen.

"Doug?" she answered the phone.

"Aunty Penny?" Trevor's shrill voice came through the speaker and Penelope smiled.

"Yes, Trevor."

"I woke Uncle Jay-Jay up and asked him his questions. He was grumpy."

"How did he do?"

"He got five gold stars."

"Did he remember all the words?"

"Yep."

She could hear his smile through the phone. Trevor was a little ray of sunshine.

"What words did you give him?"

"Cat . . . and pen . . . and shoe . . . and book . . . and truck. He remembered them all!"

"That's great little buddy. Can I talk to Uncle Jay-Jay?"

Trevor yelled something and handed the phone to Jacob without saying good-bye.

"Hello?" Jacob's voice crackled, and the knot in Penelope's stomach untangled. The video footage had reduced her to a twisted mess of nerves and fear, but hearing Jacob's voice was soothing, like the sun breaking through the clouds after a storm.

"How are you feeling?" she asked.

"Tired," he said, stifling a yawn. "Trevor made sure of that. But I'm feeling fine. How are things going over there?"

"It's going alright. I've seen the footage, but there's little to go on. I feel like I'm missing something."

"When will you finish up?"

"Soon. I'll be staying in Doug's upstairs guest bedroom so I'll check on you at midnight."

"Okay," Jacob said, already sounding like he was falling asleep again. "Don't work too late. Save some of that energy for wedding planning next week."

She had almost forgotten she was supposed to be on vacation next week. "I will. I promise."

"I love you," Jacob said.

"I love you back," she answered.

Penelope hung up and returned to the small security office. She found Donny rubbing his eyes behind the computer screen.

"Find anything else?" she asked.

Donny shook his head. "I think we should wrap this up, call it a night. It's getting late."

Penelope glanced at the screen. What good would it do to watch it again? She was sure she'd seen it all. But still, what if she missed something? Something that she could use.

Donny must have known what she was thinking. "Come on, Penelope. It's ten thirty," he said. "Unless you're hanging around me for another reason?"

Penelope wondered what defense she could plead for smacking a fellow officer who flirted too much.

Finally, she nodded and said, "Fine, let's wrap it up."

"We'll get these guys, Penelope."

She hoped he was right.

PART 2

CHAPTER 19

EARLY SATURDAY MORNING, PENELOPE woke from a troubled sleep. She had spent the night in Doug's upstairs guest bedroom, and it took her a few seconds to become oriented. She'd had a nightmare about yesterday's robbery.

In her dream, Jacob was in a coma and wouldn't wake up. His doctor wore black and looked a lot like Nurse Bonnie. Penelope suspected she was keeping him in a medically induced coma and just as she was about to confront her—she woke up. She didn't feel rested at all. Her eyes were gritty, and a dull headache pulsated between her temples.

Just a dream, that's all.

Her cell phone vibrated on the nightstand. The caller ID read *Dr. Wonderful*, her pet name for Jacob.

"You're up early," she said. "Is everything okay?"

"I'm not going to lie. I feel like a train hit me. But I'm lucky and grateful to be alive."

"I'm grateful too, Jacob." Her eyes welled up with tears. Jacob was right. All that mattered was that he was alive, and everyone was safe. "How did the rest of your night go?"

"I remember you checking on me at midnight, but that's about it. I think everyone conked out after that."

"No one else checked on you?"

"If they did I don't remember."

Penelope sat up in bed. "Is Trevor downstairs with you? I'd like to thank him for taking the first shift."

"I don't know. I'm not at Doug's."

Penelope stilled. "You're not downstairs? Where are you?"

"I'm at the Franklin Clinic." Jacob's voice sounded distant.

Her chest constricted, and her jaw clenched. "At work? Jacob, you need to be resting! You were shot, and you sustained a severe concussion," she said, her voice rising. She made a conscious effort to calm down.

"I know that, Penny. I'm not here for work."

"Then why are you there?" Unable to sit any longer, Penelope got out of bed and paced the room.

"That's what I was calling to tell you. Someone returned my stuff."

"What do you mean someone returned your stuff? Someone from the police department? They caught the guys?"

Why hadn't Donny phoned to let her know something

had come up? He'd promised to call—night or day. Why had she been left out of the loop?

"No, I don't think so. When Belinda arrived this morning, she found a package addressed to me at the front door. She called, and I asked her to open it."

"Addressed to you?"

"Well, it had my name written on it. Belinda thought it might be important. That's why she called."

None of this made sense. If the police had found anything, they would have logged it into evidence and then notified the owner.

"And it contained everything that was stolen yesterday?" Penelope asked.

"Yeah, everything. When Belinda told me what was inside, I called Genny and she gave me a ride on her way into work."

Penelope closed her eyes and took a deep breath. "You called Nurse Taylor? Why didn't you wake me? I would have given you a ride."

"Because, I knew Genny would either be getting ready or she would be on her way into work . . . and I knew you worked late last night. I wanted you to get a few more hours of sleep."

Penelope grabbed her overnight bag from the guest closet, clamped the phone between her shoulder with her cheek, and began to pull out clothes. "Don't touch anything. I'm on my way."

As she got dressed, she processed the information. Something didn't fit. She added it to the puzzle that was slowly forming in her mind.

Who had returned Jacob's belongings and why?

There had to be more to the robbery than a simple smash and grab for narcotics.

CHAPTER 20

Penelope's cell phone rang to life as she got into her car. She glanced at the caller ID. "Donny, I was just about to—"

"Chance, you got a minute?" he interrupted. There was a strange edge to Donny's usually casual voice.

"Sure, I was just about to call you. I've got some new evidence."

"About that, Chance. I know you're close to this case because of the doc's injuries, but I'm wondering if you're too close." Donny paused as if he thought Penelope would interject or argue, but she bit her tongue, and when she didn't speak, he said, "Penelope? You still there?"

"Yes, Donny. I'm still here," she said as neutrally as possible. Inside she was screaming. She couldn't get shut out—not now. "Why is this coming up now? You seemed fine last night."

"Look, Penelope, you know I'd love nothing more than

to work with you on this. You're a great cop with great instincts . . ."

"So what's the problem?"

"Detective Ballard found out the doc is your fiancé, and he has expressed some concern about you shadowing me on this case."

"Wait, I thought you said you weren't working this case."

"Ballard asked if I could assist . . . paperwork and phone calls mostly."

"Well, then you should know Jacob's belongings were returned today."

"Returned?" Penelope could almost hear the wheels turning in the detective's head. "What do you mean returned? Where were they? Who found them?"

"Belinda Crowe, the office manager at the Franklin Clinic. She found an envelope addressed to Jacob when she opened the clinic this morning."

"Addressed to him personally?"

"Yep. She called Jacob and then Jacob called me."

"I'll send a uniform over to take statements and collect the evidence."

"I'm on my way there now. I can take preliminary statements, bag the evidence, and drop it off in a couple of hours. You going to be around?"

"Sure. I'll see you in a couple of hours. I'll let Ballard know that your involvement will be kept to a minimum." There was an awkward silence before Donny finally asked, "So, we're all good then?"

"We're good, Donny." Penelope ended the call and

tossed the phone in her purse. She'd been coping with the stress of Jacob being shot by rushing headlong into a case she wasn't supposed to be investigating.

Donny was right.

This case did hit too close to home. Maybe it would be best for her to focus on other things—like planning her wedding.

CHAPTER 21

PENELOPE PULLED INTO THE Franklin Clinic lot and parked in a spot labeled *Jacob Gordon, M.D.*, near the front of the building. The former Presbyterian church looked more like a vacation lodge than a clinic, with its peaked roof and four stone pillars.

She grabbed her spare evidence kit and walked through the lobby to the reception desk, where Belinda's auburn hair, cropped in a pixie cut, was visible above the computer monitor. A royal blue chunky necklace matched her vibrantly painted fingernails, which flashed across the keyboard. She looked up and stopped typing at once.

"Morning, Penelope," she said, flashing her infectious smile.

"Morning, Belinda."

"How are you holding up? I can't believe Dr. Gordon was shot!"

The words sent shivers down Penelope's spine. *How am I holding up? Not well at all.* She plastered a business smile on her face and refused to show emotion.

"I didn't hear the news until this morning," Belinda continued. "I used to work there. I can't imagine what I would have done."

Penelope nodded politely. "Jacob said you found his wallet?"

"And his watch and cell phone too," Belinda said, opening a drawer of her desk. Do you want them? Dr. Gordon said you'd be by and he had me put them in a plastic bag."

"Not yet. I'll grab them on my way out. Is he here?"

"Oh, yes, of course. He's in his office. Nurse Taylor is checking his head wound and changing the bandage on his shoulder. He was banged up pretty bad, huh?"

Penelope offered a polite smile as she walked through the double swinging doors marked *Staff Only* and into the administrative area of the clinic. The faint smells of floor polish, printer toner, and coffee wafted in the air. As she walked down the short hallway, she passed two offices and only one window. The lack of sunlight left the narrow corridor dark. Fluorescent lights were set in the ceiling at regular intervals, but they could never replace the natural light. She focused on her breathing instead of the fact that the walls seemed to be closing in.

Stay focused, Penny.

At the end of the hallway were two additional rooms—Jacob's office and the break room. Penelope knocked twice on Jacob's door, waited for a reply, and then pushed the door open.

Jacob sat at his desk. His shirt was off, and Nurse Taylor hovered over him. Her fingers quickly worked on his bandages. Penelope's chest constricted. She didn't like seeing Jacob hurt. She also didn't like seeing him being taken care of by another woman.

Was she jealous? She'd had the same reaction the previous day with Nurse "Bunny." Why was she feeling these feelings? She had no reason to be jealous. "That's my man," she wanted to say, but she swallowed her words before she put her foot in her mouth.

Genevieve Taylor was a capable nurse and one of Jacob's closest friends. They'd served in Afghanistan together. Bonds like those held fast. Jacob had been a combat surgeon, and Genevieve "Genny" Taylor had been a flight medic. She flew into battle in a helicopter to pick up wounded soldiers and bring them home.

During a pick-up, Taylor's team got caught in enemy crossfire, and she took a bullet to the chest. They managed to get her back on the helicopter, but everyone was sure she was going to die. If it hadn't been for Dr. Gordon, she might have. He saved her life on the operating table, pulling her through against all odds. They were friends before, but that incident had brought them closer. There was nothing as strong as a friendship that grew out of a near-death experience.

Penelope took a deep breath.

Jacob would always have friends like that, even when they were married. She had a different part of him, even though Nurse Taylor often said, "He touched my heart."

It was a joke. She died on the operating table, and Jacob massaged her heart back to life with his hands. Well, Jacob might have literally touched Genny's heart, but he had romantically won Penelope's.

Jacob was honorably discharged from the U.S. Army and took over at the Franklin Clinic in 2009. Nurse Taylor was the first person he had called to help staff the facility, and she'd moved from her home in Baton Rouge. "I would do anything and go anywhere for this man," she'd often said.

Penelope shook her head.

She had to snap out of the jealous fiancée routine. Everyone could do with more friends like Genny Taylor. It must be the stress of the trial and almost losing Jacob.

Penelope looked Jacob up and down, noting his uncomfortable posture. "Shouldn't you be in bed? You're not looking too well."

Jacob gave her a half smile. "Thanks, Penny. Just what a guy wants to hear."

"He had a black eye and I wanted to make sure it wasn't something serious," Taylor said, giving Penelope a smile.

"Genny noticed it when she picked me up this morning." He turned his head toward Taylor and gave her a wink and a smile. "Am I going to live?"

"I think you'll survive."

It wasn't surprising that Taylor didn't express much sympathy for Jacob's injuries. The dedicated nurse practitioner was focused on her job, and she was good at what she did.

"Well, let's get your stuff," Penelope said. "I'm taking

you back to my place. I want to make up for not checking on you the rest of the night."

"Thanks, Penny, but Dr. Bishop pulled an all-nighter helping out with a multi-car accident on State Road 20 last night. I'm going to stick around here for a while."

She looked him in the eye and saw he wasn't going to fold. Usually, she admired his work ethic, but today she felt it was getting in the way of his wellbeing. "I could make you some of my garlic chicken soup."

"I know you're worried about me, Penny. But I've had much worse injuries than this. This isn't my first concussion or even the first time I've been shot." His eyes were earnest. "Do you trust me?"

"Of course I do!"

"Then let me go to work," he said with a warm smile. "I love your soup, but I'll go stir crazy if I spend another minute in bed."

Penelope flashed a look at Genny.

The nurse's brown eyes met Penelope's and she smiled a smile that was neither warm nor cold. "Don't worry, Penelope," she said, flicking her shoulder length hair away from her face. "I'll make sure he behaves."

No one could get Jacob to do anything he didn't want to do, even if it was for his own sake.

"Okay," Penelope finally conceded and then asked, "What about your car? Is it still at Grace Memorial?"

"It is . . ."

"At least let me take you to get it. I can drop you off on my way to the Gainesville station."

"Deal." Jacob extended his right hand as if to shake on

it, then grimaced and clutched his shoulder. He looked up at Penelope's concerned face. "I can still drive, you know."

"With one hand?"

"It's just a little stiff. I'm not taking any pain medication."

Penelope sighed. "Let's grab your stuff."

"Sure. Belinda has it up at the front desk."

Nurse Taylor excused herself and Penelope helped Jacob put his shirt back on. He took her hand and together they walked to the reception area.

CHAPTER 22

BELINDA HAD JUST FINISHED a phone call, and Penelope asked, "Can I grab Jacob's things?" She may have been a touch rude, but she needed to get everything to the Gainesville forensics team for processing.

"Yes, of course." Belinda fished the belongings from the bottom drawer of her desk and handed Penelope a clear plastic bag.

Penelope emptied the wallet, cell phone, and watch onto the desk. Jacob reached for the watch and she grabbed him by the wrist. "Hold on Jacob, that's evidence."

"Oh, yes . . . of course. Sorry, Penny."

Penelope removed a pair of blue nitrile gloves from her evidence kit. "Belinda, did anyone else touch these or just you?"

"No one touched them, and I used gloves."

"You did?"

"I told her to," Jacob said. "When she told me what was inside the envelope, I asked her not to touch anything and to put everything into a plastic bag."

"That was good thinking." Penelope picked up the wallet and handed it to Jacob. "Can you see if anything's missing?"

"Don't you want to dust it for prints first?" he asked in a teasing tone.

Penelope stared at him with her best cop's stare. He smiled and picked up the wallet, holding it carefully by the edges. He opened it and pulled out the contents, laying them on the counter next to the watch and cell phone.

Penelope flipped open her notepad and looked at Belinda expectantly. "Were you the first person to arrive at the clinic today?"

"I usually open the clinic in the morning. Some mornings Nurse Taylor opens up, but it was my turn today. The envelope was sitting there right in front of the main entrance."

"Where's the envelope?"

"Oh . . . I think I left it in the break room." Belinda looked a little worried. "It is probably still in there."

Penelope jotted down a couple more notes and said, "Okay, then. Let's go look."

"Penny, wait." Jacob sounded alarmed. "There's something missing from my wallet."

Penelope's stomach tightened, and her pulse sped up. "What is it? What's missing?" The contents of his wallet were spread on the counter. Penelope poured over his driver's license, credit cards, and insurance card. It looked complete. There was even some cash.

"The photo booth picture we took at Doug and Camille's wedding. It's missing!" He frantically looked through the little pockets of the black leather wallet as if he thought the photo would simply reappear if he kept looking. "And the fortune . . ."

"Fortune?" Penelope asked.

"You know, from the wedding. The fortune cookie fortune."

Penelope and Jacob had met at Doug and Camille's wedding six years earlier. Jacob was a good friend of Camille's, and she had wanted to set him up with Penelope. Camille made sure they were paired up in the wedding party. Doug and Camille handed out personalized fortune cookies at the rehearsal dinner and each person read their fortune aloud. Most of them were humorous, but Jacob and Penelope's were the same.

The love you seek is closer than you think.

Penelope and Jacob dated for a month before his last deployment and had been exclusive since his return.

"You kept that?" she asked.

"I did. In my wallet with the picture."

A curl of dread turned in Penelope's stomach. "Why would anyone want that?" She studied the contents of his wallet again. "Why would someone leave the cash and take the photo and the fortune?"

Jacob set the empty wallet down next to its contents. "I guess it's possible that I took it out."

The look on his face told a different story.

Was he trying to convince himself or keep her from

worrying? Penelope suppressed any worry this revelation had spawned and stayed focused on the facts. Collect the evidence. Focus on the task at hand. Worry could wait until later.

She removed a couple of evidence bags from her kit. She needed to bag Jacob's belongings and get that envelope. The more evidence they had, the easier it would be to track whoever dropped it off.

"Belinda, you want to show me that envelope?"

Belinda stopped typing and looked startled. "Oh yes . . . the envelope." She stood and said, "Follow me."

CHAPTER 23

THE FRANKLIN CLINIC WASN'T a large building. The small medical facility could deal with emergencies, but it was by no means a fully equipped hospital. With three hospitals in nearby Gainesville, Franklin didn't require a hospital of its own.

Penelope followed Belinda into the administrative area of the clinic. They stopped outside the small employee break room across from Jacob's office. There was no door—just a door-sized opening. Inside, next to a well-worn recliner was a wooden table and three chairs.

"It was right here," Belinda said, pointing at the table. "You're sure?"

"Yes. I left it right here." Panic rose in Belinda's voice. "Oh, no! Someone must have thrown it away." Belinda looked at Penelope apologetically, and then her eyes widened. "I was supposed to empty the trash last night because the garbage men come today, but I forgot. Nurse Taylor must have emptied them when she got in this morning." Belinda looked as if she might cry.

Penelope looked down at the empty trash can with a fresh liner inside and flipped open her notebook. "Why did you leave the envelope in the break room?"

"I brought donuts in for the staff and my hands were full. I set the envelope on top of the donut box, and I called Dr. Gordon from here." Belinda pointed to a phone on the break room wall. "Dr. Gordon asked me to open the package. Then he told me to bag his stuff. I got busy and forgot about the envelope."

"So, if Nurse Taylor took the trash out, the envelope could be near the top of the dumpster, correct?"

Belinda shook her head. "I heard the garbage truck about thirty minutes ago. It's long gone."

The loss of evidence was disappointing, but Penelope didn't want Belinda to beat herself up over it. "We'll probably find the evidence we need from the wallet, cell phone, and watch. Thanks for your help."

That did not seem to cheer Belinda up at all and she morosely walked back toward the lobby. Penelope hardly noticed. She was lost in thought, running through the evidence in her mind. The robbery . . . the security footage . . . the mysterious return of Jacob's belongings.

"Would you call Nurse Taylor for me?" Penelope asked Belinda when they got back to the reception desk.

"Sure." As she spoke, Belinda hit one of the red buttons on her desk phone, and a series of beeps sounded on the intercom.

Moments later, the sound of measured footsteps echoing in the hallway announced the arrival of Nurse Taylor. She always walked at a pace that was more than a stroll, but not quite a run. She seemed to get where she was going when she wanted to, and not a moment sooner.

Nurse Taylor nodded at Penelope and turned to Belinda, "Yes? What is it?"

"Actually, Genny," Penelope said, opening her notepad and uncapping her pen. "I asked Belinda to page you. Just a couple of quick questions, if you don't mind."

"Sure."

"Did you take out the garbage in the break room this morning?"

Taylor glanced at Belinda, who looked away and quickly resumed typing. Her eyes returned to Penelope. "I did."

"Did you happen to see a manila envelope in the break room?"

"I did. I threw it away. I heard the garbage truck and emptied the trash. No one took it out last night." That last comment was apparently intended for Belinda.

Jacob picked that moment to join them. "Are you finished with my nurse?"

"I am," Penelope answered. "Are you ready to head over to Gainesville?"

"Sure," he said, and then turned to Nurse Taylor. "Penny is going to drop me off at my car. I won't be gone long."

Taylor gave Jacob a nod and then went about her business.

"Do you need your phone?" Penelope asked. "I can dust it for prints here."

"No, I have my backup. You have that number, right?"

"I do."

"Any idea when I can get my stuff back?"

"I'm not sure, but I'll ask."

Jacob smiled and kissed Penelope on the top of her head. "Shall we go?"

"After you, Superman," she said.

CHAPTER 24

AFTER DROPPING JACOB OFF at his car, the drive to the Gainesville Police Station gave Penelope time alone with her thoughts. She ran through the facts, determined to piece together the puzzle that was forming in her head, but around every corner more things popped up that didn't make sense . . . and she didn't like it.

She drove to the Northwest 6th Street station, only to find construction equipment where the police headquarters once stood. It had slipped her mind that they'd demolished the old building a couple of months earlier to build a modern facility. She pulled up to the curb and texted Donny.

A moment later her phone chirped with the address of the temporary location.

The downtown office building on Northeast 1st Street housed the Criminal Investigations Division; the squat building looked like it had sat down on itself. It was top heavy, a row of thick glass windows set upon a bottom story of pale brick. It was as if the building had sunk into the ground, forced down by its own weight. She walked up to the glass double doors and pushed them open.

Donny found her in the lobby. Today he wore a light lavender silk dress shirt open at the collar. If he'd worn that shirt with a white suit he could have passed for something out of *Miami Vice*. But Donny classed it up with a dark gray Italian suit jacket and matching pants.

"Glad you found it," he said, taking her hand in a toned down version of a handshake. "Sorry about the mess down here. We're still moving in. The whole relocation is a bit of a headache."

"What's wrong with crime these days? It won't wait for you to get settled?" Penelope joked.

Donny paused and rubbed the back of his neck. "I spoke with Ballard . . ."

"And?"

"And he's okay with you working with me if I'm okay with it."

"Are you?"

Donny shifted in his polished black oxfords. "I already said I was . . . as long as you do what I say."

Penelope nodded her affirmation.

"So, what've you got for me?" he asked.

Penelope handed him the evidence bags, and Donny examined the items through the plastic bag.

"A Breitling Duograph. Beautiful watch," he said.

"It was a gift from Jacob's father when he graduated

med school. Anything new with the case?"

"Not on our end. Let's hope the doc's belongings turn up a clue," Donny said, holding up the evidence bag. "Detective Ballard is meeting with the County Sheriff's Department Joint Drug Task Force. There's been a string of these types of robberies at pharmacies and drug stores in the Gainesville metro area. Each robbery had the same MO—two armed assailants, one with a shotgun, the other with a handgun."

Images of Jacob getting shot flashed through Penelope's mind.

"The robberies always occur at the end of the month," Donny continued. "Ballard has a theory. He thinks it's so they can get cash for rent, or something."

"You think it's as straightforward as that?"

Donny shrugged. "You'd be surprised at the lengths people will go. The hospital was their biggest hit. It looks like they're getting more aggressive."

"Any idea why?"

Donny shook his head. He was right. Nothing they'd learned was useful. They didn't have any leads.

"None of this makes sense," Penelope said. "The robbery I can understand, but returning Jacob's belongings? That's got me stumped. I spoke to the receptionist. She said the envelope was in front of the door when she opened up this morning. Addressed to Jacob."

"And no indication as to who returned them?"

Penelope shook her head and handed Donny her interview notes. "These are the statements I took. Have you ever heard of a thief returning his victim's belongings?"

"A thief with a conscience? I don't think so. Perhaps a good Samaritan found them and returned them?" Donny offered.

"Maybe." Penelope was not convinced.

Donny flipped through Penelope's notes, paused, and then looked up. "I appreciate your taking the notes and collecting evidence—"

"But what?" Penelope interrupted.

Donny put his hand on Penelope's shoulder. It was supposed to be an act of kindness, showing friendship, but to Penelope, it felt like he was trying to soften a blow.

"But . . . what I was going to say was, I have a mountain of paperwork and some follow-up calls to the robbery victims to make. Probably not the best day to shadow me, unless you'd like to help me by typing up your notes?" Penelope shook her head, and Donny chuckled. "I didn't think so. I'll keep you updated, okay? I'll let you know when Jacob can collect his belongings."

Penelope nodded and forced a smile. She said good-bye and walked purposefully to her car. It was easier than trying to explain that she couldn't sit by and wait.

"Lord, please guide me. If I can assist in this investigation, please help me to find a way, without being in the way. And please give Donny, Detective Ballard, and their capable team the wisdom they need to find suspects and bring them to justice. Amen."

CHAPTER 25

FIFTEEN MINUTES LATER, PENELOPE found herself back at Grace Memorial Hospital. It was busier than usual on a late Saturday morning. A fire had struck a local greasy spoon, and several customers and employees were being treated for smoke inhalation and minor burns.

She paused in the main lobby across from the clinic. There was no sign of yesterday's struggle. Even the wall where three bullets had come to rest was patched and painted. She didn't see Sylvia or Tina. Those poor women probably deserved a few days off after what had happened.

Deborah Thompson, the pharmacist, was apparently made of tougher stuff. Penelope could see her distinctive hairstyle bobbing up and down behind the counter, bustling around and pulling bottles off the shelves. Deborah was a married mother of three grown children. She had been at the hospital for decades and everyone, even those who didn't know her by name, knew her by her 1970s-style Farrah Fawcett hairdo.

Penelope traced the route the robbers would have taken when they fled—through the clinic's double door, into the lobby, and out the automatic front door. The clinic was the ideal target for a smash-and-grab job. It was a wonder the pharmacy hadn't been hit before.

Her eyes wandered around the spacious main lobby. Two women in white uniforms sat at a U-shaped desk in the center of the entry area. A sign above the station read *Reception/Intake*. Penelope looked for additional security cameras. She had only seen the videos from the hospital clinic's three angles. There were at least two additional cameras in the lobby. The video from these cameras may not be of use, since the ceilings were vaulted, but it wouldn't hurt to take a look.

"Chance?" a voice called from behind.

Penelope was so absorbed in her thoughts that she jumped when she heard her name. Her heart sped up, and a twinge of guilt shot through her.

"Oh! Professor. You startled me . . ." She looked at the professor and tried to reconcile his face with his attire. The same professor that she had always seen in Oxford shirts and khakis was now standing in front of her in dress pants, dress shirt, tie, and a white lab coat. "What on earth are you doing here?" she asked.

"I told you Penelope to call me Gabriel. My office is on the fourth floor."

"You have an office here? You didn't mention that yesterday," Penelope said, genuinely confused.

"I didn't? I was sure I mentioned it when I drove you here last night." Gabriel looked confused too. "Well, either way, I still have a private practice. I'm between consulting cases, so I spend more time with my patients."

Penelope knew Gabriel could be a little spacey, so even though she found it odd that he had forgotten to mention that he had an office at the hospital, she accepted it as another one of his idiosyncrasies. He once gave a speech to her graduating class and had forgotten his notes. He had rambled on about video games' positive and negative effects on behavior. She supposed his brilliance in his field made up for his odd behavior.

"How's your fiancé? Are you here to visit him?"

"He's okay and back to work at the clinic in Franklin today."

"So you're not here to see him?"

"No, I'm just looking around."

"Looking around? Looking around as in investigating the robbery, looking around?"

"I'm here unofficially." Penelope tried to keep her face blank.

"Unofficially?"

"With Jacob involved, I'm . . . interested."

"From what I heard, a couple of junkies robbed patients, snatched pills, and brute-forced their way out of the hospital, isn't that right?"

"Yes, but I'm afraid there's more to the story." Penelope glanced around to make sure no one would overhear. "Jacob's belongings were returned to him this morning."

"So they caught the suspects?"

"No. That's what I thought at first. It looks like someone may have found the belongings and returned them. I don't know for sure." Gabriel nodded in agreement. "I dropped the belongings off with Gainesville PD to be processed," Penelope continued, "but here's the odd part . . . there was something missing from Jacob's wallet."

"Like money? Credit cards?"

"No, a photo he carried of us and a fortune . . . from a Chinese fortune cookie."

Gabriel looked surprised and interested. "And everything else was returned to the clinic where your fiancé works in Franklin?"

"Yep."

"How did they know to return it to the Franklin Clinic? Why not return it here or to his home?"

Penelope was silent for a moment. "I hadn't thought about that." She knew Gabriel could offer new insight.

"Was there anything in his wallet with the Franklin Clinic address?"

"No. Just his driver's license, credit cards, insurance card, and some cash. Nothing with the clinic's address."

"A business card perhaps?"

"Maybe . . ." Penelope thought for a moment. "His cell phone! Maybe they got the address from his cell phone? He doesn't have a passcode on it."

Gabriel rubbed the stubble on his chin with his thumb and forefinger. "You know . . . if they accessed his address book, there's a possibility they have all his contacts."

"I'm in his address book," Penelope said.

"I don't think it's anything to worry about."

"But what about the missing photo and fortune?"

Gabriel's face contorted. "I think the most likely scenario is like you said . . . a good Samaritan found the belongings. The photo and fortune could have fallen out when that person was looking for identification." Gabriel was obviously attempting to set her mind at ease.

How did they know Jacob worked at the Franklin Clinic? And why wouldn't they come forward? If she had that envelope, she might have been able to analyze the handwriting. A possible key piece of evidence—gone!

CHAPTER 26

"...ISN'T THAT RIGHT?"

Gabriel's catch phrase jarred her back to the present. "I'm sorry, Gabriel, what were you saying?"

"I said it looks like we have a mystery on our hands." His eyes lit up. "I have a light caseload. Maybe you could use a consultant. Say, a forensic psychologist?" Gabriel wasn't insensitive—he just loved a good mystery.

Penelope's cell phone rang and she glanced at the caller ID. "Excuse me, Gabriel. It's my chief. I should take this." He didn't look like he was going anywhere. "Hey, Chief. What's up?"

"Chance. I heard about yesterday. How are you holding up?"

"I'm good, Chief. Thank you."

"I would have called yesterday, but I figured you'd be busy taking care of that fiancé of yours. I heard they released him from the hospital. How's he doing?"

"He's good. He's back to work today if you can believe that."

"Back to work? Already?"

Penelope paused for a moment. "Well, he went in because his belongings were returned to the Franklin Clinic."

"Items that were stolen in the robbery?"

"Yes."

"But not returned by Gainesville PD?"

"No, we don't know who returned his belongings. I went in this morning and collected the evidence and took preliminary statements for Detective Greene."

Jackson was silent for a few seconds. Penelope cringed as she imagined the look on his face. "What are you doing collecting evidence and taking statements for Gainesville PD? You're supposed to be on vacation." Penelope could hear the frustration in his voice. When he spoke again, he sounded tired. "Well, Chance, I suppose how you spend your vacation is your business. You find out anything . . . you tell me."

"You got it, Chief."

Jackson hung up without another word. Even though the chief was irritated with her for getting involved, he still trusted her enough to continue. He was giving her the benefit of the doubt, and she appreciated that.

She ended the call, and her eyes met Gabriel's. He was looking at her with interest and genuine, professional curiosity.

"So what do you say? Could you use a consultant?" he asked.

"This isn't my case and I don't want to interfere with Gainesville's investigation."

"We wouldn't be interfering. We'd be looking at the case from a different angle. They hire me to consult on cases all the time."

"I couldn't hire you." That wasn't what he meant, but she wanted to be clear.

"That's fine with me. I'll be your *unofficial* consultant." Gabriel smiled. "When do we start?"

Penelope's stomach answered him with a growl. She hadn't eaten all day.

"What does your schedule look like Monday?"

"Monday? What's wrong with right now?"

Despite Gabriel's enthusiasm, Penelope needed time to think. There were no clues and she had to figure out where to start. "I have to check on Jacob this afternoon and I have church tomorrow. It's the only full day Jacob and I get to spend together. You and I could get a fresh start on Monday, the official start of my vacation."

Gabriel looked disappointed. Penelope was always surprised by how he acted like an excited child one moment and a respected scholar the next.

He held his hand out to her. "Monday, then. Eight o'clock?"

"Yes, eight o'clock Monday morning would be great," she said, shaking his hand. "I'll meet you here."

She was touched. Surely he had important work to do. She thanked God for her many loyal friends and for showing her a way to assist in the investigation—unofficially.

CHAPTER 27

SUNDAY MORNING PENELOPE SLID open the door to her closet and took out a dark navy dress, a pair of champagne leather wedge sandals, and a wide beige belt. She laid the dress on her bed. The floral print on the short sleeved, modest outfit reminded her of spring after a storm. It was also Jacob's favorite. She turned to the mirror, arranged her hair, and started her makeup.

It was nice to get dressed up for a change.

With her makeup done and her hair in loose curls over her shoulders, she looked like a refined version of herself. The stress of the Findley trial had taken its toll. Her typically athletic frame had begun to look slightly stooped but now seemed taller and more relaxed. But the usual spark in her green eyes was replaced with an intensity that only appeared when she had a lot on her mind.

Her cell phone ring tone startled her.

Franklin PD? *Why would the station be calling?*

Sunday was her day off, and she was supposed to be on vacation. Perhaps they had information on the robbery and were calling to inform her. She pressed the answer button and held the phone to her ear.

"This is Chance."

Judy Preston's voice crackled over the speaker. "Penelope, I'm sorry to be calling on your vacation."

"No problem, Judy. What's up?"

"The 9-1-1 dispatch just routed us a call. A man jogging the Franklin River Trail discovered a body. I haven't been able to reach the chief. I dispatched DeBose to the scene. He thought we could have a murder on our hands and I wanted you there to confirm."

"Of course. Thank you, Judy. What part of the trail?"

"Near the Southside Bridge, out by the Last Chance Tavern."

Penelope closed her eyes for a moment. She heard the crackle of fire and saw the crooked shadows the flames cast on the walls. She heard the screams, her lungs burning, the smoke smothering her . . .

"Penelope? You still there?"

Judy's voice pulled her back to the present. She blinked away the memories of the fire that claimed the lives of her mother and father.

"Yes, Judy. I'm still here. Keep trying the chief and radio DeBose. Tell him to secure the scene. I'm on my way. And call the county sheriff. We'll need their forensic assistance on this."

"Will do, Penelope."

Penelope hung up and put the dress back in her closet. She grabbed her uniform from another hanger and finished getting dressed.

CHAPTER 28

FIFTEEN MINUTES LATER, PENELOPE grabbed her keys and opened the front door, just as Jacob came walking up the steps to her porch.

She'd forgotten to call and tell him she had to cancel. She'd been forgetting a lot of things lately. She was often on call and Jacob had a tight schedule that divided his time between the Franklin Clinic and Grace Memorial Hospital. It didn't make for much quality time. Sunday was their day to recharge. They drove to church together and then went to Spanky's Grill for brunch. They needed this time without the many distractions.

Jacob looked her up and down before he gave her a quick peck on the lips. "Not exactly Sunday attire, Penny. Why are you in uniform?"

Penelope shook off the guilt brewing in her stomach. It was her sworn duty to serve the people of Franklin. She reached up and touched his bandaged head and caressed his cheek. "I'm sorry, Jacob." She stepped in closer to him and gave him a gentle hug. He wrapped his arms around her and she leaned against his chest. It was warm, and she savored being close to him. There were days when it seemed he was miles away, even when he was standing right next to her.

"Is everything okay? You're starting to worry me."

"A jogger found a body out by the Southside Bridge, and dispatch couldn't reach the chief, so she called me."

"And no one else could take the call? I understand that you're high up in the ranks there, but if it's a dead body, they aren't going anywhere."

"Jacob! A person is dead. Possibly murdered."

"I don't mean any disrespect. You know I don't. But it's Sunday . . . your day off. You're supposed to be on vacation." Jacob looked at her, and she fought the urge to squirm under his gaze. His eyes drilled through her. "Why does it always have to be you?"

"You know they wouldn't call unless they needed me," she said. "DeBose is there now, but he's still a rookie. I need to supervise until Judy can reach the chief."

Jacob opened his mouth to speak but closed it again. Finally, he sighed. "You're not going to let this go, are you? I've seen that look before."

Penelope frowned and took a step back from Jacob. "What look?"

"The look you get in your eyes when you've made up your mind about something. When you get that look, you don't take *no* for an answer, and there's nothing anyone can do about it."

"It's my job," Penelope said in her defense—and it was the truth. "We can ride over together and go to church afterward. I don't want to leave DeBose out there alone."

Jacob turned his face away from her and looked down the road. His eyes traveled over the objects in her front yard—the mailbox, the rose bush, the garbage can. She knew he wasn't looking at anything in particular. He was thinking about what she had said.

"Well . . . If that's the only way I'm going to get to spend time with you . . ." he said, letting his sentence trail off.

Penelope smiled tentatively, and they walked to Jacob's car.

The drive was awkward. Twice Penelope tried to start up a conversation, to talk about something arbitrary, but both times the words fell—lifeless.

She looked out the passenger window at the scenery. Should she have told Judy *no*? She was on vacation. It was a Sunday. Her relationship with Jacob didn't deserve to be put on the back burner. But Penelope was a police officer with a sworn duty. She'd dedicated nine years of her life to the Franklin Police Department, to doing what was right. It was in her blood. She couldn't refuse.

CHAPTER 29

WHEN THEY ARRIVED AT the crime scene, a line of cars was already on site. Penelope recognized some of them, like the Putnam County Sheriff Forensics Unit and DeBose's police cruiser.

"Looks like DeBose wasn't alone out here after all," Jacob said, parking behind DeBose's car.

Penelope swallowed her reply.

The scene was alive with people walking back and forth between cars and talking to each other. She prepared herself mentally for what she was about to see. Butterflies stirred in her stomach, like her first day as a rookie. She glanced down the street at the empty lot, and the memories of a night twenty-three years ago played in her mind.

Her childhood home was on fire. Her parents were running with her to the front door. The fire was blocking their escape. Her father was smashing the kitchen window, and her mom was lifting her up and out of the window. And her mom's final words, "Run, baby, run away" just before the fire whooshed up and burned her ankle—a permanent scar was a reminder of that night.

Even after releasing the guilt of surviving that night, the memories still consumed her.

"Hey," Jacob said softly, taking her by the hand. "It's going to be alright."

Penelope shook away the images and released a shaky breath. She didn't need to hide her emotions from Jacob. She'd become so good at putting on a strong face; sometimes she forgot to take it off. He was a pillar of strength. He knew she wanted to pray—needed it even. It was a relief to know that he was on the same page. Any tension between them vanished.

She nodded, and he closed his eyes, holding her one hand in both of his.

"Lord," he began, "may the soul of this person rest in Your capable hands, and may the family of the victim be eased through this terrible time. If this person was murdered, please give Penny and her fellow officers the knowledge they need to find the person that committed this crime, so justice may prevail."

"By Your will and strength alone," Penelope added.

Jacob squeezed Penelope's hands. "And Lord," he continued, "even though she'd never admit it, I know Penny has a lot on her mind . . . being here today . . . at this location . . . so close to where she lost her parents. Please watch over her and take care of her. In the name of Jesus Christ. Amen."

"Amen," Penelope echoed.

It felt good to know she could hand this kind of stress over to the Lord, and He would guide her through it. God and Jacob got her through so much. She said a silent prayer of thanks for Jacob. Nothing he needed to hear, just a rush of gratitude that she still had him.

When they both opened their eyes, Penelope took a deep breath, trying to work oxygen around the tightness in her chest. "Thank you for that, Jacob."

"A word of advice," he said. "Don't look at it as a dead body, look at it as a mystery . . . a mystery that needs to be solved. It's horrible that someone died, but they're gone now, and they'll need someone to speak for them. You're that person."

Penelope flashed a smile, hoping she looked more confident than she felt, and gave Jacob a quick kiss on the lips. "Thank you," she said and steeled herself. She was about to open the car door when she glanced back at Jacob. "Will you wait here?"

"Huh?" He looked taken aback.

"I won't be long."

"I might be able to help."

Penelope shook her head. "I'll come get you if I need you."

CHAPTER 30

PENELOPE WALKED THE SHORT distance from the trailhead to the crime scene and tried to shake off the tension of the day.

The Franklin River Nature Trail was an old fire service road that ran parallel to Franklin River. Joggers, hikers, and dog walkers used the road. The trail was usually peaceful, with birds chirping in the canopy of branches overhead. Today the chirping was absent. The wind rustled through the trees and the smell of damp moss and undergrowth traveled on the breeze. Penelope took a deep breath. She was wound up tight, and she wanted to handle her encounter with the body with grace.

Penelope rounded a short bend in the road and spotted Officer Alex DeBose. Yellow crime tape already marked the scene. The county sheriff's forensics unit was on-site taking photos and marking evidence. Death was never private. Every inch of the person and the scene would be photographed, documented, labeled, and discussed. It was all very clinical. The usually quiet area hummed with activity, a slight buzz in the air.

DeBose was talking to a taller man with an athletic build—probably the caller. The man had his back to Penelope, but with his short graying hair, she placed him in his late forties. He was wearing black sweatpants, a blue sleeveless T-shirt, and black Nike running shoes. He appeared to be a little shaken up. Discovering death was never pleasant, no matter how involved you were.

When DeBose spotted Penelope, he excused himself and walked over to greet her. "Just your luck. Great way to start your vacation . . . huh, Chance?"

"It's not a matter of luck."

DeBose shrugged and handed Penelope a clipboard. It was standard operating procedure for all persons entering or leaving a crime scene to sign in and out. Judging by the list of names, DeBose had done a good job of securing the scene. Penelope printed her name, badge number and signed in.

DeBose took the clipboard and handed her a pair of blue latex gloves.

"Looks like you've got everything under control here," Penelope said as she ducked under the crime scene tape.

"The county forensics team arrived about ten minutes ago. I was just wrapping up with our caller."

Penelope took a deep breath through her nose. "What've we got?"

"Victim was a Caucasian male, late twenties, early

thirties. Haven't touched the body, so no ID yet. A Mr. Tony Egland found the body. He was out for a run with his dog—" DeBose paused and flipped through his notes.

"Kona," Penelope said. "Tony's dog's name is Kona."

DeBose glanced up from his notepad. "Yeah . . . that's right. You know him?"

Penelope looked over DeBose's shoulder, caught the eye of the jogger, and gave him a smile and a wave. "I almost didn't recognize him out of uniform. Tony's a volunteer with the Franklin Fire Department."

"That's right," DeBose continued. "Kona ran down into the river and found the body. Mr. Egland called 9-1-1. And when I arrived, he helped secure the scene."

"Where's the body?"

"Over here . . ."

Penelope followed DeBose across a small wooden footbridge to the west side of the river. A half dozen yellow evidence tents marked what looked like blood drops. The medical examiner wasn't on site yet, so no one had disturbed the body. It was on a dark patch, lying cold and lifeless, at the bottom of the slope that led toward the river.

Penelope snapped on the blue gloves and stretched her fingers until the gloves fit snugly. Franklin River was more like Franklin Trickle. If the water had been any deeper, it might have taken longer to find the body. Small blessings.

A forensic technician passed and Penelope gave a respectful nod.

From where they stood on the edge of the river, the victim looked to be about six feet tall and was face down in the muck of the stream. He was wearing black pants, a black T-shirt and a pair of black basketball shoes. The victim's legs were crossed at the ankles, and his arms were sprawled.

"Looks like a dump job," Penelope observed.

"How can you tell?"

"See the way the legs are crossed and the arms are flailed to the sides? He was probably rolled down the embankment."

DeBose frowned, considering it. "So he wasn't killed here?"

"That would be my guess. We'll know for sure when the M.E. has had a chance to examine the body."

They watched as the forensics unit methodically took pictures of the body from various angles. One of the photographers looked up, gave them a polite smile, and continued taking photos. Penelope lifted her hand in a half wave.

The idea of lost life was getting to her. Maybe it was because she'd nearly lost Jacob, and she knew that someone else, somewhere, hadn't been so lucky. Somewhere a mother had just lost a son. She paused for a moment and said a silent prayer.

A rustling noise from behind pulled Penelope's attention back to the job at hand. She turned to see Jacob and Dr. Tammy Harris, Gainesville's Chief Medical Examiner, walking cautiously but quickly across the wooden bridge.

"Jacob?"

"Sorry, Penelope. I was waiting in the car, and Dr. Harris asked if I'd give her a hand."

The medical world wasn't a big one, and the two

worlds—medical and law enforcement—often rubbed shoulders. Penelope turned back to the body and tried not to let her emotions show.

DeBose signed in Dr. Harris and Dr. Gordon and headed back to the trailhead.

Dr. Harris made her way down to the body and began her preliminary examination. She worked systematically, starting at the head and working her way down, following a mental checklist. Jacob stopped next to Penelope, and they watched side-by-side. No matter how much she wanted him to be far away and safe, his presence was soothing.

CHAPTER 31

FIFTEEN MINUTES LATER, CHIEF Curtis Jackson arrived on the scene with Officer Bill Peterson.

"Chance," Chief Jackson said, sounding surprised, "you're the last person I expected to see today."

Peterson raised his eyebrows, confusion showing on his stern face. "Aren't you supposed to be on vacation?"

"It's no use, guys," Jacob said. "She wouldn't even listen to me."

Penelope rolled her eyes. "Tony Egland, a volunteer firefighter with the Franklin Fire Department, found the body while jogging this morning. Judy called me when she couldn't reach you, Chief. I wanted to give DeBose a hand. Murder isn't something we come across in Franklin every day."

Jackson nodded and watched the medical examiner while Penelope filled him in on everything they knew so far.

"Dr. Gordon, will you come down here?" Dr. Harris called. "I need help rolling the body over. You guys can come down, too."

Peterson excused himself and Jacob made his way down the embankment. Penelope and the chief followed. Jacob squared his shoulders and moved toward the body. He had to stand in the trickle of water to reach the body.

"Let's flip him over," the examiner said.

Jacob closed his eyes for a moment and nodded. For someone who worked with death and illness every day, he was a shade too pale. He gripped the body by the shoulder and heaved. Emotion flickered across his face too fast for Penelope to read. It took a bit of force to manipulate a dead body. It was almost as if the soul had been replaced with lead, and none of the limbs cooperated the way they needed to.

The body flopped over, the arms splashing in the bit of water in the river. The face was revealed, and despite a smear of mud and a couple of smudges of dirt, the face was surprisingly young and unblemished.

Jacob's face went pale. His eyes were glued to the face of the victim. He looked like he might fall over. "It's him," he said so softly it was barely audible, but none of them missed it.

Penelope reached for Jacob's hand as he stumbled backward, trying to scramble away from the body. "You recognize this guy?" she asked.

Jacob looked at the corpse for a moment. Penelope saw him mentally flipping through every face he knew. His eyes widened slightly when he found a match.

"It's one of the guys that robbed the pharmacy," he said.

It was as if something had sucked all of the air out of the space around them, and they stood in a vacuum.

"Are you sure?" Penelope asked.

Jacob nodded. He pointed to the face. "The scar on his left eyebrow. It's him. I'm sure of it." He looked up, and his eyes showed concern when they met Penelope's. "But how did he get here?"

Penelope exchanged glances with Jackson before they both looked back at the body. They were thinking the same thing: the two crimes had to be related.

"Good question," Penelope said, still holding Jacob's hand. She gave it a reassuring squeeze and then let go.

Chief Jackson knelt to inspect the body and Penelope joined him. He moved slowly and calmly as if he examined dead people all the time—which wasn't far from the truth. The chief had been in law enforcement for thirty plus years and had probably seen much, much worse than this.

With the body flipped over, the wound was apparent. Despite the dark T-shirt, Penelope could see the large, brownish stain of dried blood on the abdomen.

"Single gunshot wound," Dr. Harris said, confirming what everyone was seeing.

"Now we need to find out who *he* is," Jackson said. "Is it okay to check for ID, doctor?" Dr. Harris nodded, and Jackson searched the body. "Nothing," he confirmed.

"Caliber, Doctor?" Penelope asked, leaning in to get a closer look.

Harris shook her head. "A .45 perhaps? I'm not sure. I'll know more when I get him back to the morgue."

"Time of death?" Jackson asked.

"Based on liver temp and lividity, I'd say your TOD is sometime in the last thirty-two to thirty-eight hours."

"So what's that? Somewhere between eight o'clock Friday night and two Saturday morning?" Jackson asked.

"Correct. I should be able to narrow that window after my examination."

Chief Curtis Jackson stood up and flexed his back. He stared into the distance, not looking at anything in particular. Penelope knew what was happening. The chief was thinking, cogs turning, perhaps accessing an old memory.

She looked at the body again, searching for clues. "Come on, there has to be something," she said under her breath, "any clue about what happened to you and how you got here."

The only sounds around them were the trickle of the stream and the clicking of the cameras several officers were using to collect evidence.

"Looks like we may have a drug deal gone wrong," Jackson said, breaking the rhythm of the sounds around them, and then he fell silent again.

Penelope looked at Dr. Harris, who shrugged. She wasn't going to offer any more input until she'd had a chance to study the body.

They stood together in silence.

CHAPTER 32

THE DISTANT SOUND OF cars approaching caught Penelope's attention. She looked to Jackson. "News media?"

"Gainesville PD," he said. Penelope's frown deepened, and she pushed herself up with her hands on her knees. Her body was stiff from squatting in the awkward position.

"Gainesville?" *This is Franklin's jurisdiction, isn't it?*

"They're better equipped for this kind of case, Chance. I called them on the way over. With you on vacation, I'm not going to have the manpower to take on a murder case. Besides, the body is on their side of the river."

Penelope was a little hurt that Jackson had called them, but the chief was right. Even though they were in the middle of nowhere, in an unincorporated part of the county, the Franklin River was the imaginary line that separated the two cities. The east side was Franklin and the west side was Gainesville.

"If Jacob is right, and this is one of the suspects from the robbery, Gainesville would want to work them together," Jackson added, saying it more to himself than to her.

Penelope nodded without answering. Jackson was the boss and she swallowed the lump of rejection that had risen in her throat. Gainesville had more resources than Franklin, but she wanted to help. It was getting personal again. Jacob was directly linked to this now, and she wanted to protect him. And the only way she could do that was by being a part of the team and being aware of what was happening.

The engines shut off, and boots crunched along the trail and through the leaves. Detective Donny Greene was the first to emerge from the trees. Two of Gainesville's finest uniformed officers followed.

Chief Jackson greeted Donny with an outstretched hand. "Detective Greene."

"Good to see you, Chief," Donny said, shaking Jackson's hand.

"Thanks for coming. Sorry to call you out on a Sunday."

"No problem. Crimes don't have office hours." He tipped his head at Penelope and then asked, "What've we got?"

Jackson and Dr. Harris filled Detective Greene in on what they knew so far. Penelope stayed out of it.

After the facts had been relayed, Donny scratched his head and asked, "Any sign of the stolen drugs?"

"He doesn't have anything in his pockets. No wallet, no ID, no pills. Nothing," Jackson said. "To me, it indicates that someone emptied his pockets before they dumped him here. I also think he was killed at another location and brought here. There's a blood trail across the bridge, so I think he did most of his bleeding somewhere else."

Donny looked to the medical examiner. "So the murder took place in a different location?"

"That would be my opinion as well," Dr. Harris confirmed. "The victim had lost a lot of blood, but there's very little blood here at the river. The rest of it has to be somewhere else."

"The stream couldn't have washed it away?"

Harris shook her head and pointed at the body. "The torso wasn't in the water. Only the lower half of the body."

"What about rain? It rained Friday night," Penelope offered.

"That's a possibility, but I still think your primary crime scene is elsewhere."

"Any sign of the murder weapon?" Donny asked.

"Not that we've been able to find," Penelope said.

Donny nodded at Harris and thanked her and Jackson for what they'd done so far. He turned to one of his men who looked like a rookie. The young-looking cop stood frozen behind Greene clutching a roll of bright yellow caution tape. Poor kid had probably never seen a body before.

"Officer Meeks, go relieve officers DeBose and Peterson, and keep the scene secure." Officer Meeks didn't move. The detective snapped his fingers in front of the officer's face. "Caleb, secure the scene."

Officer Caleb Meeks snapped out of it. "Yes, sir." He adjusted his glasses on his nose and sprang up the hill, apparently elated to be away from the corpse.

Donny spoke for a moment longer with Dr. Harris and then started up the slope. He paused and turned to Penelope. "Chance. Walk with me?"

"Sure." Penelope motioned to Jacob and Jackson. "I'll be right back."

Jackson nodded, and Penelope followed Donny up the hill.

"I have the doc's belongings in my car," Donny said.

"That was quick. Any prints?"

"Only the doc's. The guys at the lab said the watch and cell phone were both clean."

As they crossed the wooden bridge and walked back to the trailhead, Penelope's mind raced. Was the victim murdered for the stolen drugs? Was that why the drugs were missing from the crime scene?

"Got any theories?"

"I don't want to speculate too much. It does appear that the cases are related. I'll be coordinating with Ballard, and we'll have to see where the evidence leads. However, I'm still not sure how Jacob's belongings being returned factors into this. I mean I get the robbery and the murder being related. Could be a drug deal gone wrong. But who returned Jacob's belongings and why?"

"I was wondering the same thing. I'm a little concerned for Jacob's safety. If our vic was the one that returned Jacob's stuff, the killer might come after Jacob."

"I don't think it's anything like that. Besides, they have no reason to go after the doc."

Detective Greene retrieved a paper bag from his trunk

at the trailhead parking lot and handed it to Penelope. "Look Chance . . . I know this case is personal."

"More so now that this murder might be related."

"Look, I'll let you know the moment something happens, but for now, we need to focus on finding a killer." Donny put his hand on her shoulder. "We're doing what we can, but these things take time. You know how the system works. We'll get to the bottom of this, and when we do, you'll be one of the first to know, okay?"

Penelope nodded. No matter what her argument was, Donny was right. As much as she didn't want to sit back and watch, she trusted Donny. She always had. They had to follow procedures.

She let out a shaky breath and walked with Donny back to the crime scene.

Penelope looked back down toward the river. The M.E. was putting the body in a body bag for transport to the morgue. Jacob stood off to the side, looking lost.

The investigation no longer mattered. Penelope knew what she had to do—take care of Jacob. She made her way down to him and took his hand. Her touch seemed to jerk him out of a different world and back into hers.

"Are you alright?" she asked.

He looked at the body as they zipped it up. "I was thinking how close it came to being me inside that bag."

His voice was hoarse and for the first time since the robbery, it looked like it was getting to him.

"You're safe now. That's all that matters." She put a hand on his cheek and turned his face toward hers. "I can't tell you how grateful I am that you're safe and we still have our future together."

Jacob nodded. "I'm going to go back to the car," he said, walking away as if he were on autopilot.

Chief Jackson stepped next to Penelope and spoke without looking at her. "I want you to take that man of yours home and stay away from this case. He needs you more than we do."

She opened her mouth to say something, but Jackson spoke before she could.

"Go home," he said. "Take care of yourself. We'll be fine without you. We need you healthy and well after your vacation more than we need you on duty twenty-four seven."

The chief wasn't often this blunt and she didn't know how to respond.

She turned and walked back to Jacob's car, trying to shut off her brain . . . but she couldn't do it.

CHAPTER 33

THE LITTLE SLEEP PENELOPE got Sunday night was full of disturbing dreams.

She couldn't stop thinking about the events of the past couple of days. The robbery and homicide had to be related. Coincidences were a novelty. Usually, if something looked related, it was.

Penelope sat up in bed as dawn finally flooded her bedroom with golden light. The dark tendrils of the night slowly slipped away.

Still in her pajamas, and too exhausted to prepare breakfast, she poured herself a cup of coffee and reviewed her duties for the day. Later that afternoon she'd have time to take care of the house for a change, do some laundry and send her uniform in for professional dry-cleaning. Her uniform got a break about as often as she did—which was seldom. First order of business for the day was her eight o'clock meeting with Gabriel.

Her cell phone rang, and she half expected it to be Gabriel calling to get an early start on their unofficial investigation. Jacob's ID flashed on the screen and Penelope smiled.

"Morning, Officer Beautiful," he said when she answered. He almost sounded like his old self again.

"How are you feeling?" she asked.

"Better," he said, upbeat and cheerful. There was no trace of the run-down Jacob.

"Are you working today?" She already knew the answer.

"Yes. I'm in Gainesville, but I have a light morning. I was just about to go for my run."

"You're going for a run? Are you sure that's wise?"

Before work Jacob liked to run the Gainesville-Franklin Trail. The scenic route weaved through tall trees, and leaves whispered overhead. It was the kind of place that transported you in time and took you back to nature. Penelope had run with him once or twice, but she wasn't much of a runner.

"I'll take it easy," he said.

"I'm concerned about you running after suffering a concussion."

"Don't forget the part about me getting shot."

"That's not funny, Jacob!"

"I'll be fine. I'm a doctor, remember?"

"Promise me one thing, Dr. Gordon."

"Anything . . ."

"Watch out for gators?"

"I will," he said with a chuckle. "I saw a big one last

week. Don't forget we have our wedding cake tasting appointment this afternoon at Ambrose & Sons."

She did forget. She also forgot she was supposed to take care of some preliminary wedding planning while on vacation. Even though the wedding was still a year away, with their busy schedules, her vacation was probably the only time they'd have to take care of the big stuff.

"I'll see you this afternoon," she said.

"I love you, Penny."

"I love you back." Penelope hung up smiling, ready to start her day.

She took a quick shower, threw on a pair of jeans, a white T-shirt, her black-and-white Converse Chucks, and a gray pullover hoodie. Not being in uniform felt strange, but it was a pleasant change.

She relaxed in the comfort of her civilian clothes.

CHAPTER 34

THE DRIVE TO GAINESVILLE took less than twenty minutes, and Penelope was running early for her eight o'clock meeting with Gabriel.

She stopped at The Coffey Shop, and LeeAnna greeted her with a warm smile. Since the trial, Penelope had become a regular.

LeeAnna's blonde hair was pulled into a bun, and her blue eyes sparkled from a constellation of freckles. "I almost didn't recognize you out of uniform, Penelope."

"You and me both," Penelope said, feeling a little untethered.

"Regular today?"

"Let's change it up." Penelope scanned the chalkboard menu against the back wall. "Make it a large vanilla latte."

"You got it."

"Speaking of uniforms, is Travis on patrol today?"

Penelope asked over the *whoosh* of the milk steamer.

"He is. Crime never stops."

"Don't I know it," Penelope said as her cell phone chimed in her purse. She excused herself and checked the message.

It was from Gabriel. **Sorry, last minute appointment. Can we meet at 9 instead?**

Penelope replied, **sure**, and slid the phone back into her purse. "LeeAnna, may I also get a large regular coffee and one of your homemade brownies?"

With an hour to kill, she'd swing by and see Donny for an update. He had a sweet tooth, and a little bribe would be better than showing up empty-handed.

CHAPTER 35

PENELOPE'S MIND WAS BUZZING when she got to the Gainesville Criminal Investigations Division building. The desk sergeant, Catherine McPhie, recognized her and gave her a nod and a smile.

"Is Detective Greene in?" Penelope asked, returning the smile.

"I'll give him a buzz."

A moment later Donny appeared in the lobby.

"I come bearing gifts," Penelope said, offering him the coffee and brownie.

"Something tells me you're not here just to drop in and say hello."

He'd seen right through her attempt to soften him up.

"How are things?" she asked, attempting to make small talk.

"I thought you were on vacation," Donny said, taking a

bite of the brownie and a sip of the coffee.

"I am. Can't you tell? Anything new in either case?"

Donny took another sip of coffee and let out a sigh. "You're not going to let this go, are you?"

Penelope stood silent.

"I didn't think so," Donny continued. "Well, with the robbery, there's still no sign of the drugs on the street. Ballard has a couple of uniforms checking the pawn shop merchandise registration database in case the perps . . . or I should say perp, tries to pawn the stolen goods. Nothing so far."

"Tell me you've got some good news."

Donny smiled for the first time. "I thought you might be coming by today. We got an ID on our vic," Donny took another bite of his brownie and handed Penelope a sheet of paper. "His name is Kevin Scott. Age twenty-eight. No felonies. A couple of juvie busts for shoplifting. That's his file."

"No B and E? Nothing more recent?" she asked, scanning the page.

"Nope. Nothing. He either cleaned up his act, or we just didn't catch him."

"Based on the recent string of robberies, I'd say it's the latter."

"We're running a full background for next of kin and any known associates. I'll keep you posted."

"Thanks, Donny."

Donny paused and then asked, "Is the doc working today?"

"He is."

"At Grace Memorial?"

"Yeah. Why?"

"I wanted to ask him a couple of follow-up questions on our vic. Standard stuff . . ." His sentence trailed off as if he weren't being entirely honest. "I'll let you know if anything new pops up." Donny nodded to someone over Penelope's shoulder and said, "Look, I have to go. Thanks for the brownie and coffee."

Penelope nodded, and Donny rushed off.

Was she missing something?

CHAPTER 36

PENELOPE PARKED HER CAR in one of the empty spots in front of Grace Memorial Hospital and sent Gabriel a text. **In the parking lot.**

As she waited for a reply, she glanced around the lot, looking for Jacob's car. He drove a yellow 1965 convertible Mustang—impossible to miss. There was no sign of his car. He was probably still on his run.

Her cell phone chimed, and she read the message from Gabriel. **Suite 406. Come on up.**

The hospital was bustling with activity and Gabriel was on the phone when she poked her head into the small reception area. He waved her in.

"Yes. That's fine. Yes. Good-bye." Penelope had forgotten how gruff the professor was on the phone, another one of his quirks. He stood and pulled on a blue windbreaker. "Ready to go?"

"Ready," she said. "There have been quite a few developments, but I'll only be able to do half-day with you. I'm meeting Jacob this afternoon."

Gabriel had a twinkle in his eye. He looked eager. "That's fine. That gives us plenty of time. Let's get started."

He held the door for Penelope. She stepped out of the office, and he followed.

As they walked down the stairs to the lobby, Gabriel said, "I've been thinking about your fiancé's belongings being returned, and I think we should—"

"A body was found at the Franklin River yesterday," Penelope interrupted.

"A body? Really? Related to the robbery?"

"Yes. Jacob identified the body as one of the suspects."

"Hmm. That is an interesting development."

Penelope nodded. "The victim was shot somewhere else and dumped. Gainesville is handling the investigation," Penelope said, trying to sound more neutral about it than she felt.

Gabriel frowned.

"I met with Detective Donny Greene earlier," she continued. "He's the lead detective on the homicide case."

"So they haven't ID'd the victim yet?"

"They did." Penelope handed Gabriel the rap sheet printout that Donny had given her. "Low-level criminal named Kevin Scott."

Gabriel paused at the first-floor landing. "This changes our *unofficial* investigation slightly. You want to show me the dump site?"

"Sure. I hope you've brought hiking shoes."

Gabriel was known for wearing the same ratty pair of tennis shoes every day at college. During the trial, he had forgone his usual footwear and wore fancy shoes. Since then, he had returned to his grubby sneakers.

"We'll take my car," Gabriel said as they exited the stairwell and entered the hospital lobby.

It wasn't a question.

Penelope followed him into the parking lot.

"Well, that is—something." Penelope didn't know what else to say. She hoped her jaw hadn't dropped.

Gabriel's car was a giant, beige Hummer H2 with dark tinted windows, a monstrosity of a truck. It struck her as funny that the stuffy academic with the dirty tennis shoes and the windbreaker from a thrift store, drove this vehicle. The only thing that would make this more ludicrous would be fuzzy dice hanging from the mirror and plush velvet seats.

There were neither.

CHAPTER 37

AS THEY DROVE TO Franklin, with Gabriel's eyes on the road and Penelope's on the passing landscape, they discussed what had happened so far. Talking to someone and putting events into words helped Penelope to sort things out. She was grateful for Gabriel's presence and the fact that she could trust him with this information and he wouldn't scold her for her involvement.

"The robbery occurred early Friday afternoon," Penelope said, starting with the first event. "Drugs and valuables were stolen. Detective Edward Ballard is working with the county's drug task force, but there's no trace of the drugs on the street yet."

"Any of the other victims have their belongings returned?"

"I hadn't thought of that. I'll check with Donny." Penelope sent Donny a quick text message and then continued. "On Saturday morning, Jacob's valuables were returned to the Franklin Clinic, but the picture and fortune cookie fortune he kept in his wallet were missing. Then on Sunday one of the perps turns up dead."

Gabriel tapped his thumbs on the steering wheel. "Hmm. Did the M.E. give a preliminary time of death?"

"Sometime late Friday night to early Saturday morning."

"So approximately eight to twelve hours *after* the robbery occurred? That's a pretty wide timeline," Gabriel said. "I wonder if the partner killed him or if it was a drug deal gone wrong? But that still doesn't explain why your fiancé's belongings were returned. And why dump the body in Franklin?"

Penelope nodded, but she didn't have any answers. So much didn't add up yet.

Fifteen minutes later, Gabriel parked close to the Franklin River trailhead. Everything was quiet and deserted now compared to the bustle when the officers surrounded the crime scene the day before. The crime scene tape was gone, but Penelope was still nervous. She wasn't there on official police business.

The river burbled softly and looked much the same as it had the morning before, minus the dead body. It was a brisk morning by Florida standards with the temperature hovering around fifty-nine degrees. The thought of the murderer disposing of the body gave her another kind of shiver, and the little forest became sinister to her. Aside from the faint murmur of the river, there were no sounds. No birds, no cars on the road . . . nothing. There was nothing obvious to further her understanding of the case. But Gabriel often saw things that other people overlooked.

Penelope watched Gabriel as he quickly and carefully made a pass through the east side of the river. Even though she knew he was good at what he did, it was still impressive to see him work. He pointed to a steeper part of the west bank. "That's where the body was dumped," he said bluntly.

"That's right," she said.

They started to cross the wooden bridge to the west side, where the body was discovered, and Gabriel paused to inspect the blood trail.

He looked up at Penelope. "The killer dragged the body across the bridge."

"How can you tell?"

"See these scuff marks in the wood?"

Penelope pulled out her cell phone and snapped a couple of pictures of the area where Gabriel was pointing. "I don't see anything."

"Come closer," he said, and she bent down beside him. "See how every couple of boards has a scuff in the wood?"

He was right. They were faint, but they were there. How did he notice that?

She took a few more pictures. "I don't know if the forensic unit caught this yesterday."

"I'm sure they did. They're trained to spot stuff like this."

"So the killer dragged the body out here?" Penelope said, thinking out loud as they continued across the bridge. "But I didn't see any other footprints or drag marks. Not in the dirt . . . nowhere."

Gabriel picked up a leafy branch and pretended to swipe it across the dirt. "They covered their tracks. Look here," he said.

The area seemed disturbed—as though someone had dragged a branch across it.

"So the killer knew what he was doing."

"She . . ."

"Huh?"

"She," Gabriel said. "I think you're looking for a woman."

"What makes you say that?"

"The body was dumped down there," he said, pointing to a spot at the bottom of the embankment. "Isn't that right?"

"That's correct."

"And when the forensics technicians and the medical examiner accessed the body, they walked down to the water over there." This time Gabriel pointed to an area a few yards away that looked heavily trafficked.

"Right. So no one disturbed the area where the body was rolled into the river."

"And no one walked in this area near the embankment? Not you, not forensics, not the M.E.?"

"No one. This section was all taped off."

Gabriel rubbed his chin with his thumb and forefinger. "I suppose someone could have walked by since then, but tell me, what do you see?"

Penelope watched as Gabriel stepped closer and

pointed to a spot in the clay-like mud. "Mud and leaves?" she answered.

He cleared away a few leaves. "Now what do you see?"

"Whoa! A heel print."

Gabriel had revealed what looked like the imprint of a wedge heel from a woman's shoe. Penelope took several pictures of the print. She held her foot as close to the print as she could without touching it. The print appeared to be a size or two larger than her own size eight. She took another photo for comparison.

"She leaned her body here on the bank and either rested or used it to brace herself or gain leverage." Gabriel pantomimed the motion he described.

"And her heel dug into the side of the embankment when she did."

"That's right." Gabriel stood and dusted himself off.

Penelope marveled at the way he spent moments at the scene and discovered details that may have eluded several trained forensics experts after hours of investigation.

"Did they find the murder weapon?"

"They did not."

They continued to look around a bit longer, fanning out in a circle to see if they could find anything else that might have been missed. Penelope kept an eye on Gabriel, who worked systematically. Maybe his hawk eye would spot something else.

"You know, Penelope," Gabriel said looking off into the distance. "With this Kevin Scott guy turning up dead, I've been thinking."

"About what?" Penelope prompted.

"I think we should consider the possibility that the person that killed Kevin Scott and the person that returned your fiancé's belongings could be the same person. Maybe even someone your fiancé knows."

"I was thinking the same thing yesterday. But I don't know, Professor. Someone Jacob knows? A murderer? It seems a little farfetched."

"It could explain why they didn't return his belongings openly . . ."

"Because they murdered the person that stole them?"

"Right. Otherwise, they would have taken the credit for finding them. It could also explain why the body was dumped in Franklin."

"Why is that?"

"Because they knew your fiancé would hear about it, isn't that right?"

Penelope looked at Gabriel. "I don't know . . ."

"I know it sounds crazy and a little scary," Gabriel said in a calm voice, "someone your fiancé knows being a murderer. But if I'm right, we're probably looking for someone with a troubled mind."

"Well, I agree with you there. We're definitely looking for someone, possibly a woman, with a troubled mind."

Penelope looked around. Everything was quiet; only the sound of the wind in the leaves was audible. Could Gabriel be right? Could someone Jacob knew be a murderer?

Gabriel gestured with his head toward his truck, an invitation to head back. Penelope followed without a word. She kept her eyes on the ground, lost in thought, when a tire track caught her eye. A tire track she hadn't noticed before, and it ran close to the dump site.

"Hey, look at this," she said. "This is a track that hasn't been documented."

Gabriel squatted to look at it more carefully. "Are you sure? Could be from a service vehicle," he offered. "This is a service road, and there were quite a few cars here yesterday, weren't there?"

"I didn't see any of the cars come down this way," she said. "Everyone parked at the trailhead. Even the M.E."

She was sure they hadn't used the service road in any part of the crime scene investigation. And the track was in the mud. Friday had been the first time it had rained that year, and it hadn't rained since.

"Well, get a picture of it," Gabriel said. "You never know."

Penelope nodded and took a photo of the tire track. She would get it to Donny, along with the rest of the photos, and let him know what she found.

When they got back to the SUV, Gabriel asked, "What time do you want to meet tomorrow?"

"I'm going to stop at the Franklin Clinic and see Jacob tomorrow. We'll have to play it by ear. Is that okay?"

"Sure. Do you have time to make one more stop?"

Penelope glanced at the time on her phone. It was eleven forty-five.

"Sure," she said. "What are you thinking?"

Gabriel pointed down the road. "Do you know if they questioned anyone at the Last Chance Tavern?"

"I'm not sure."

"I say we head over there. See if the victim was a regular or if anyone saw anything. Do you still have that printout?"

"I do, but let me call Officer Sanders and have him pull a recent DMV photo."

CHAPTER 38

THE LAST CHANCE TAVERN was the only establishment within three miles in either direction from the Franklin River trailhead, and it made sense to check there next. Maybe someone had seen something that night.

They drove the short distance instead of walking, and parked in a space in front of the one-story cinderblock structure. The words Last Chance were written in red neon script across the front face of the uninviting beige building. That was new.

Penelope's phone chimed as she slid out of Gabriel's SUV.

Saunders had come through with Kevin Scott's DMV photo. She showed the photo to Gabriel and motioned for him to follow her into the bar. A handwritten sign on the front door indicated that the establishment was open from 10:00 a.m. until 2:00 a.m.

Penelope opened the door, and the smell of cigarette smoke and stale beer assaulted her nose. The dimly lit watering hole was built in the early 1950s to cater to the farmers of the citrus boom that never arrived. It hadn't changed much over the decades and it was one of the few bars in Florida that still allowed smoking. It was paneled with dark wood that had a musky smell. A lone pool table stood in the middle of the rectangle-shaped room, with a dartboard against the far wall, and a forgotten jukebox. The more modern upgrades were a pair of thirty-two-inch flat panel TVs that hung at either end of the bar. A handful of customers—regulars that had made The Last Chance their second home—sat at the bar, while Terry O'Brien, the owner, stood behind the bar polishing glasses.

Penelope gave Terry a nod, and he sauntered over to the end of the bar, dishcloth over his shoulder.

"Well, good afternoon, Officer," he said, leaning against the bar on one elbow. "Almost didn't recognize you without your uniform. Special occasion?"

Penelope shook her head. "We just want to ask you a couple of questions about the body found in Franklin River. Do you know this man?" She held up her phone with Kevin's DMV photo. "His name is Kevin Scott."

Terry looked at the photo with a blank expression, then at Penelope, and finally at Gabriel. "Who's your boyfriend?"

"He's not my boyfriend. He's a consultant. He's assisting on the case."

Gabriel held out his hand. "Dr. Gabriel Pike . . ."

Terry looked at his hand but didn't take it. Instead, he

raised his eyebrows and nodded at Penelope. "A doc, huh? You like them doctor types, don't you?"

Penelope took a deep breath. Terry was trying to get under her skin. She'd had the pleasure before. "Just answer the question, Terry. Do you know this man?"

Terry shrugged. "Why do you need a doc consulting? I hear the guy is already dead."

Penelope fought the urge to roll her eyes. Calm. She would stay calm, and patient. Maybe a different approach would work. "So you knew the deceased?"

"Now, I didn't say that," Terry said, finally getting off the elbow he was leaning on and shifting his weight to his other leg.

"Well, what are you saying, Terry? Because you haven't given me a straight answer yet. Perhaps you'd be more comfortable in a formal setting?"

Terry looked back at his customers, seeing if anyone needed a top off. When he was satisfied that they were taken care of, he turned back to Penelope. "Yeah, alright. I don't know the guy, never seen him before."

"Not even as a customer?"

Terry shook his head. "This isn't exactly the kind of place the younger crowd comes to, you know? We're more of a . . . mature joint. But I don't see why I have to answer all your questions again."

"Again?"

"Yeah. Two of your cop friends were here yesterday afternoon, asking me the same questions. Only the guy didn't look that good in the picture they showed me."

Penelope glanced at Gabriel.

"Don't you guys talk to one another?" Terry asked, shaking his head. "Some police work."

Terry knew how to rub Penelope the wrong way. "Why didn't you say so in the beginning and save us both some time?"

"Now, what fun would that be?" he said with a laugh.

Penelope rolled her eyes. "Thanks, Terry. You don't mind if we ask your patrons a few questions, do you?"

"Knock yourselves out."

Penelope and Gabriel approached each customer individually, making small talk before they got into the serious questions. In a town like Franklin, almost everyone knew each other, and it was polite to ask about their lives before getting down to business.

After almost twenty minutes, they hadn't learned anything new. Somehow she'd hoped something new would come up.

"Don't worry, Penelope, we'll get to the bottom of this," Gabriel said once they were back in his SUV. "This is the first piece of the puzzle. The picture will become clearer in time."

Penelope nodded and turned her head toward the window, trying to make sense of all the loose ends as they drove back to Gainesville.

CHAPTER 39

AFTER GABRIEL DROPPED PENELOPE off at Grace Memorial Hospital, she drove back to Franklin to meet Jacob for their wedding cake tasting appointment at Ambrose & Sons Bakery. With the convertible top down on her MGB, she tried to shut off the cop part of her brain so she could focus her full attention on her fiancé.

Five minutes early, she found a parking spot right in front of the building. She waved to Jacob as he waited by the double doors that led to the bakery.

The almond-colored, two-story building was multipurpose with a shop front downstairs and an upstairs apartment with two large bay windows that looked like they belonged on a Brooklyn brownstone. The bakery sat just feet from the curb on the busy street and was wedged between F.D. Minucciani Insurance and the Franklin Travel Agency.

As Penelope exited her car, Donny's number came up on her cell phone. She looked at Jacob and held up a finger to signal, "One moment."

"Hey, Donny, what's up?" she asked.

"Chance, I got a couple of updates for you."

"Good news, I hope."

"I think so. First, I got your text. I called the other victims Saturday after you dropped off the doc's belongings, but none of their stuff had been returned."

So only Jacob's stuff was returned. "It was worth a shot."

"I was thinking the same thing."

"What else you got for me?" Penelope asked, urging Donny to continue as she watched Jacob's strained expression.

"We found out Kevin Scott worked at the Chevron station off of East University. The owner said Mr. Scott worked there for a little over a year and never had any trouble. Said he had a girlfriend . . ." Penelope heard Donny shuffle through his notes. "A Denise Wilson. She was his emergency contact. We're trying to locate Ms. Wilson."

"That's great news, Donny. Maybe she can offer some insight into his behavior. Thanks for the update."

"There's more."

"More?" she asked as she turned slightly away from Jacob, not wanting to feel the heat of his glare.

"Yeah. We have the last known . . . an apartment complex off of South East 24th Street. I got a warrant, and I'm headed there now with a couple of officers. You want to meet us there?"

Penelope turned to look at Jacob waiting as patiently as

he could by the front door. She wanted to meet Donny, but Jacob would kill her if she canceled. "I'd love to, but I have a cake tasting with Jacob."

"You have what?"

"Cake tasting."

"Is that like some fancy brunch thing?"

"Wedding cake tasting."

"That really is a thing?"

"Yes, it's a thing, Donny."

"So, let me get this straight," said Donny. "You can actually eat the cake before the wedding to be sure it is exactly the right one?"

"Yes, Donny," she said, holding back her exasperation. "Did the background check turn up anything else?" she asked, determined to change the subject.

"Just his last known residence. We can't find any next of kin on this guy. Both his parents died years ago. There's no siblings, no nothing."

"I appreciate the call, Donny. Keep me updated?"

"I have you on speed dial."

Penelope chuckled. If police officers could maintain a sense of humor, even when they saw the gruesome side of life, there was still hope.

CHAPTER 40

"Everything okay?" Jacob asked as Penelope walked over to greet him.

Still dressed in his work slacks and blue dress shirt, Jacob appeared to be getting his energy back. The light had returned to his chestnut colored eyes, and a small white gauze bandage taped over his wound replaced the one that had been wrapped around his head. Despite everything that had happened, Jacob still managed to look like a soap opera star with his broad shoulders, wide smile, and chiseled jaw.

"Everything is perfect," she said, standing on her tiptoes and giving him a kiss on the cheek. "Just Donny being his usual annoying self."

"I saw him a few hours ago . . ."

"At the hospital?" she asked.

"Yeah. He stopped by to ask me a few follow-up

questions about the victim."

"Anything else?"

"Nope. That was it."

Jacob held the door, and Penelope stepped past him, feeling calmer and more relaxed already. The smell of fresh baked pastries hung in the air and filled her senses as she walked over to the counter with Jacob. She took a deep breath and inhaled the delicious aroma of Belgian chocolate, butterscotch, and cinnamon.

Ambrose & Sons Bakery was the oldest family-owned bakery in Franklin. The current baker and owner, William Ambrose, was the grandson of Lawrence Ambrose, who founded the bakery in 1909. With recipes passed down through generations, the bakery retained its strong Italian identity, offering everything from bread, to cookies, to cakes for all occasions. If you were getting married, Ambrose & Sons was the place you went for a cake.

Amanda, William's oldest daughter, recognized Penelope and Jacob and motioned for them to take a seat. Penelope let her eyes wander a moment longer on the overstuffed cannolis and homemade cheesecakes before she turned and followed Jacob.

The bakery was warm and cozy, and they sat at a table close to the window. The view of the street wasn't particularly good, but she had Jacob to stare at, so the view was perfect. The white bandage on his forehead stood out in sharp contrast to his brown hair, but his eyes were twinkling, and he was ready with a smile every time her eyes met his.

"This is nice," she said. "We need to do this more often."

"What? Cake tasting?" he teased.

Penelope chuckled and put her hand on his. He inter-linked his fingers with hers.

"I mean spending time together in the middle of the afternoon, silly."

They'd been together for six years, and Penelope still felt butterflies like the first day they met.

"I know," he said, and then flashed a warm smile.

It was contagious.

"How was your run this morning?" she asked.

He groaned. "Not my best idea. I didn't even get halfway before I started feeling light-headed and walked back to my car. I sat there for a while, watching the other runners, feeling like a complete newbie."

"Even superheroes deserve a break."

"Look who's talking," Jacob said with a grin.

Penelope smiled back.

"So, what are your plans for the rest of the week?" Jacob asked.

Well, let's see, I've got a pretty busy week. First, I'm going to find out who robbed Grace Memorial, who shot you, and who returned your belongings. Then I'm going to find out who killed Kevin Scott and why they dumped his body at the Franklin River.

"Penny? Are you still with me?"

"Oh yes. Sorry . . ." She wanted to tell him everything she was thinking of doing, but he'd probably be angry with her for getting more involved than she already was, so she told him what she'd most likely be doing instead. "I'm going to take some time for planning the wedding. Look into florists, catering, photographers, videographers, DJs, accommodations for guests, rehearsal dinner locations. Oh, don't forget we have a meeting with a potential wedding planner in Gainesville on Friday." She paused and glanced up to see if he remembered. He nodded, sure of himself. He hadn't forgotten. She was the one who forgot things when work got in the way. "I'm also looking into reception locations Thursday."

"That sounds like a great vacation."

Apparently, Jacob didn't know much about planning a wedding if he thought it was like a vacation.

CHAPTER 41

WILLIAM AMBROSE WALKED OVER to Penelope and Jacob's table, carrying a large silver platter that held a dozen tiny squares of various cakes for them to taste. He wore black-and-white houndstooth pants and a white chef's coat with Willie embroidered in red above the left breast pocket.

For a man who had spent his entire life surrounded by sweets, Willie was surprisingly thin. His face was creased with laugh lines, and both his dexterous hands, and his gray hair never seemed to stay in one place for long.

"So, I hope you're hungry," he joked as he sat down at the table. "These are some of my finest creations. First, we have the red velvet, white truffle cake."

Penelope and Jacob looked at each other as Willie jumped right into explaining each concoction on the platter. Penelope's stomach let out a rumble and her mouth began to water.

When Willie finished explaining, he looked at Penelope and smiled. "This one is my favorite," he said. "In fact, it's the same cake that I made for your parents on their wedding day." He glanced out the window and continued, "I guess would be about thirty-five or thirty-six years ago. It was one of the first ones I did with my dad, and it has been my favorite ever since."

Penelope looked at Willie. "You did Gerald and Irene's cake?" she asked, referring to Doug's parent. Not everyone knew that Doug's parents, Penelope's godparents, adopted her when her mother and father died.

Willie smiled softly. "No, your real parents, sweetie."

A wave of sadness washed over Penelope.

"As a matter of fact, hang on just a second." Willie set the tray on the table and motioned for Penelope and Jacob to start eating. He got up, disappeared into the back of the bakery and returned a moment later. His hands tightly gripped a photo.

"See," he said, showing them the old black-and-white photo. "Here's the one of me making the cake with my dad." Willie sat down and looked at the picture with nostalgia. "Oh, wait, of course!" He jumped up again and ran to the wall and grabbed a framed photo. "Here, here's the finished cake." He held the framed picture out for Jacob and Penelope to see. "This is after we finished it, on the table at their wedding."

Penelope leaned in afraid to breathe too hard for fear of damaging the picture. The cake stood center stage, a seven-tier masterpiece of white buttercream garlands and latticework sitting atop royal fondant.

"We used star and C-scrolls," Willie continued, "It was my dad's way of teaching me over piping, something we do to give each layer depth. And these bands . . ." he said, pointing to several of the delicate decorations on the cake, "these were inspired by the lace of your mom's bridal gown."

Penelope searched the picture feverishly hoping to catch a glimpse of her mother or father in the background, but she couldn't. Instead, her eyes rested on the confectionary bands and she delved into her memory, trying to recall the wedding pictures her parents had hung in the front hall of their home before they died in the flames that destroyed every photo on that terrible night.

"It's beautiful," Jacob said. "I think we've found the perfect cake. Willie, could you create one just like it for our wedding?"

"Of course! Splendid idea."

"What do you think, Penny?" Jacob asked.

Penelope let one tear slide down her cheek, and she nodded to Jacob. Then, she turned her face to Willie. "May I get a copy of that photo?"

Her parents weren't in the picture, but it was the closest reminder she had. This picture was taken at their wedding. This was the cake that they ate. She needed something of them, and if this was all she could get, she would take it.

"You can have that one, my dear," he said, and left them alone to sample the cakes.

Penelope looked at Jacob across the table and smiled. Soon this was what life would be like. They would be married and share moments like this one. It was a little thing, but sometimes the small things were the most powerful.

They'd almost finished the tasting when Jacob's cell phone rang. He looked up at her apologetically. She nodded knowing that he needed to answer, and that such responsibilities would be a part of their life together, as well. She would have to share him with the people who depended on him.

"Dr. Gordon," he answered curtly. He was all business now, and Penelope watched in awe at the change in his demeanor from loving fiancé to the no-nonsense doctor. "Really? Yes, I'll be there soon." Jacob's eyes focused on nothing as he listened. "No, no. I'm all right. I'll see you shortly." He ended the call without saying good-bye. "That was the hospital—"

"Go," she said. "I've got this."

He rose and gave Penelope a kiss on the cheek. "I love you, Penny."

"I love you back, Jacob."

Jacob thanked Willie on his way out and turned to wave to Penelope as he walked to his car. She returned the wave with a smile.

CHAPTER 42

First thing Tuesday morning, Penelope stopped at the Franklin Clinic to check on Jacob. When she arrived at eight thirty she spotted two Gainesville police cruisers in the parking lot.

What's GPD doing here?

She parked her car and ran into the clinic. Nurse Taylor's expressionless face greeted her in the reception area.

"Morning, Genny," she said in a rush. "What's Gainesville PD doing here? Is everything okay?"

"I told him not to hire her," Taylor said, shaking her head slowly.

"Who? Not to hire who?"

"Belinda. I knew it was a mistake to hire her."

More confused than ever, Penelope asked again, but got the same answer. She tried a different approach, hoping for a more definitive answer. "Where is everyone?"

Taylor gave her head a sharp nod to the left.

Penelope flashed a tight-lipped smile and then hurried into the administrative area of the clinic. She walked past a uniformed officer standing by the receptionist's desk; another officer milled about the hallway just past the double swinging doors. Neither officer tried to stop her.

What's going on here?

Had the Clinic been broken into?

Please, God, let Jacob be okay.

Penelope walked to the end of the hall, and to her right she saw Jacob sitting at his desk. Detective Donny Greene stood next to him with two uniformed officers. She recognized Officer Caleb Meeks from the Franklin River crime scene. He looked a much better shade than he had the day they found Kevin Scott's body. The older, female officer, she hadn't met. Her silver nameplate identified her as *G. Watson.*

When Donny noticed Penelope, he ushered Meeks and Watson out of Jacob's office and motioned for her to come in.

"Donny, what is going on? What are you doing here?" she asked in a clipped tone.

Jacob looked up at Penelope and raised his eyebrows. Two butterfly bandages had replaced the large white bandage on his head. The reminder of how close he had come to death was as strong as ever. Even though she was concerned about the news she might hear, she was grateful to see that Jacob was okay.

Donny flashed Penelope a smile. "Hey, Chance. We caught a break in the case."

Penelope looked at Donny with hard eyes. "What type of break? How come you didn't call me? You promised to keep me in the loop."

Donny raised his hands as if to calm her, but she was having none of it. "Okay, listen, we didn't have much until last night." He saw her eyes grow wide, and he continued before she could say anything. "*We*, meaning the Gainesville PD," he said, reminding her of jurisdiction. "We located the vic's car yesterday at the apartment complex. There was a lot of blood in the stall opposite his car. We think he was shot during a drug exchange. Forensics is going through the car now."

"So you've located and processed the primary crime scene?"

"Yep. Finished up late last night."

"That's great, but what does that have to do with Jacob and the clinic?"

"After we located the vic's car, we searched his apartment. There was no sign of the drugs, but we did find a few dozen blank prescription pads."

Penelope looked at Jacob.

"They were from the clinic," he said. "And they had my name on them, but they were old."

"Old?" Penelope asked.

"Yes. As I was explaining to Don, we switched to tamper-resistant pads a couple of years back—a Medicaid mandate."

"The pads we found were plain white pads," Donny said. "I couldn't tell you last night because of your relationship with the people here at the clinic."

Penelope let out a sharp breath. "I understand what you're saying, Donny. But you're way off base here. No one at the clinic's involved. Not in this. They're probably counterfeits."

"Maybe. But this is exactly why I didn't call. I knew how you'd react."

Heat rose in Penelope's skin. He was right. She was anything but objective when it came to the people at the clinic, especially Jacob. "Go on," she said.

"So, I showed up here at seven o'clock this morning to see if I could get some more information and I ran into Nurse Taylor. I told her about the prescription pads we found at the vic's apartment, and asked her if she knew where the prescription pads were kept and who had access to them, and if any were reported stolen."

Penelope nodded and Donny continued. "The doc arrived around 7:20. He showed me where everything is kept. That's when he noticed that one of his prescription pads was missing."

"The pads are sequentially numbered, similar to how banks number checks," Jacob explained. "I keep them in order and that's how I knew a pad was missing."

"I asked if he could have left one in an exam room or lying out somewhere," Donny said.

"I keep them locked up or in my pocket."

"So together we did a quick search of the clinic and questioned the staff."

"And?" Penelope prompted.

"And," Donny said. "When we got to Belinda's desk, we found several bottles of the same drugs that were stolen during Friday's robbery."

Belinda? How could she be involved in something like this?

"You were looking for the missing prescription pad and found drugs? In Belinda's desk?" Penelope asked.

"That's right," Donny said.

Penelope looked at Jacob and saw the same disbelief on his face. "There's got to be some sort of mistake," Penelope said, voicing her opinion out loud. "Belinda can't be involved."

Donny rolled his eyes slightly. "We have enough to conduct an interrogation."

Even though she didn't want to believe that someone who worked so closely with Jacob could be involved, she couldn't shake the gnawing words in the back of her mind. The words Gabriel spoke at the Franklin River crime scene: "I think we should consider the possibility that the person that killed Kevin Scott and the person that returned your fiancé's belongings could be the same person. Maybe even someone your fiancé knows."

Could Belinda be that person? Was Belinda a cold-blooded killer?

"What about the missing prescription pad?" Penelope asked.

"It was in my spare lab coat pocket," Jacob said, looking a little guilty and pointing to the coat hanging on the back of his office door.

Donny went on. "The doc told me Belinda started work at eight o'clock, so I radioed for a transport unit. We were just wrapping up when you arrived. I was going to call you on my way back to Gainesville."

Penelope's expression didn't change.

Donny added, "And to see if you want to *observe* the interrogation?"

Jacob's kind eyes pierced Penelope's heart as she looked at him across the room. "I don't think that's a good idea, Penny," he said.

Penelope shifted her weight and looked at Donny. "Where's Belinda now?"

"Officers Watson and Meeks are getting her ready to take in," Donny said as he began to walk out of Jacob's office. "She's been read her rights."

Jacob walked around his desk, joined Penelope, and they followed Donny down the hall.

"Did you find anything else?" Penelope asked.

"Like the murder weapon and a typed confession? No, not yet. But we're gonna keep looking."

They walked into the lobby where the rest of the clinic staff had gathered. Nurse Taylor and two other nurses stood silently, watching as Officer Watson handcuffed Belinda.

"I didn't do this!" Belinda cried out, tears spilling onto her cheeks. "Those are not my drugs! I don't know how they got there."

"Please, Officer," Jacob said, hands outstretched toward Belinda like he physically wanted to help. "No handcuffs. She'll go quietly. Won't you Belinda?"

His eyes were warm and reassuring. He was that way with patients when he did something that would help them but might also hurt them.

Belinda nodded slowly.

"It's okay, Gail." Donny said motioning for Officer Watson to remove the handcuffs.

Belinda dropped her head and followed Meeks, Watson, and the two other officers out of the clinic to a waiting Gainesville police cruiser.

Donny walked out behind them and then turned back. "Chance. You coming?"

CHAPTER 43

TWO HOURS LATER, PENELOPE stood in the observation room behind a two-way mirror. On the other side of the glass, Belinda Crowe sat slumped in a chair at a table in the middle of the interrogation room. She looked as if her life had ended.

This was not the cheerful lady that welcomed everyone to the Franklin Clinic. Her cheeks were pink, her mascara was smudged, and hair was tousled and out of place—presumably from the same jittery hands that were now picking at the remnants of her glossy red fingernail polish.

In the movies, and on TV, interrogation rooms were usually big, well lit and some even had windows. Interrogation Room 2 at the Gainesville Special Operation Division Headquarters was small. The floors were plain concrete, and the cinder block walls were painted an impersonal, institutional green. The room had no windows, and the low ceiling gave the space a cube-like feel. The furniture consisted of two, straight-back metal chairs and a six-by-four-foot metal table anchored to the floor.

Detective Donny Greene entered the interrogation room, and Belinda glanced up, her eyes wide and wild, like a trapped animal.

"Ms. Crowe, you've been read your rights?"

Belinda nodded in small, quick movements. "This is crazy. I didn't kill that man," she said, her voice hoarse from crying.

Donny placed a manila folder and a notepad on the metal table and took a seat across from Belinda, with his back to Penelope.

"We just want to get to the bottom of this, Ms. Crowe," he said in a reassuring tone.

"This is all a big mistake," she said.

"You have a chance to come clean here. If I were you, I'd take it."

"I didn't do it," she pleaded.

Penelope's cell phone vibrated, and she glanced at the caller ID. It was Gabriel. She let the call go to voice mail and turned her attention back to the interrogation.

"Belinda, tell me about your relationship with Kevin Scott," Donny continued.

Belinda shook her head. "I didn't know him."

Donny didn't argue. Instead, he tapped his fingers on the folder in front of him and looked at Belinda with a blank expression. It was an interrogation technique Penelope knew well. If you kept quiet for long enough, the right answer would come out. People tended to keep filling the silence if they had the chance.

"I don't know Kevin Scott," Belinda finally said, breaking the silence.

Donny remained silent, opened the folder in front of him, and one by one slid a DMV photo, a crime scene photo, and an autopsy photo of the victim, across the table in front of Belinda. She gasped and pushed the photos away.

Donny pushed the DMV photo back and said, "Look carefully, Ms. Crowe."

She paused, "Maybe a patient at the Franklin Clinic? I can't say for sure. Not a regular. I know that."

The door to the interrogation room opened, and Officer Gail Watson stepped in. She handed Donny a couple of sheets of paper and left the room.

Donny scanned the contents and then looked up. "Ms. Crowe, have you ever been a patient at the Gainesville Recovery Center?"

CHAPTER 44

BELINDA CROWE DENIED BEING a patient at the Gainesville Recovery Center and then clarified. "I worked at the Gainesville Recovery Center. I was never a patient."

Donny glanced at the stack of papers in front of him. "During your employment at the Gainesville Recovery Center, you didn't meet Mr. Scott?"

"Mr. Scott? No."

"Well, that's interesting Ms. Crowe, because the center's records indicate that he was a patient the same time you worked there."

"A lot of people were patients the same time I worked there."

"It says here you were a clinical associate for a Dr. Teresa Behrmann."

"That is correct."

"And you assisted Dr. Behrmann . . . monitoring client

and program activities?"

"I did."

"So you got to know Dr. Behrmann's patients pretty well?"

"Most of them, yes."

"Well, Ms. Crowe, Mr. Scott's medical records indicate that he was a patient at the Gainesville Recovery Center and he was in Dr. Behrmann's group therapy class. A class you assisted."

"I don't re—" Belinda stopped, and her eyes went wide as if a distant memory had finally resurfaced. She took another look at Kevin Scott's DMV photo, and her eyes filled with tears.

"Ms. Crowe, I'll ask again. Do you know Kevin Scott?" the detective pressed.

"Yes . . . sort of," Belinda sobbed. "Only he had a beard back then . . . and he didn't have that scar across his eye and eyebrow. He was in Dr. Behrmann's group. I only knew him by his first name. I can't believe it's the same Kevin. I didn't know him very well. I can't believe he's dead."

Donny nodded. "Were you and Mr. Scott partners?"

"Partners? No, that would have been unprofessional."

"I'm not talking about an intimate relationship, Ms. Crowe," Donny interrupted. "When did you last speak with Mr. Scott?"

"Must have been three years ago . . . at the rehab center."

"And no contact since?"

Belinda shook her head. "No."

"Not even as a patient at the Franklin Clinic?"

"No. I don't think so."

"Which is it, Ms. Crowe? No, or you don't think so?"

Penelope watched as Donny switched to bad cop.

"No."

"Were you and Mr. Scott dealing drugs?"

Belinda gripped the edge of the table so hard her knuckles went white. "I said I never saw him again, and I certainly wasn't dealing drugs."

Donny flipped to another page. "You used to work at Grace Memorial Hospital. Is that correct?"

"Yes."

"As a medical receptionist in the clinic?"

"Yes."

"The same clinic that was robbed last Friday?"

"Yes."

"And why were you let go, Ms. Crowe?"

Belinda sat silent.

"Ms. Crowe? Why were you let go?" Donny pressed.

"They did a random drug test, and I tested positive for pain medication. But that was for an ankle injury," she quickly added. "What does this have to—"

"Was that the only reason for your termination?"

Belinda looked flustered. "No."

"Medication also went missing during your shifts. Is that correct?"

"But that wasn't me. I didn't steal those drugs."

"That drug test wasn't random, was it, Ms. Crowe? The hospital tested everyone that worked at the free clinic, but you were the only one that tested positive. Positive for the same medication that went missing."

"That was a—"

"A what, Ms. Crowe?" Donny interrupted. "Another big mistake?" Belinda looked visibly upset, and her eyes welled up again. Donny was not going easy on her. "You had a pretty good operation going there for a while. Until the hospital caught on and you were terminated."

Belinda's eyes shot up and met Donny's. "It wasn't like that."

"Yet, somehow you managed to get a job at the Franklin Clinic."

"Dr. Gordon gave me a job at the Franklin Clinic because he knew I wasn't stealing drugs from the hospital."

Penelope's skin prickled. Was that true? Jacob never mentioned anything about Belinda's past to her or why he gave her the job.

"So Dr. Gordon . . . he's a pretty great guy," Donny continued.

"Yes. He gave me a second chance. He believed in me."

"Is that why you returned his belongings?"

"Someone else returned his belongings. I found them when I got there."

"It's convenient that you were the one that found them, isn't it? And isn't it also convenient how the envelope just happened to get tossed in the trash?"

"It's the truth."

"Here's what I think happened, Ms. Crowe," Donny said leaning forward and resting his elbows on the table. "I think you have a little crush on your boss, Dr. Gordon.

I'm not an expert on this sort of thing, but I understand he's a pretty good-looking guy. A real sweetheart, too. So it was only natural that when you found out your drug dealing friend and his partner shot Dr. Gordon, you got upset. So upset you killed Mr. Scott and dumped his body in the Franklin River."

"That's not true! That's not true at all! None of it . . ."

"What about Mr. Scott's partner? Did you kill him too?"

"I didn't kill anybody. I didn't do this."

"You had last Friday off, Ms. Crowe. Where were you between the hours of twelve o'clock and three o'clock?"

"I was home until two thirty."

"Can anyone confirm that?"

"No."

Penelope took a deep breath as she watched. No alibi for the time of the robbery. This was not looking good for Belinda.

"What about after two thirty? Where were you then?" Donny continued.

"I didn't do this," Belinda sounded more determined. "Look, I know I made mistakes in my past, but theft and murder aren't included."

"Then how do you explain the drugs in your desk drawer? The same drugs Mr. Scott and his partner stole from the pharmacy where you used to work."

"Someone put them there. Not me," Belinda said with conviction. "Everyone has access to the reception desk."

"We'll find out the truth, Ms. Crowe. This is your last chance. Come clean now. Where were you Friday afternoon?"

"I was driving to The Villages to visit my grandmother. I spent the night and drove back early Saturday morning. You can check."

"We will, Ms. Crowe. We will."

CHAPTER 45

AFTER A FEW MORE questions, Donny gave Belinda one more stare, stood, and then left the interrogation room. Penelope watched as Belinda lowered her head, rested it on the edge of the table and started to cry.

Detective Donny Greene stepped into the observation room. "That was a tough one," he said, rubbing the back of his neck and flexing his head from side to side. He strode up to Penelope and looked through the window. "What do you think?"

"She doesn't seem like the type," Penelope answered.

"They rarely do."

Penelope turned to face Donny. "Do you really think she was involved somehow?"

"Until we confirm her alibi, she's our best suspect."

"Only suspect," Penelope said.

"I'm not ready to convict her of murder yet. But, Officer

Watson did confirm the drugs are from the same batch stolen from Grace Memorial. It's a long shot, but I'm going to have the bottles run for prints."

"If Belinda's alibi checks out, how did they get into her desk?" Penelope asked, thinking out loud.

"Well, they didn't crawl in there on their own. We'll know more once the fingerprint results come back."

Donny excused himself and left the room. Penelope turned and looked back through the two-way mirror to the crying Belinda. Her head was still down, but her sobs had slowed to a soft whimper.

Penelope's heartstrings ached for the woman. She had only known Belinda for the past year, but she liked her. Jacob had never mentioned anything about her past, but she hadn't asked, either. It was just like him to give someone another chance. He saw the good in everyone and never judged. Those were qualities that she loved about him. Maybe Jacob hadn't confided in her about Belinda's termination as a courtesy to Belinda, and she respected that.

Penelope's phone rang and when she saw Jacob's number, she answered immediately.

"Have you finished interrogating my office manager?" he asked.

Penelope immediately felt a bit defensive. "Donny had to bring her in, Jacob. You saw what was in her desk. He had to talk to her."

"I can't believe this," Jacob said, sounding frantic.

"I know," Penelope agreed, "but it's going to be alright. God will look out for her, and if she's innocent, it will come to light. Don't worry. Just trust Him. I have a feeling it's going to work out."

Jacob sighed with a shudder.

Penelope understood the feeling. It was a shock when someone you knew got arrested for a crime you never thought they were capable of committing. "As soon as I know more I'll let you know," she added.

"Can we get together for dinner tonight?"

"I'd love that," Penelope said.

"Pick me up at the clinic?"

"Sure. And Jacob . . ."

"Yes, Penny?"

"Remember . . . I love you."

"I love you back, Penny."

Penelope hung up and looked through the glass. Belinda was wiping her eyes with the palms of her hands. She had only been in the interrogation room for a few hours, but it looked like she had aged a decade. Penelope looked for any signs of guilt and spoke to the glass. "If you didn't put the drugs in your desk, someone else put them there. But who else had access to the clinic and your desk?"

PART 3

CHAPTER 46

EARLY THAT TUESDAY EVENING Penelope's car sat idle in the Franklin Clinic parking lot. After the day she just had, a pair of fuzzy slippers and a giant cup of hot cocoa with the man she loved would be the perfect way to end the day.

It would also help to vent to someone. Penelope didn't usually have so much to unload—she was normally pretty good at compartmentalizing her emotions. Then again, under normal circumstances, she was able to distance herself from a case. But this case was different. It was about Jacob.

Lately, it seemed like all her cases were getting personal. First the case with Doug and now with Jacob. Her emotional reaction to the events—because they were so personal—wasn't always professional and that bothered her. She had always prided herself on how well she did her job.

She took a deep breath and let it out slowly. She had to keep it together. There were still a lot of missing pieces to this puzzle. As soon as they were revealed, she would figure it out, and this emotional rollercoaster could come to an end.

"Dear Lord," she prayed, "please give Donny the wisdom he needs to do his job. And if it is your will, please allow me to assist him so we can put the pieces together quickly, without anyone else getting hurt. Amen."

Penelope massaged her temples in small circles and glanced at the time on her phone: 5:58 p.m.

Right on time, Jacob swung the passenger door open and hopped in. By looking at him you'd never know that he'd been shot and knocked out four days earlier.

"Thanks for the ride, Penny."

"Anytime. What's wrong with the Mustang?"

"Oh, nothing. I drove home for lunch and decided to jog back . . . to clear my head."

"I hope you took it easy."

"I've been careful, Officer," he said, a smile playing around his lips. "You hungry?" he added quickly.

"I had a late lunch. But I could eat." She wasn't that hungry, but she needed to spend some time with Jacob and make sure he was doing okay. Just seeing him now was reassuring, and for the first time all day, she felt at peace.

"We could go to my place. I'll make us some spaghetti."

Penelope was familiar with Jacob's spaghetti and meat sauce. He wasn't much of a cook, having been a bachelor most of his adult life, but he had managed to master his mother's pasta.

CHAPTER 47

AFTER A MOSTLY SILENT, though not uncomfortable, drive to Jacob's house, Penelope sat on a high stool in his kitchen. She watched as he made the meat sauce and told her about an interesting study he had read in the *Army Medical Department Journal*.

Although honorably discharged from the U.S. Army, Jacob still liked to read up on the latest advances in battlefield medicine. She couldn't always follow his explanations of the more complicated medical terms, but it was how he blew off steam, so she was happy to listen. It helped to take her mind off of crime so she could enjoy this time with her fiancé.

She watched him deftly combine the ingredients for the sauce, mixing cans of stewed tomatoes with oregano, rosemary and a pinch of sugar. Even with an injured shoulder, Jacob's movements looked practiced and professional, but his cooking prowess was limited to pasta and steak.

Most of the time, Penelope cooked, or they ordered takeout, but she enjoyed watching him take control in the kitchen. The way his broad shoulders bent over the mixing bowl and how he was able to do three things at once.

Penelope hopped off the stool and took two plates out of the cupboard. She rummaged in the drawer for knives and forks and set the dining room table.

She knew where everything was, and they moved together like long-time dance partners. The past six months had been so busy that she'd forgotten how comfortable it was being with him. Once this whole mess was over, they could get back to what mattered—being together.

When the utensils were in place, Jacob brought out the bowl of pasta and set it in the middle of the table.

They said grace and Penelope didn't waste any more time. "So how was the rest of your day?" she asked, trying to keep her voice neutral.

"Nothing out of the ordinary." Jacob swallowed a bite of spaghetti and asked, "So how did it go with Belinda?"

"Well," Penelope began slowly. "Donny did a full interrogation and based on the information he has so far, it appears Belinda may be innocent. Donny is checking her alibi so he can exclude her as a suspect. I know that she had problems in the past." Penelope kept her eyes focused on the spool of spaghetti on her fork. When she looked up to gauge Jacob's reaction, he was looking at her and slurping a long string of spaghetti. She was about to continue when he spoke.

"Yeah, I know she had her problems over at Grace

Memorial, but I believe she was innocent. And everyone deserves a second chance, right?"

Penelope smiled. The thought of how Jacob treated her brother when the rest of the town turned their back on him flashed through her mind. Doug was a drunk and had done nothing but skate by the past few years. When he became the prime suspect in his ex-wife's murder, everyone assumed the worst. Not Jacob—he was skeptical, but he kept an open mind.

"Yes, they do," Penelope agreed. "What I don't get though . . . is if Belinda is innocent . . . and she didn't know about the drugs in the desk drawer, how did they get there? Someone had to put them there. Someone connected to the robbery. Someone who had access to the receptionist's desk."

Jacob studied Penelope. His thoughtful face was handsome. He looked sure of himself even when he had questions. That was probably what made him a good doctor. No one would doubt him, even if he silently doubted himself.

"We'll find out who did this," Penelope reassured him after some moments of silence.

Jacob looked up at her, frowning. "We? Are you working this case?"

His words stung. They were a reminder that she wasn't. She pushed her offense away. "Well, I'm not . . . but Donny's been keeping me up to date and he's been allowing me to assist." She paused to read Jacob's face. The last time she'd talked about getting involved in the robbery case, they'd had a falling out.

His face was neutral.

It was a little unsettling—a cop that couldn't figure out what someone was thinking? It was like having to write with your left hand when you were right-handed.

"Is this going take a lot of time out of your day?" Jacob asked.

"I hope not."

"And you're still going to do wedding stuff?"

Her mind hadn't been on wedding planning at all. "Well, I was going to—"

"You still want to get married, don't you?"

Where did that come from? The question hit her like a punch to the stomach. "Of course, I do! Did I ever give you the impression that I didn't?"

"You told me you were going to take time this week to scout locations, call florists, find out about DJs, that kind of thing. It's a lot of work."

"I'm worried. You could be in danger."

"Penny, the Gainesville guys are good at what they do. Don is on the case and from what he tells me, this Detective Ballard fellow is good at his job, too. You don't have to be worried about me." His voice was gentle and assuring, but it did nothing to calm the storm that had risen inside her.

She stared at her plate, no longer hungry.

"I want to make sure my fiancé is still alive by the time the wedding rolls around," she said, and her voice cracked. The surge of emotion surprised them both, and there was a void in the room.

"Penny, I'm still here." He reached across the table and took her hand. "I'm not going anywhere."

She fought to squelch the tears that had popped out of nowhere. She bit her cheek, trying to get the feelings to go away. "I'm sorry. I'm just a little rattled. Things have been rough . . . you know? And with the robbery, you getting shot, your belongings returned, one of the suspects turning up dead . . . it's made everything a little—"

"Weird?" Jacob asked.

"Yeah. Weird."

"But we're a team. Remember? We'll get through this together."

Penelope sat silent.

"You're making that cop face," Jacob added.

She tended to zone out as her brain put together a picture of the events surrounding a crime. This picture was incomplete and troublesome considering the possibility that Jacob might know the suspect.

"I have some cop thoughts," she admitted. "But I'm shelving them for now. What do you say to a movie and a cup of hot cocoa?"

"Sounds perfect."

Penelope put aside thoughts of the investigation and focused on spending a pleasant evening with her fiancé before she had to head home.

Jacob collected the dishes and quickly washed them. She was pretty sure that he only had two plates in his house, and they were always clean. She thought about the merging of their homes and what would happen when they married. At least the dishes would always be clean. She let out a slight giggle.

"What's so funny?" he asked.

"I'm just happy."

And she was. She really was.

She put a kettle on to boil, hoping that her feeling of security would last.

CHAPTER 48

WEDNESDAY MORNING THE HOSPITAL cafeteria at Grace Memorial Hospital was quieter than usual. Penelope sat with Gabriel at a round table in the corner. She looked into her coffee as she stirred it with the plastic stick.

Gabriel smiled at Penelope like a kid who had just gotten an early peek at his Christmas presents. "So, what is the status of the case? Unofficially, of course."

Penelope stopped stirring and looked around the cafeteria, making sure that no one else was listening. "Well, Detective Greene searched the victim's apartment Monday afternoon. They found his car in the parking lot. There was a lot of blood, and they think that may have been where he was killed. Forensics is going through his car."

"That's big," Gabriel said.

Penelope nodded and curled her fingers around the hot cup of coffee. "They also found several blank prescription pads in his apartment."

"Prescription pads?"

"Yeah."

"Whose prescription pads?" Gabriel asked, eyes narrowed.

"Jacob's, from the Franklin Clinic," Penelope said.

"Do they have any idea how they got there?"

"Jacob said they're older . . . a type he doesn't use anymore. He never had any stolen, so they may be counterfeit." She paused and took a sip of her coffee. "The office manager, Belinda Crowe, might be connected. It seems she may have a connection to the victim."

Gabriel sat looking at Penelope intently.

His gaze caused her to shift uncomfortably in her seat. "Anyhow," she continued. "Yesterday morning, when Donny went to the Franklin Clinic to ask Jacob about the prescription pads, Jacob noticed that one of his new pads was missing. He found the missing pad in a spare lab coat, but while they were searching, they found drugs from the robbery in the reception desk."

"The drugs from the Grace Memorial robbery last Friday? In the desk Belinda uses?"

"That's right. Donny brought Belinda in for questioning and let me observe. That's why I couldn't take your call yesterday."

"You said Belinda had a connection to the victim?"

"Yes. She worked at the Gainesville Recovery Center during the time that Kevin Scott was a patient. She was a clinical associate for a Dr. Teresa Behr—"

"Behrmann." Gabriel finished. "Dr. Teresa Behrmann?"

"That's right. You know her?"

"Yes. I know Dr. Behrmann very well. She's the colleague I was telling you about—the one that was supposed to consult on the Michael Findley trial, but got called away on a family emergency. I might even know Belinda. Did she work here at Grace Memorial before she got the job at the Franklin Clinic?"

"She did."

"Short brown hair with a smile that lit up a room?"

Penelope smiled. "That's Belinda."

"Wow. It would be too bad if she's mixed up in all of this."

"Well, Donny's not sure how she's involved, if she's involved at all. He's checking her alibi."

Gabriel sat back and processed the new information.

"This can't be comfortable for your fiancé."

Penelope was confused for a moment before she realized what Gabriel meant. Of course! From a purely procedural view, Jacob was an obvious suspect. It hadn't occurred to her for one second that he could be involved somehow. "I hadn't thought of that," she said. An uncomfortable feeling wedged itself between her ribs, and she exhaled around it.

"Of course, you didn't. You are a fiercely loyal person, Penelope. You could never see the people you love in a negative light. Why, look at how you defended your brother, Doug Foster, when he was accused of murder. All signs pointed to him, yet your belief in his goodness was so strong that you were able to solve a rather convoluted case and exonerate him. Why should this be any different?"

"This time is quite different," Penelope said in a tone that was a little harsher than she intended. "There is no way that Jacob could have done it. He was badly injured."

"Could be motive."

Jacob's facial expressions from the murder scene replayed in Penelope's mind. "He was genuinely shocked to see the robber's body there in the river. I think he felt bad for him and was sad that he lost his life."

"I believe you, but the Gainesville police are going to be looking at him pretty closely."

As he said the words, Penelope knew he was right. She would be suspicious of Jacob too if she didn't know him. He certainly had a motive to kill the robber. A weak motive, but still motive.

"And, they'll look closely at the time of death. Which was when?"

"Late Friday night or early Saturday morning," Penelope said, her thoughts reeling.

"They'll probably think he had a partner to help him dispose of the body," Gabriel continued.

"Well, it's doubly impossible because I know where Jacob was the whole time. He was at Doug's place sleeping downstairs, while I was upstairs."

Gabriel leaned in conspiratorially. "All night?"

Nervousness bunched in Penelope's stomach. "No, not all night . . ."

"When was the last time anyone checked on him?"

"I checked on him at midnight, Friday."

"And what time did you hear from him the next morning?

"About seven o'clock . . ." Penelope's voice trailed off as she realized where Gabriel's line of reasoning was going.

"So he has no alibi from midnight to seven a.m.?"

Penelope felt her face crumple as she made the connection. "But . . . Jacob wouldn't . . ." Even as she protested, she knew that Jacob essentially had no alibi. When she analyzed the evidence with the cop part of her brain, she arrived at the conclusion that Gabriel had reached. Donny soon would think the same thing.

Jacob was the prime suspect.

When she considered the events through the eyes of love, the room began to spin.

Not again. Please Lord, not again.

Just months after she had cleared her brother of murder, it now appeared that her fiancé could be a suspect in a homicide case. She was certain of his innocence, as she had been with Doug. The truth would be known, but at what cost? A life had already been taken—what else would be lost or ruined in the wake of this crime?

She took a deep breath and blew it out slowly.

Gabriel looked concerned. "Penelope, are you okay?"

"I don't know what to do," she admitted.

"We follow the clues and re-examine the evidence."

Penelope nodded. A steely resolve began to solidify inside of her. She needed to do everything she could to protect Jacob and prove he wasn't involved. She wasn't going to let anyone she loved get hurt on her watch.

CHAPTER 49

"WHERE TO FIRST?" GABRIEL asked, looking at Penelope rather intensely across the vast interior cabin of his Hummer.

"Head down University Avenue. I want to check out the victim's apartment."

Gabriel looked at Penelope and nodded. "You think Detective Greene may have overlooked something?"

"No, not at all. I just want to have a firsthand look at the primary crime scene."

She wasn't sure what she was looking for, but she felt compelled to see what the victim saw in his day-to-day life. Being a cop meant viewing things from every angle. You never knew what would lead to the next development in an investigation.

"Kevin Scott's apartment it is," Gabriel confirmed.

They rode the short distance in silence, and a light drizzle began to fall. As they drove east on University Avenue, Penelope noted a distinct change in the atmosphere and the architecture. This would've been a tough neighborhood to grow up in.

"Turn right on 24th Street," she told Gabriel. "His apartment complex is a couple of blocks up on the left." Penelope paused. "I want to see the world through his eyes. See what he saw . . ."

Gabriel chuckled.

"What's so funny?" she asked.

Penelope had been lost in thought—contemplating her next move—and she hadn't realized she'd been thinking aloud.

"It's incredible to watch you work. It's not often that I get to spend time with students that are now law enforcement professionals. Some investigators wouldn't think of looking at the world from someone else's perspective. They gather evidence. They analyze the evidence, they conduct interviews, and that's it. But a good investigator knows that you need to submerge yourself into the world of the crime. You have to see things the way your subject saw them. In this investigation, we are trying to figure out the motivation for a man to commit robbery as well as to determine why he was murdered and by whom." He chuckled again. "I guess I'm laughing because you had the same idea as I did. Let's see the world through his eyes."

Penelope was flattered to hear Gabriel compare her to himself. She had few role models in her life, and Gabriel was certainly one of the most important. She didn't know what to say, so she didn't say anything.

Gabriel appeared lost in thought. His eyes scanned the surroundings, taking in old buildings and a handful of small businesses that appeared to be thriving in spite of the general dilapidation of the area. They passed a small liquor store that served as the local hangout for a group of scruffy teenagers, and Gabriel pulled up to a large multi-building apartment complex. Penelope hadn't told him the exact address, but he stopped right in front of Kevin Scott's building and cut the engine.

"How did you know which complex?" Penelope asked.

"The orange spray paint markings on the pavement," Gabriel said, pointing over his left shoulder.

Penelope was familiar with the brightly colored symbols. She used them often with traffic accidents to document things like vehicle location, direction, and skid marks. They were also used at crimes scenes to mark victim, vehicle, and evidence locations, to assist investigators in reconstructing the scene at a later date, if needed.

She got out of the SUV and walked over to one of the marked parking spaces. Gabriel followed close behind.

"Okay, so the victim's car was parked here," she said, talking herself through the crime scene. It was her way of working through something and seeing if everything added up.

"And someone came up from behind and shot our vic in the stomach," Gabriel said, standing behind Penelope, his voice in her ear.

She jumped, and Gabriel grinned.

He'd stepped into her reenactment, playing the part of the killer.

Penelope shivered. "That's pretty gruesome, but no. According to Donny and these markings, our vic was shot over there." Penelope pointed to a large bloodstain on the pavement in the opposite parking space. "He was parked here, but shot there."

Gabriel stepped back and nodded. "So, possible drug deal gone bad?"

"It looks that way. The vic was probably taking the drugs out of his trunk and putting them in the trunk of the buyer," Penelope said, piecing together the different bits of evidence. It was magic when a crime investigation came together like this—one of the things about her job that she loved.

"And then the buyer shot the vic, put his body in their trunk, and dumped him in the Franklin River?"

Penelope nodded. "That's what Detective Greene suspects."

"But why not just take the drugs? Why move the body? And why dump the body in Franklin?"

"That's what I'm hoping you can help me figure out."

CHAPTER 50

PENELOPE TOOK A STEP back, physically doing what she was doing in her mind—distancing herself from the crime scene and the victim's point of view. "I want to get a feel for how this guy lived."

"What floor?" Gabriel tilted his head upward as if trying to see into the windows of the building. Small beads of water formed on his forehead from the mist that wasn't quite rain.

"Third floor. Apartment 323," she said, a little worried they might be recognized as police, but people walked by and didn't give them a second glance. It didn't hurt being in civilian clothes.

A call box was located next to the heavy front door. Penelope gave the door buzzer an experimental push, but nothing happened. She pulled the door handle and was not surprised to find the lock was broken. It looked like someone had taken a screwdriver and hammer to the locking mechanism and the landlord had never fixed it.

"No telling who's been in or out of here," Penelope muttered in Gabriel's direction.

They entered a gloomy hallway lined with metal mailboxes. A staircase with a scarred metal banister led up to the upper-floor apartments. She turned back to see if Gabriel was following. Her eyes met his and he nodded. She did her best to act like she belonged there in case they should run into a resident.

"No elevator?" Gabriel asked from behind.

"I've never minded taking the stairs," she said with a smile.

She didn't usually work with a partner, but she found that she liked having him around. It made this building a lot less spooky.

They didn't cross paths with anyone as they moved up the three flights of stairs. As they exited the third-floor stairway, Penelope looked up and down the long hallway. It appeared that the paint on the walls had started off as light beige. It was ending its life as a dingy gray marked with black and brown scuffs from people moving furniture in and out over the years. A lone window at the end of the hall, near apartment 323, allowed light to filter in from outside.

Penelope headed for the window.

The view was dismal. A giant warehouse across the street dominated the view. Chain-link fencing surrounded empty lots, and several abandoned vehicles dotted the landscape.

A creaking sound came from behind.

Penelope turned to investigate and saw Gabriel pushing open the door to apartment 323.

"Hello? Anybody home?" he called out.

Before Penelope could react, Gabriel fell backward and a young white or Hispanic woman pushed past him. The woman ran for the stairs and, without thinking, Penelope gave chase.

"Wait!" she called out after the rapidly receding figure of the frightened woman. "We just want to talk." Penelope estimated the girl to be in her early twenties. She was wearing dark blue jeans and a blue, University of Florida sweatshirt. Her long black hair bounced as she ran for the stairs. She was fast. Penelope ran up to the stairwell and looked over the banister in time to see the girl disappear down the last flight of stairs and around a corner.

Penelope walked back to the victim's apartment where Gabriel was dusting himself off. How could this professional criminal psychologist walk right into a potentially hostile situation, without any form of protection, when a couple of days earlier he'd dissected a crime scene with surgical precision?

"Are you okay?" she asked, trying to remain calm. "What were you thinking?"

"I-I don't know. The door was open." Gabriel sounded bewildered and surprised.

"We're here to observe only. We aren't officially working this case, remember?"

"I just got wrapped up in the idea that someone was in there, someone who could tell us what happened." He held his hands in front of him and shrugged. "I know it doesn't help now, but I'm pretty sure I was right."

How often did the professor get out into the field for actual investigation work? Not very. He probably spent most of his time treating patients, reviewing crime scenes, and testifying in court. He undoubtedly spent more time reading reports than questioning witnesses.

"What if she was the killer?"

"Are you mad at me?" Gabriel asked.

"You're my responsibility. What if something happened to you?"

Gabriel stood silent.

Penelope didn't know how she sensed this, but she could almost feel prying eyes all around them. They may have gotten in unseen, but they certainly would be watched closely as they made their exit. It would be best to get out of there as soon as possible. "We shouldn't be here. We need to leave . . . now," she said, grabbing Gabriel by the arm.

"Don't you want to look inside?"

"No. Now let's go before we're spotted."

Gabriel wrenched his arm out of Penelope's grasp. "I'm sorry," he said, eyes clear and piercing. "You're right. It was foolish. It won't happen again." He turned away and started gracefully down the stairs.

Penelope shook her head and followed.

In the entryway, a little girl with wild, curly blonde hair stood in front of the rows of battered mailboxes; she stared at them with wide, blue eyes. A tall woman with chestnut colored hair and brightly painted fingernails stood nearby checking her mail. The woman's eyes tightened at the sight of Penelope and Gabriel.

So much for going unnoticed.

CHAPTER 51

GABRIEL DIDN'T SAY A word as they walked back to the Hummer. He opened the door for Penelope, and as she climbed inside, her cell phone rang, breaking the silence.

"This is Chance," she answered.

Gabriel shut her door and walked around to the driver's side.

"Chance, it's Donny. I thought you might like an update."

Gabriel settled into the driver's seat and Penelope put the call on speaker. "An update would be great, Donny." Gabriel nodded, acknowledging the nature of the call, and Penelope continued, "What've you got for me?"

"I had Officer Watson follow up on Belinda's alibi. She confirmed Belinda was in The Villages volunteering at the Loving Care Assisted Living Facility Friday afternoon. Watson also confirmed with Belinda's grandmother that she spent the night there."

"What time did she leave?"

"Her grandmother says she left at four thirty that morning."

Penelope looked at Gabriel and then asked Donny, "What was her grandmother doing up that early?"

"Apparently making her granddaughter some breakfast. Bacon and eggs. You know old folks. Early bird dinner at five, in bed by nine, up at four. She knew Belinda had to work early the next day and she didn't want her granddaughter going to work on an empty stomach. That's what she said. Bottom line . . . Belinda's not the killer."

"But still no alibi for the time of the robbery?"

"I have Watson and Meeks following up with Belinda's neighbors. But I think she's telling the truth."

Penelope sighed. She didn't think Belinda was guilty, but at this point, any clue would have been better than nothing at all. "What about the drugs in her desk? Do you think they were planted to make her look guilty?"

"That would be my guess."

"Which means it could be someone at the Franklin Clinic."

Penelope looked to Gabriel and he appeared deep in thought.

"It's looking that way," Donny said. "I have a feeling the reception desk is often left unattended, and it's open to the public."

"So we're back to square one?"

"Not completely. I'm going to do some follow-up interviews with everyone at the Franklin Clinic and check alibis. I'm not ready to rule Belinda out yet. She may not have committed the robbery or killed Kevin Scott, but that doesn't mean she's not involved. She used to work the reception desk at the Grace Memorial clinic, so she had intimate knowledge of the comings and goings of staff."

"So you're going to hold her?"

"I'm not holding her, but she is still a person of interest."

"Anything on the fingerprints on the bottles?"

"Nothing yet. I might have something by the time you stop by this afternoon."

Penelope and Gabriel looked at one another. "Who said I'm stopping by?"

Donny laughed. "I know you, Chance. You're coming. You can't stay away. And bring me a coffee when you do."

Penelope rolled her eyes. "Good-bye, Donny."

"Oh . . . and one of those brownies, too. Those were really good. Did you make those yourself?"

"I'm hanging up now, Donny . . ."

"Coffee and brownie. Thanks, Chance!"

Penelope ended the call and Gabriel asked, "Is he always that witty and charming?"

"Pretty much," was her answer.

There was an awkward silence before Gabriel spoke again. "Look, about earlier—at the apartment. I really am sorry, Penelope."

Penelope held up a hand. "No, I'm sorry for yelling at you. After what happened to Jacob . . . I just didn't want you getting hurt. Lately, everyone close to me seems to end up hurt or accused of murder."

"So," Gabriel said, changing the subject, "what's our

next move?"

"With Belinda's alibi checking out and the possibility that someone planted the drugs, I honestly don't know. If this were my case, my next step would be questioning the clinic workers. But it's not, so we can't."

"I have a suggestion."

"I'm open to anything at this point."

"You're not going to like it . . ."

"As long as it doesn't interfere with Donny's investigation. I don't want to have another incident like we had today."

"We wouldn't be interfering," Gabriel said, starting the SUV. He pulled out of the apartment complex parking lot and spoke as he drove back to Grace Memorial Hospital. "We'd only be observing. I think we should revisit the possibility that the person responsible is someone Jacob knows. Especially if Detective Greene is leaning toward the drugs being planted."

"Given what we know so far, I'd agree that the person responsible is probably someone Jacob knows. And there's an even greater possibility that it could be someone that works with him at the clinic."

"Not necessarily someone from the clinic."

"No?"

"No," Gabriel said, stopping at a red light before making a left onto University Avenue. "Someone from the clinic would be the obvious assumption and a smart one, but I think there's more to this case than we're aware of."

"How do you figure?"

"Hear me out . . . I have a theory."

Penelope shifted in her seat, turning her body toward Gabriel. "I'm listening."

"I think this person might have an infatuation with your fiancé. It could be a casual acquaintance, a co-worker, or a patient. Someone that knows his schedule and has been admiring him from afar. The crush was probably quite innocent until she saw him get shot. Then she acted in rage."

"So you think we should be looking for someone with a crush on Jacob that saw him get shot? Someone that may have been there at the time of the robbery?"

"Right. Your fiancé may not even know this person exists."

"I don't know," she said hesitantly. "That's quite a theory."

"Like I said, it's just a theory. But if I'm right, the infatuation is no longer a fantasy for this person . . . it's becoming a reality. And the sooner we find the person responsible, the better. For your safety and the safety of your fiancé."

"So how do we find this person? Between Grace Memorial and the Franklin Clinic, that's a lot of potential suspects. And we can't question them all. We can't question any of them."

"You're still thinking like a cop. Think smarter, not harder. Remember what I taught you."

The professor was using this as a teaching opportunity. He did the same thing with his students in college; he challenged them to look at situations from all angles and to explore all of the possibilities.

Penelope thought about it for a moment longer.

"Narrow it down to the people that were at Grace Memorial at the time of the robbery?" she asked.

Gabriel stopped at another red light, as University Avenue became Newberry Road. "You're on the right track," he said.

"We still can't question them, though . . . not without interfering or possibly compromising the investigation."

"We don't have to," Gabriel said. "We let the person come to us."

"And how do we do that?"

"By observing the observer," he said. "We follow your fiancé and watch the people in his life."

"You mean spy on him?" Penelope asked.

"No, not spy. We'd simply watch the people he interacts with and how they interact with him. See if we notice anyone suspicious."

"Ah . . . We'd be observing the observer and observing the observee."

Gabriel chuckled. "Precisely. Of course, it'd be better if he didn't know about it. That way he would act natural, and we can see if anyone stands out."

"But I know Jacob and his friends."

"I know you do. I'm talking about his life away from you. You each have your independent lives, and if we follow him, keep an eye on him, we might find a few likely suspects."

Penelope nodded. Gabriel was right. If the actual perpetrator was around and Jacob didn't know he was being followed, he couldn't give himself away. She didn't have anything else to go on, so how else was she going to find the individual responsible?

"What's your fiancé's schedule like?" Gabriel asked, pulling into the Grace Memorial Hospital parking lot.

"He's in Gainesville Monday, Wednesday, and Friday and at the Franklin Clinic on Tuesday, Thursday, and sometimes Saturday. Aside from that, the only time he has to himself is on Sunday, and we usually spend that day together."

"We could start tomorrow morning. If he's working in Franklin, I could swing by and pick you up," Gabriel offered. "What's his morning routine like?"

"He runs the Gainesville-Franklin State Trail most mornings and is usually to work by eight."

"So pick you up at seven o'clock?"

"Better make it six. Jacob likes to get an early start. I'll text you my address."

She didn't like the idea of spying on Jacob without his knowledge, but she liked the idea of an admirer secretly watching him even less.

CHAPTER 52

LATE THAT AFTERNOON, WHEN Penelope walked into the Gainesville squad room with coffee and a brownie from The Coffey Shop, Donny's face lit up. "Chance!" he said, acknowledging her and gesturing for her to wait one moment while he walked a guest to the exit.

A sharp breath hitched in Penelope's chest at the sight of the person with Donny. *What is she doing here?*

The woman Donny was escorting out was the same woman Penelope had chased at the victim's apartment that morning. The woman didn't look at Penelope as she loped down the hall toward the exit.

Penelope's mind filled with questions. Was she reporting Penelope and Gabriel for being at the victim's apartment? What was she doing at the victim's apartment? Was she related to the victim?

"I was beginning to wonder if you were going to show,"

Donny said, motioning for Penelope to follow him.

She handed him the coffee and brownie and followed him to his office. Before he could continue, she asked, "Who was that woman?"

Donny shut the door to his office and took a seat behind his desk before he responded. "That was Denise Wilson, our vic's girlfriend. Detective Ballard is going to take her to ID the body." The way Donny's eyes were shining, Ms. Wilson must have given him useful information. "She confirmed that she was with him the morning of the robbery," Donny continued.

"Is she a suspect?"

"Not at this point. She seemed pretty upset and genuinely surprised to hear that her boyfriend was dead."

"How did you finally track her down?"

"She found us. Mr. Scott was supposed to meet her Friday afternoon with money—money to help with her rent. But he never showed. She hadn't seen or heard from him since Friday. She was following up on a missing person report she filed."

"When did she file the report?"

"Sunday morning. Our systems just hadn't connected the cases."

Penelope had so many questions, she couldn't ask them quickly enough. "Did she know about his criminal past or the robbery?"

"That's where things get murky," Donny explained, leaning back in his chair and looking off into the distance, as though trying to picture the scene. "Ms. Wilson claims she didn't know about the robbery. She knew Mr. Scott had a record, but she said he'd cleaned up his act. He'd been helping pay her rent, and she said he claimed to have a job that paid enough to buy them whatever they wanted."

"Did she ask what the job was or who he was working for?"

"Yep. And he wouldn't tell her. She didn't like that. Ms. Wilson didn't want him going to meet some mystery person, but he did anyway. She waited for him all day Friday. Obviously, he never came back. When she couldn't get a hold of him Saturday or Sunday, she filed the missing person report. She did have something interesting to tell us."

"Like what?"

"She went by Mr. Scott's apartment today to see if he was there. But when she arrived she said a man was trying to break in. He frightened her pretty bad and she ran."

She hadn't just arrived; she was already in the apartment. Why would she lie about that? And why would she lie about Gabriel trying to break in? What else was she lying about?

Penelope's lips did not move. She wanted to explain to Donny that the man Ms. Wilson saw was Gabriel, but Donny continued before she could speak.

"Ms. Wilson said there was a woman with him, but she didn't get a good look at her."

"That's right!" Penelope said. "There probably is a woman involved. I forgot to tell you I went to the Franklin River scene Monday with Gabriel, and he discovered a heel print. He thinks it's a woman's." She pulled her phone out to show him. "I don't think these were documented by forensics. We also spotted tire tracks." She swiped the screen to show him the pictures, which were not as impressive as she remembered.

"Gabriel?" Donny interrupted.

"Oh . . . sorry," Penelope said, remembering that Donny didn't know about Gabriel's unofficial involvement. "Dr. Gabriel Pike," she clarified and then hurried to continue. "He was an expert witness in the Michael Findley trial."

"The forensic psychologist?"

"Yeah, you know him?"

"By reputation only. The department consults with him on occasion. What I don't understand is why he is consulting on my homicide case?"

"That's my fault, Donny. He was with me when I got the call about Jacob being shot. He drove me to the hospital. Then I ran into him Saturday after I dropped off Jacob's belongings here. When I told him about the belongings being returned, he offered to help."

"You should have asked me first, Chance. We don't have the budget to hire someone with Pike's expertise on this case."

"Oh, he's not charging a consulting fee."

Donny tilted his head to the right and raised a single eyebrow.

"He was my professor in college, and with Jacob being injured, he considered it a personal favor to me." Maybe if she left it at that, he wouldn't question her further. "I'm sorry, Donny. I should have consulted you first," she added.

"E-mail me the photos and I'll send them to the lab," he said, squinting at the photo of the heel print. "We probably caught those marks on film." Donny didn't say anything else about Gabriel's involvement.

"So any other updates?" Penelope asked, changing the subject.

"I'm still waiting to hear from the lab guys checking the bottles and prescription pad for prints. And Ballard is still working the drug angle. Maybe we'll get lucky."

"Let's hope so."

"How's the rest of your week look?" he asked.

Penelope thought of her conversation with Jacob. She was supposed to look at reception venues tomorrow, and then she remembered her commitment to Gabriel to follow Jacob tomorrow morning as part of their unofficial investigation. Friday she had an appointment with a potential wedding planner. "I'm . . . somewhat flexible," she finally said. "What's up?"

"Tomorrow I'm going to interview a couple of the staff members that weren't at the Franklin Clinic yesterday. Then on Friday I'm following up with the Grace Memorial staff that was working the day of the robbery. You want to join me?"

Penelope wanted to join him both days, but she didn't want to cause a rift between her and Jacob. "Sure," she said, trying to sound normal. "I have some wedding stuff to do tomorrow, but I could meet you Friday for the Grace Memorial interviews."

"Two o'clock work for you?"

"Two o'clock Friday works," she said.

Donny walked Penelope to her car, and as she sat in the parking lot, she thought about the new developments.

She now knew the woman at the victim's apartment was Kevin Scott's girlfriend and that she probably wasn't involved. Donny agreed that Belinda probably wasn't the killer either. But the drugs were definitely in her desk. Even though she didn't want to believe it, it was looking more and more like someone at the Franklin Clinic must have been involved.

She drove out of the parking lot with her head full of questions. She could use some family time. Spending time with Trevor would help lighten her concerns, and Doug was always a good sounding board for her theories. As she headed toward Doug's house, she thanked God for keeping her and Gabriel safe and for allowing her to be more involved in Donny's investigation.

CHAPTER 53

WHEN PENELOPE PULLED UP to Doug's house that evening, she saw her brother smiling as he watched Trevor push his cars around on the brightly painted porch. Camille had picked the color, back when she and Doug had been married. Doug hated that shade of yellow, but since Camille's murder, he had stopped talking about it. He had the time to paint over it, but never did, and Penelope knew her brother well enough to know that he never would.

Doug waved as Penelope parked and Trevor looked up to investigate; he jumped up and pointed at her.

Penelope couldn't help but smile at the little guy's enthusiasm. This was the closest thing she had to a family. She shut off the engine and grabbed the burgers and fries she had picked up on her way over. Trevor almost tackled her as she got out of the car.

"Hey there, buddy!" She tried to hug him without

dropping the bag of food.

Doug laughed and grabbed the bags before she dropped them. "Thank you for bringing dinner, Penny," he said and looked pointedly at Trevor.

"Thanks, Aunty Penny."

"You're welcome, Trevor. Tell you what. Let's go inside and see if there's some french fries in the bag."

"French fries!" Trevor waved his arms over his head and ran toward the house.

Doug grabbed him by the shirt. "Not so fast. Pick up your cars, and then wash your hands."

Trevor grumbled for a bit and then picked up his toys with gusto.

Doug held the door open for Penelope. "After you."

Together they walked into the kitchen and sat at either end of the small table. Penelope fondly remembered Trevor's high chair, and the first time he had spaghetti. There was still a small stain on the ceiling.

She handed Doug a burger. "Got you a double cheeseburger, extra onions." She pulled out a smaller burger and put it on the table. "Kid's burger for Trevor," she said. She found her burger and unwrapped it.

"Aren't you going to say grace?" Doug asked, with a twinkle in his eye.

"Yes, I am. Do you want to say it with me?"

"No, thanks." He took a huge bite of his burger.

She didn't mind that Doug didn't pray—he might want to someday. She bowed her head. "Dear Lord, bless this food to the nourishment of our bodies and us to Thy service. In Christ's name we pray, Amen."

"Where's mine?" Trevor asked, bursting into the room.

"Hands," Doug said with his mouth full of burger.

Trevor presented his hands. Doug nodded and pointed to the small burger.

"What about the fries?"

"Eat half your burger, then you get some fries," Doug said calmly.

Trevor looked like he was going to complain, but thought better of it, and then took a bite of his burger. He didn't take his eyes off the fries. Penelope marveled at the way Doug kept the rambunctious six-year-old in line. He had been a single father for a while now, but since they lost Camille, things had gotten even tougher. He took it in stride.

"How's work?" Penelope asked.

"Busy. Cars always need fixin'," Doug said with a smile. He looked happy.

"I got two new cars," Trevor added.

"What color?" Penelope asked.

"A red one and a green one. The green one's a truck." Trevor kicked his legs under the table as he ate.

"You'll have to show them to me."

"Right now?"

"No, later," Doug said.

"Okay." He took a big bite of his burger and held it up for Doug to inspect. "See? I ate half."

Doug gave him a small pile of fries and a squirt of ketchup.

"Thanks, Dad!"

"You're welcome."

Doug looked at Penelope and lifted his eyebrows.

She laughed. He had grown into such a confident parent.

Trevor told his dad about a field trip he had taken with his kindergarten class. As he described the small local train museum, Penelope remembered doing the same thing at his age. Doug asked him about the different things he learned while he was there. She beamed as she watched the two bantering and joking around with each other.

Trevor cleared the table when they were through.

"Can I go watch the Disney Channel?" Trevor asked.

"Sure," Doug said.

And just like that, Trevor was gone. The room was still and quiet.

"He's getting so big," Penelope said, breaking the silence. "I was thinking about when he was a baby."

"Yeah. He's doing pretty well, considering."

"How are things going?"

"They're going. I couldn't do it without Jacob's Aunt Jess, though."

A year earlier, Jessica Gordon had stepped in to help care for Trevor when Doug was being investigated for Camille's murder. Jess and Trevor became inseparable, and now she insisted on watching Trevor for free while Doug was at work.

Doug stuffed a few fries in his mouth and went on. "He's still seeing a therapist in Gainesville once a week. It gives him someone to talk to, and the therapist gives me parenting tips. Turns out he needs a lot more structure than what I was giving him before."

"You've always given him everything, Doug. We both know that."

"Oh, I'm not down on myself for not knowing everything about being a dad. I'm learning about it now, and that's all right with me. Plus, his therapist isn't bad looking . . ."

"Oh, Doug, you couldn't date Trevor's therapist!"

He laughed at her reaction. "I haven't asked her out or anything." He paused for a second. "No, I don't think I'm ready to date. I still miss Camille."

His face darkened a little, and the two fell silent. Despite the joviality of the visit, Camille's death weighed on both of them.

"Don't be sad, Daddy," Trevor said, suddenly appearing in the doorway. "Mommy's in Heaven now, with the angels."

"I know she is, Trev," Doug told him as he opened up his arms for a hug.

Penelope watched them hug, and her eyes welled up.

"Don't cry, Aunty Penny!" Trevor said and then gave her a hug, too.

"I'm not crying because I'm sad," she said, patting his back. "I'm crying because I'm glad to have you and your dad as my family. I don't have any other family but you two. Did you know that?"

"Yeah, I know that," Trevor said.

Doug burst into laughter. Neither of them had told Trevor about Penelope's past. He was just at the age when kids pretend to know things.

"Are you guys laughing at me?"

"No, Son. We're just in a good mood."

Trevor seemed to accept that. Penelope hugged the boy until he wiggled away.

"Go finish your show," she said. "I want to talk to your dad."

"Okay."

Trevor ran off, and the silence returned.

CHAPTER 54

"LISTEN, DOUG," PENELOPE FINALLY said, "it's been a strange week for me."

Doug gave Penelope a wary look. "I'm listening . . ."

"Did you hear about the body discovered in the Franklin River Sunday?"

"Yeah, I saw it on the news."

"Well, I got the call. Donny Greene assumed jurisdiction. The victim turned out to be one of the robbery suspects."

"Friday's robbery? That wasn't on the news."

"It wouldn't be," Penelope told him. "Details like that aren't usually released this early on. Also, Jacob's belongings were returned sometime Saturday morning, and something was missing from his wallet."

"His stuff that was stolen? Who returned them?"

"I don't know yet."

Penelope went on to explain how the stolen drugs were

found in Belinda's desk, and how that led to her arrest.

"Is she their prime suspect?" he asked.

"Well, she has an alibi, but Donny hasn't ruled her out as being involved." Penelope hesitated as her heart got heavy, and then added, "I wanted to let you know that Jacob might come under suspicion."

Doug didn't respond right away. He looked across the table at her with unblinking eyes. She saw the disbelief on her brother's face.

"What? Jacob? Why? How could anyone think that?"

"It makes sense, from an investigative standpoint. With Belinda's alibi checking out, someone had to have put the pad and the drugs in her desk—someone connected to the robbery. What with Jacob's belongings being returned and prescription pads with his name turning up in the victim's apartment, it's only a matter of time before Donny comes to the same conclusion. Jacob is the only connection between the two crimes."

"You don't believe it, do you?" Doug was incredulous.

"Of course not! He was in the hospital after the robbery and he stayed here with you until he went to work the next day."

Doug ran his fingers through his disheveled hair. "I can't believe it."

"I've been working with Donny, but if Jacob becomes a suspect, he'll probably shut me out of the case."

"What? You're the best! You see things others don't." Now Doug was even more indignant.

Penelope reached out and put her hand on her brother's arm. "It would only make sense, Doug. I'm too close to the suspect. But that would just mean I couldn't investigate openly."

"What do you mean . . . *openly*?"

Penelope sat back in her chair. "Well, that's the other thing I wanted to tell you. You know I'm on vacation this week.

"Yeah . . ."

"Well, I've been working the case unofficially."

She gave Doug a few moments to process the information.

"You said there was something missing from Jacob's wallet. What was it?"

"A picture of us from the photo booth at your wedding and a Chinese fortune slip . . . from the cookie you and Camille gave us."

"They took that and a picture of you and Jacob? Nothing else was missing?"

"Nope. Just the picture and fortune."

"Why would someone take those?"

"I don't know. But Gabriel and I have a theory."

"That psychologist from the trial?"

"Yeah. He was my advisor in college. He has an office at Grace Memorial and he's been helping me investigate this . . . unofficially."

"What's his theory?"

"When I told him about Jacob's stuff being returned, he thought it was a bit unusual as well. He suspects that whoever returned the belongings probably knows Jacob."

"Like a patient?"

"Or a coworker."

"But how did they get his belongings in the first place? Did they find them? And why didn't they say anything?"

"That's been bugging me all week. We think the same person killed one of the robbers and returned Jacob's belongings."

"Are you in danger, Pen?"

"No, but I think Jacob is."

"You think they'll come after him? Why would they do that after they returned his belongings?"

"We think this person might have a crush on Jacob."

"Like a secret admirer?"

"Exactly. And when they found out about the robbery, they took the law into their own hands."

"What did Jacob say about all this?"

"I haven't told him. Gabriel and I are going to follow him tomorrow. I want to make sure he's safe, and I want to see if we can spot this person."

"You need to tell him, Pen."

"I don't want to worry him if we're wrong."

"You still need to tell him," Doug insisted.

"I will. If nothing pans out tomorrow, I'll run the theory by him."

"I don't like this, Pen. It sounds dangerous."

"I'll be careful."

Doug was much more upset than Penelope thought he would be. She didn't say anything for a while. Sometimes Doug needed a few minutes to calm down. His reaction made her see things in a new light, though. Was she in danger? Why on earth would someone want a picture of her and Jacob?

Doug had only recently lost his ex-wife, and his seemingly strong grip on things might be deceiving. Losing Penelope would crush Doug. She was his only sister; even though they weren't related by blood, they were still family.

"I want you to text me your location while you're unofficially working. I don't want you to get caught up in this any more than you have. I'd go with you, but—"

"Doug, you know I can take care of myself," she interrupted. "I'm a cop, Doug. Dangerous is what I do. I'm careful. I'm professional, and I'm armed. Besides, Gabriel is going to go with me, so I'll have a bodyguard after all."

She meant to lighten the tone, but Doug only got more serious.

"Text me. Can you do that, please? I want a running report of where you are going." He rubbed his temples. "This worries me, Pen. I want to know you'll be safe."

She was touched. "I promise. I'll let you know where we are going. It should only take a few days to find conclusive evidence that Jacob couldn't be involved."

"Donny should take your word for it," Doug grumbled.

"If Jacob does become a suspect, Donny would just be following procedure. It's all part of the investigative process." Penelope liked being a part of the process, but she disliked where this one seemed to be headed. The sooner it was solved, the better.

Trevor walked into the room. He looked subdued. "Are you guys fighting?"

"No way, Trev. Your Aunt Penny and I never fight. We debate."

Penelope and Doug put their smiles back on, though

there was slightly less joy than before.

"Promise?" Trevor asked.

"I promise," Penelope said with solemnity and authority.

Trevor seemed appeased.

Penelope and Doug joined Trevor in the living room. Doug turned off the TV and pulled out a puzzle he and Trevor had completed a hundred times. Penelope spotted the corner pieces and pointed them out to Trevor. Once they found the four corners, they began searching for the edge pieces. Penelope's eyes darted across the scattered pieces as she fit the puzzle together in her mind—she worked criminal cases in the same manner.

As they completed the edges, they each picked up various pieces and tried to place them in position, placing one piece at a time until the picture became clear.

CHAPTER 55

THURSDAY MORNING, GABRIEL PULLED into Penelope's driveway at 5:59 a.m. She hopped into the passenger seat and Gabriel offered her a cup of coffee. It was quiet and misty outside, but being inside the tank of an SUV gave Penelope a distinct feeling of entombment.

She greeted Gabriel with a smile, took a sip of coffee, and then sent Doug a quick text, **With Gabriel. Continuing our unofficial investigation.** She hit send and put her cell phone on the enormous dashboard. She took another long sip of her coffee and punched Jacob's address into the vehicle's navigation system.

They drove to the beautiful, well-developed Franklin neighborhood of comfortable homes on large lots. The houses were built in the 1990s, but had been updated over the years and kept in meticulous condition. Landscaping trucks lined the streets and teams of workers dotted the lush lawns as Gabriel drove through the winding, tree-lined streets.

The voice navigation system alerted them of the upcoming turn onto Jacob's street, and a knot tightened in Penelope's stomach. She slid down a few inches in her seat as they rounded the corner and began the crawl up the rain-splattered street she had driven hundreds of times.

They parked at the neighborhood playground parking lot a few houses away from Jacob's. The location gave them a perfect view of his house, garage, and driveway.

Fifteen minutes later, Penelope watched as Jacob emerged from his front door and locked it behind him. She held her breath as the man she loved waved to his neighbor Justine, a woman in her mid-fifties that Penelope had met a few times.

Jacob walked to car. From the corner of her eye, Penelope noticed Justine still standing on her front stoop, in her silk bathrobe, eyeing Jacob as he walked away. Her eyes lingered on Jacob and Penelope felt a sting of jealousy.

"I never realized that Jacob's neighbor looked at him like that," she said aloud, forgetting for a moment that she wasn't alone in the car.

Gabriel watched in silence. If he had an opinion, he kept it to himself.

Jacob got in his car and backed slowly down the driveway. Gabriel put the Hummer into drive and pulled out of the park after Jacob made the turn onto the main street. Penelope sat up taller. She knew where he was going.

Jacob worked in Franklin on Thursdays and usually jogged the trail that passed behind the Franklin Clinic.

His usual routine was to park at the Franklin Clinic, run five miles toward Gainesville and then run back. After his run he would head into the clinic, shower, and then start his day.

As they neared the clinic, Penelope felt a loosening of the vice grip around her stomach. But it was quickly replaced with fear when Jacob stayed on State Road 20 and drove past the Franklin Clinic.

He wasn't sticking to his normal schedule.

Penelope's mind raced. *Where's he going?*

"Isn't this exciting?" Gabriel asked. He gripped the steering wheel tighter and stepped on the gas.

Exciting? That wasn't the word she would use. "He probably got a call from Grace Memorial," she said defensively. "That happens quite often."

"I'm sure it's something like that. Or maybe where he's going will help us learn more about why your fiancé was targeted."

Targeted? Was Jacob targeted?

CHAPTER 56

TEN MINUTES LATER, AT 8:06 a.m., Jacob's car pulled off the main road and into the Boulware Springs parking lot—the beginning of the Gainesville-Franklin State Trail.

Gabriel found a space in the shade of a water oak tree with a view of the picnic benches and the trailhead. It was getting increasingly hot despite the light rain. Gabriel turned the engine off, but let the air conditioner run.

Penelope pulled out her phone and read a text from Doug. **Thanks for the update. Keep me posted.**

At Boulware Springs. Jacob is starting his run. Nothing so far, she replied to Doug, and then sent Donny a text. **How are the Franklin Clinic interviews going?**

A few moments later Donny's reply came. **On our way to the clinic now. Starting interviews at 9. You still good for tomorrow?**

"Who's that you're texting?"

Penelope jumped. Gabriel had been so quiet she had

almost forgotten he was there. She was slightly put off by his directness, but she knew it was simply his way of cutting to the chase. When she wasn't mad at him, it was something she liked about him.

"Detective Greene," she answered Gabriel as she typed a reply to Donny. **Yep. Still good. I'll meet you at the station.** She pressed send and continued out loud, "It's strange . . . how far we've come."

"How far who has come?" Gabriel asked.

"Donny and I. I mean . . . we studied together, graduated together . . . and now he's a detective . . ." She didn't have to add the rest, that she was still a beat cop when he'd gotten so much further.

"You've learned other things that you wouldn't have learned if you were a detective," Gabriel said absently. He was distant, his mind somewhere else, but what he said hit home. Penelope had learned so much. The path the Lord had taken her on had shaped her as a person. "You'll make a great detective one day, you know," Gabriel added, glancing at her.

Penelope smiled tentatively. Once upon a time, she might have been confident enough to think that, but lately she'd been emotionally involved in the cases. It had not been as easy as she'd hoped to piece this case together. Nothing matched up.

Jacob got out of his car and Penelope took a deep breath, trying to release some of the tension.

Gabriel saw the change in her expression and followed her gaze. "There's the good doctor," he said.

Penelope watched Jacob and her heart filled with love,

the type of love she had never experienced before she met him. She admired his posture and his bearing. He walked to one of the picnic benches and went through a series of stretches. A moment later he sat down and started tapping on his cell phone. Penelope had seen him do this countless time. The e-mails, the phone calls, the frantic texts from nurses at both the hospital and the clinic.

As she watched him with admiration, a figure approached. It was hard to see clearly through the thick, moist air. The drizzle had picked up slightly, and the sky had darkened. The figure was clearly female, but she wore a hooded coat.

Jacob clearly knew the woman. He was smiling as he shook her hand warmly.

Penelope didn't know whether to be relieved that a man was not attacking him or to be upset that a woman was talking to him.

The woman sat next to Jacob on the bench responding to his welcoming gesture. When she laughed at something Jacob said, her hood fell back to reveal her face.

A chill of recognition flashed through Penelope.

It was Tina Shifflett, the medical receptionist from Grace Memorial Hospital.

For the next ten minutes, Jacob faced Tina and listened to her, nodding sympathetically. Penelope sat frozen, not letting on that she knew the woman, afraid of the conclusions that Gabriel would jump to and trying to avoid jumping there herself.

Gabriel, seated next to her in the richly appointed captain's seat of his tank, seemed to be perplexed. It was certainly not what either of them had expected. She was a little embarrassed that he should see her fiancé in what could be a compromising situation. Of course, this was nothing but an innocent visit between friends. Jacob would never do anything to hurt Penelope, and she didn't need anyone else involved in his or her private business if it was something untoward.

For a moment, she became irrationally angry with Gabriel for judging, even though he had said nothing. The next moment, she felt that she needed to apologize.

"He is giving her some type of advice," Gabriel said calmly.

He pointed out the key indicators of their body language to Penelope, using the most clinical language and deconstructing the scene scientifically. She could see what he meant about the way their bodies were facing and how their heads were tilted in relation to each other. It was too misty and far away to see their facial expressions, but Gabriel's analysis appeared to be correct.

"You see, now that she is leaving," he continued, "she is tilting her face away from his. If this were romantic in nature, she would press against his cheek, isn't that right? And her arms . . . you see how she keeps one arm at her side and uses the other to pat his back? I believe this to be a coworker, someone with whom he has no romantic entanglements."

It was impressive the way that he broke down the situation. The stress left Penelope's body as he explained each movement and its psychological significance. She was confident that everything had happened exactly the way

Gabriel described it.

Tina walked away, and she and Jacob exchanged friendly waves. She drove off in a gray sedan and Jacob disappeared into the wooded trail at a light jogging pace.

A wave of guilt washed over her. Was she doing the right thing by following the man she trusted with her heart and soul? It was in his best interest, but something didn't feel right.

CHAPTER 57

PENELOPE GAZED INTO THE woods. She no longer liked the idea of following Jacob. It made her feel sneaky, calculating, and untrustworthy. The last thing she wanted was a reason to create any distrust in their relationship.

"I'm not sure how I feel about this," she finally told Gabriel.

"About the woman your fiancé was talking to or us following him?"

"Us following him."

"Would you feel better if he knew?"

"I don't know. Maybe . . . But he'd probably say that he can take care of himself."

"This is your investigation, Penelope . . . unofficially, of course. You tell me what you'd like to do. I'm at your disposal."

Penelope thought about it for a moment. "Let's see

where he goes after the run and if we notice anything else unusual. He normally heads to the clinic and showers."

"You're sure? I don't want you doing anything that makes you uncomfortable."

"It's going to feel uncomfortable, but it's the right thing to do. If someone is stalking him, or admiring him from afar, it's going to be our best chance to catch that person in the act."

The two sat in silence while they waited for Jacob to finish his run. Gabriel busied himself by listening to a local talk radio program while Penelope checked her e-mail and sent Doug an update. She opened the Bible app on her phone and began looking up verses that would help calm her ragged nerves.

She found Philippians 4:6-7 especially reassuring. "Do not be anxious about anything, but in every situation, by prayer and petition, with thanksgiving, present your requests to God. And the peace of God, which transcends all understanding, will guard your hearts and your minds in Christ Jesus."

Thirty minutes later, Jacob emerged from the woods, sweaty and flushed. He paused to do a few stretches before hopping into his car and driving off.

Gabriel kept his distance, following five to six car lengths behind. They rode back to Franklin without saying a word. Penelope prayed that there would be no more mystery women and no more surprises.

When Jacob pulled into the parking lot of the Franklin Clinic, Gabriel turned into the church lot across the street and parked where they could catch a glimpse of the driver's side of Jacob's car.

Penelope watched across the road as her fiancé checked his phone, obviously handling urgent matters and tending to his agenda as he always did in preparation for a busy day. She still felt bad for watching without his knowledge, and resolved right then that she would tell him everything. She was about to tell Gabriel that they should leave but was interrupted when he spoke first.

"So, what does he usually do for lunch? Does he stay here or go out? Do you know if he goes straight home after work?"

"Listen, I appreciate your help, truly I do, but I don't think this is a good use of our time."

Gabriel seemed to take her decision in stride. "It's your call. I'll help in any way I can."

Penelope thought about all the things she had to do for the wedding. "Any way you can?" she asked.

Gabriel looked at her and nodded. "Yep. Do you want to go back to any of the crime scenes? Review case notes?"

"I had something else in mind."

"Like what? I'm all yours today."

"Would you mind checking out a few venues with me?" she said with a slight hesitation. It was asking a lot, but she enjoyed spending time with Gabriel.

Gabriel smiled broadly. "Of course! I'd love to. Where to first?"

Penelope sat back and relaxed. She'd finally be able to follow through on her promise to Jacob—even if a little spying had diverted her. She grabbed her phone and looked up the list of venues she had found online.

"There's the Sweetwater Branch Inn, The Hippodrome State Theatre, and the Kanapaha Botanical Gardens to start."

Gabriel laughed and punched the locations into the navigation system. "Looks like we're closest to the Botanical Gardens. Shall we start with that one?"

Penelope nodded and as they pulled out of the church parking lot, her phone rang.

She tapped *answer* and Jacob's voice boomed through the phone. "Hi, Penny."

"I was just thinking of you," she said sheepishly. "I'm on my way to take care of some wedding stuff."

"About that," Jacob said with a slight edge in his voice. "I need to reschedule our lunch tomorrow."

Penelope felt her cheeks heat up. "We're supposed to meet with Josie, the potential wedding planner." Jacob had been pressing her to make the wedding a priority, and now here he was, doing just the opposite.

"I know . . . and I'm sorry. I completely forgot about my meeting." Penelope could hear his fear of disappointing her. "I called as soon as I remembered," he added.

"Is everything okay?"

"Yeah, everything's fine. We can catch up tomorrow at dinner, okay?"

"Is there something you need to tell me?" she asked.

"Dinner tomorrow night, alright Penny?"

He was purposefully not answering her question. *Was someone nearby?* "Should I be worried?" she asked.

"No. I don't mind where we eat, as long as we're together," he replied playfully.

Penelope chuckled. "Okay, mystery man. I'll see you tomorrow night."

"See you then. I love you."

"Love you back." She hung up and shook her head. *What was he up to?*

"Everything okay?" Gabriel asked.

"I think so," was her honest answer.

CHAPTER 58

THAT EVENING, AFTER A long day of looking at potential wedding reception venues, Penelope smiled as Gabriel pulled into her driveway. Life could be so overwhelming and then something as simple as spending an afternoon with a good friend could bring her back to herself.

Penelope hopped out of the SUV and thanked Gabriel for an enjoyable day. He asked her about her plans for Friday, and she told him that she would be working with Donny doing follow-up interviews with the staff from Grace Memorial Hospital. She promised to keep him posted and then waved as he drove off.

Down the road, an engine started and Penelope paused mid-step, her pulse quickening. There were only three other homes on her block. The houses in this part of town were set back off the street, and there were no sidewalks.

She turned and spotted a light-colored SUV, with its lights off, about sixty yards away. It made a slow U-turn and Penelope squinted to get a better look. With no streetlights, she couldn't make out the model or license plate before it disappeared into the darkness.

That was odd.

Had someone been spying on her the same way she was spying on Jacob? Where they casing the neighborhood?

Penelope listened for more activity.

Nothing.

She unlocked her front door, walked into her house, and assessed the scene.

Soft moonlight shining through the front windows lit up the living room, casting eerie shadows against the white walls. The refrigerator clicked on with a whirl, but Penelope didn't flinch. One by one she checked the rooms and closets of her house. As she moved from room to room, she made sure all the windows were locked.

She almost called Gabriel but dialed the Franklin PD instead.

Officer Jim Saunders had just finished his shift and offered to drive by.

Penelope retrieved her service weapon, a Smith & Wesson Sigma Series .40 caliber semi-automatic double-action pistol, from the gun safe in her closet and waited for Saunders. As she sat in the darkness, staring out through the bushes and trees, Gabriel's words from a few days earlier rustled through her mind: "If they accessed your fiancé's cell phone and his address book, there's a possibility they have all his contacts."

CHAPTER 59

FIFTEEN MINUTES LATER, HEADLIGHTS lit up Penelope's driveway.

She put her shoulder holster on and seated her Sigma in it. The action brought her back to the present. She stood on the porch until Officer Saunders got out of his cruiser.

"Chance, is everything okay?" There was no trace of his usually laid-back and goofy demeanor. He was all business.

"I hope so. A truck was out on the road there. It left when I got here. I want to go see if there are any clues about why they were here." She paused. "It could've been teenagers, but in light of recent events . . ."

"I think you were right to call, Chance." He was taking her seriously. "You've got to follow your gut. Better safe than sorry."

"I figured you'd understand. Got a spare flashlight?"

"One step ahead of you."

Saunders held up a small duffle bag. He reached inside, pulled out a flashlight, and tossed it to Penelope. She caught it and switched it on. Saunders armed himself with a flashlight as well and slung the bag over his shoulder.

"Which way?" he asked.

Penelope pointed at the clump of trees at the top of the incline that led to her house. The bushes and groundcover were thick and tangled. She looked at Saunders, and he nodded. She pointed up the driveway, and they crunched through the gravel toward the road, shining their lights in a sweeping motion as they went.

Their flashlights shone on fresh tire tracks in the dirt road under the row of trees.

"Definitely a truck," Saunders noted. "You know anyone with a truck?"

"Just Doug. And Gabriel. No one else close to me. But acquaintances, well, I know a lot of people who drive trucks."

"Not much to go on, but I'll get pictures of the tracks. It'll help narrow it down."

Taking care to avoid stepping on the imprints of the tires, Penelope shined her light into the surrounding bushes while Saunders snapped a few pictures.

"What do you see?" Saunders asked.

"A few beer cans. They could have been there already. Let's bag them anyway."

Other than the tire tracks and the beer cans, there wasn't much to see.

"No footprints. He . . . or they must not have gotten out of the truck." Saunders finished scanning the area with his light and clicked it off. "Maybe someone pulled over to take a call?"

Was that what Saunders thought or was he just trying to make her feel better? It seemed to be a likely explanation.

"Well, I appreciate you coming out."

"You alright, Chance?"

"Yeah. Just a little jumpy."

Something rustled in the bushes as Penelope and Officer Saunders walked back to her house.

Penelope's blood froze.

Saunders took a revolver from the duffle bag and held it low.

"Who's there?" Penelope called into the bushes. She pointed her flashlight at the thick undergrowth. The rustling stopped.

"Police. Come out!" Saunders shouted as he walked toward the bushes.

The bushes heaved, and Penelope removed her gun from its shoulder harness.

Twigs snapped as someone, or something, large headed straight for them.

The next instant a broad-faced Florida panther emerged from the sea of leaves and Saunders fired a shot into the ground in front of the panicked cat. It stopped on a dime and leaped into the air as it hastily turned away from the noise and darted into the forest.

The whole confrontation lasted less than a couple of seconds.

Saunders stood motionless, and Penelope used her

flashlight to make sure the cat was gone. The gunshot spooked it pretty good. Hopefully, it wouldn't be back.

"Saunders?"

Saunders shook his head and lowered his gun.

"You all right?" she asked.

He didn't answer. Instead, he walked straight to his cruiser, opened the glove box, and removed a pack of unfiltered Camel cigarettes. He had quit months ago. His hand trembled like a wind-battered leaf as he lit one up, and took a long drag.

"I'm all right, Chance. I sure wasn't expecting that to happen." He smiled at her and must have seen something in her expression. "I know, I know. I quit, but I think that encounter warranted a smoke."

"I didn't say anything, Jim." If cigarettes didn't make her feel so nauseous, she might have smoked one, too. She let out a giggle. The adrenaline made her feel giddy, and the next thing she knew, she was laughing hysterically and had to lean against Saunders' cruiser to prop herself up.

"Aw, cut it out, Chance!" Saunders tried to maintain his composure, but failed and started laughing as well.

Once the nervous energy burned off, the two were silent for a minute or two as Saunders finished his cigarette. Penelope wondered if the panther was in her neighborhood often. She'd seen panthers before, and she probably would again.

"You need me to sign your report?" Penelope broke the silence.

"What report?"

"For discharging your service weapon. You'll have to

write it up."

"Oh," Saunders looked at the weapon. "This is not my service pistol. It's my grandfather's old revolver."

"Saunders, you know that's against the rules when you're in uniform!"

Saunders chuckled. "Jeez, this is the thanks I get for saving you from a panther. I'll remember this next time a wild animal is charging us. You'll be on your own!"

CHAPTER 60

EARLY FRIDAY MORNING, PENELOPE'S cell phone rang.

She shot up in bed and blinked hard, trying to wake up. She blinked again and glanced at the time on her phone. It read 6:12 a.m.

"This is Chance," she answered.

"Chance. It's Donny. Sorry to call so early, but there's something you should know."

"What is it? What's wrong?" Penelope held her breath.

"Our murder victim," Donny continued, "was a former patient of Dr. Gordon."

Her insides curled and tightened. Another sign pointing to Jacob's involvement. Could it be a coincidence? An even more disturbing realization hit her . . .

What if someone was trying to frame Jacob for the murder?

Donny was silent on the line, waiting for Penelope to gather her thoughts enough to speak.

"What did Jacob have to say about it?" she asked.

"He was the one that brought it to our attention."

Calm began to flow through her body. "He did?"

"Yeah. After my interviews with the staff at the Franklin Clinic yesterday I had some follow-up questions for him about Belinda. The doc told me there was something familiar about the victim and not just from the robbery. He looked through the clinic's records and found a file on Kevin Scott. The doc saw him once a couple of years ago at the Franklin Clinic."

"Did he say what he saw him for?"

"Addiction. The doc had noted that Mr. Scott grew agitated during his appointment when he wouldn't prescribe methadone. He also thought the patient might get violent. Mr. Scott didn't come back again."

Jacob did not prescribe methadone. There was a methadone clinic between Franklin and Gainesville where most people went for treatment.

Hungry for information that would help her prove Jacob's innocence, Penelope asked, "Why didn't the file show up when you pulled Mr. Scott's medical records?"

"That's the odd part. The file wasn't in the clinic database. The doc located a hard copy. It had never been digitized. The doc wasn't sure why. He doesn't input the forms to the computer. He said the office staff usually takes care of that."

"I appreciate you keeping me in the loop, and this is great information, but couldn't this have waited until I saw you in person this afternoon?"

"I wanted to catch you before you drove over . . ."

There was hesitation in Donny's voice and Penelope braced herself for more bad news. She took a deep breath and closed her eyes before she spoke. "What is it, Donny?"

Another pause.

"It's just that, well, I think it might be better if you stayed behind the scenes for a while."

"What? Now that you might have found a connection you want to shut me out? Donny, you can't. I need to clear Jacob's name and prove that he's not involved. I need to make sure I'm doing everything to protect Jacob." As soon as the words left her mouth, she realized how that sounded, how unprofessional and personally involved that sounded. "And, to help catch the killer," she added a second later, but it was too late.

"That's what I'm talking about, Chance. It's not that I don't want your expertise and your help. Believe me, I do. It's just that I don't want to compromise the investigation with personal involvement, especially if it involves digging deeper into Jacob's life so we can get closer to who's really behind all this."

Penelope's head swam. Donny was right. She was personally involved and she would have said the same thing if their roles were reversed.

She tried to approach it from a new angle. "Donny, that's what makes me valuable," she pleaded. "I can offer a perspective you wouldn't otherwise have. I need to stay involved."

Penelope gripped the phone as Donny let out a long

sigh on the other end.

"Okay," he said reluctantly. "Listen, I'll let you sit in on the hospital staff interviews today. But . . . if it starts looking more like the doc is involved . . . in any way, you're out. You hear me?"

"Okay, I know. I don't want to jeopardize the investigation. I appreciate you sticking your neck out for me, Donny. I promise to stay in the background."

Penelope hung up and noticed a text message from Josie, the wedding planner she was meeting for lunch; the message had come late last night, and she had missed it. **Sorry for the late notice. Mind if we meet at the Gainesville Hilton tomorrow? I'll be setting up for a wedding, and you can see me in action.**

Penelope typed a quick reply, **Sure. See you this afternoon**, and pressed send. She typed Jacob a message informing him of the change, but stopped when she remembered that he couldn't make it.

She set her phone on the nightstand, slid out of bed and dropped to her knees. She clasped her hands in front of her as she closed her eyes. "Dear Lord, please show me how I can help Donny prove Jacob's innocence and find the person who is really responsible."

God and God alone would mete out true justice. Her duty was to protect and serve her community, and she planned to do just that.

CHAPTER 61

WHEN PENELOPE PULLED INTO the Hilton Hotel parking lot at twelve thirty that afternoon, she saw Jacob's yellow Mustang parked near the front entrance. She parked a few rows back and immediately went into cop mode.

What's Jacob doing here?

Was his meeting at the Hilton? Maybe his meeting was canceled and he was there to surprise her.

Penelope closed her eyes and said a quick prayer of thanks for having such a wonderful, thoughtful man. She was about to step out of her car when Jacob emerged from the hotel lobby.

Seconds later, the picture became disturbingly clear.

Tina Shifflett followed Jacob out of the hotel. If it had been anyone else, a female doctor colleague, or even Nurse Taylor, she could have told herself that this was work-related. But Tina?

Penelope's mind raced as Jacob grabbed Tina by the elbow, pulled her close, and twirled her. Tina's skirt flared as she spun, and the pair laughed. Jacob tangoed Tina to her car, a gray sedan—the gray sedan from the park yesterday. Tina kissed Jacob on the cheek before she got in her car and drove off.

Penelope hunkered down in her driver's seat.

Please don't let Jacob see me.

Jacob smiled ear to ear as he walked to his car. He drove off as though he had not a care in the world. He didn't appear to notice his surroundings at all. He looked happy as he drove right past Penelope's car without seeing it, or her.

Her insides tightened like a relentless vise, and she couldn't breathe.

Oh dear God . . . what did I just witness?

Jacob had lied to her about his meeting, and she had witnessed him embracing another woman. And the tango! Jacob didn't dance. It wasn't something he enjoyed; he had told Penelope that when they met. Whenever they went out he resisted every attempt she made to get him onto a dance floor, but here he was, dancing with Tina and clearly enjoying it. He had lied about that, too. And Tina had kissed him! On the cheek—but still. She replayed the kiss over and over in her mind.

The urge to cry hit her like a physical blow. She took several deep breaths, but she had a hard time burying the swell of emotions. She forced her rational side to take over.

"What are the facts, Chance?" she asked herself.

This question usually helped her figure out what to

think, and how to proceed when things got too crazy.

"Fact one . . . Jacob told me he had a work meeting," she said aloud.

She double-checked her memory. *Had he said work meeting?*

Now that she thought about it, he may have just said meeting. That could mean anything. That could mean going to lunch with Tina.

"Fact two . . . Jacob hates dancing," she continued. "But it sure looked like he was enjoying it with Tina."

Penelope's thoughts began to work against her. While she enjoyed dancing, she had given it up since she'd been with Jacob. It wasn't his thing, and that was fine with her. But what if he just didn't want to dance with her? He clearly enjoyed the little dance with Tina. The twirl replayed in her mind and she cringed. And the tango to the car. That couldn't have been the first time Jacob and Tina had done that. It was too smooth, too polished.

A war of emotions raged within her and hot tears streamed down her checks.

How could Jacob do something like this?

None of this made sense.

The logical part of her brain was failing to come up with comforting facts to refute the obvious conclusion—Jacob was having an affair. It was almost too outlandish to believe. Jacob had a close relationship with God, and she couldn't make herself believe that he was having a fling with Tina. It was out of character for him. But there was the twirl, the tango, and the kiss, and he hadn't told her it was Tina that he was meeting. He was keeping secrets that involved another woman.

Penelope looked at herself in the rearview mirror and wiped a hand across her eyes, thankful that she hadn't worn mascara. She looked at her reflection critically. A few more lines in the face and her eyes were red and puffy from crying, but she still looked pretty good.

It had been such a long time since Penelope had experienced emotions of this magnitude; she hardly remembered what it felt like.

The weight was suffocating.

Her gut said not to give in to negative presumptions. She was jumping to conclusions too quickly. Give Jacob a chance to explain. There has to be a logical explanation— there has to.

But another part of her was a little girl, crying, watching her house burn to the ground with her parents trapped inside.

Numbness spread through her body.

She wasn't sure how long she sat there, crying silently, and mourning for everything she had ever lost. The tears kept coming long after she thought she had finished.

Slowly, Penelope became aware that life was moving on outside of her personal space, and suddenly remembered why she was at the hotel. She grabbed her phone and sent the wedding planner a text message apologizing and saying that she had to cancel. There was no way she could meet with her now.

Would there even be a wedding?

Fresh tears began to flow, and Penelope quickly turned her mind toward the case. The case was something tangible, something she could focus on until she felt real again. She welcomed the numb feeling and shoved her emotions down deep. They would hit her again later, but if she could get through the rest of the day, she might be okay.

She brushed her hair and wiped her face with a tissue from the glove box. She turned on the AC and adjusted the vent to blow cold air in her face. If her eyes were still red when she met with Donny, she could blame it on allergies.

As she regained her composure, she ran through the facts of the case—the ones she could handle now.

Kevin Scott and his partner robbed the Grace Memorial Hospital early Friday afternoon. Sometime late Friday night or early Saturday morning, Mr. Scott was shot and killed in the parking lot of his apartment complex—probably in a drug deal gone bad. His body was later dumped in the Franklin River. Jacob's—she winced at the thought of his name—and only Jacob's belongings were returned to the Franklin Clinic Saturday morning. Mr. Scott's body was discovered Sunday morning. Donny located the primary crime scene Monday evening and searched Mr. Scott's apartment. He discovered several outdated blank prescription pads with Jacob's information. Tuesday morning one of Jacob's missing prescription pads was found in Belinda's desk along with several of the bottles of drugs stolen in Friday's robbery.

What happened to Kevin Scott after he and his partner left Grace Memorial? What happened to the stolen drugs? How and why were Jacob's things returned? Why did someone keep the picture and fortune slip when everything else was returned? Who planted the drugs in

Belinda's desk? What was Denise Wilson doing at Kevin Scott's apartment?

The unknown outweighed the known. Perhaps Donny's interviews with the Franklin Clinic staff yesterday would shed light on the situation. She certainly hoped so. She was feeling pretty dark.

CHAPTER 62

PENELOPE TRUDGED INTO THE Gainesville Police Station that afternoon feeling divorced from reality. The surroundings were familiar, but the colors seemed off, as if something was wrong with the fluorescent lighting. The desk sergeant buzzed her in, and she walked straight to Donny's office.

She sank into a chair, and he jumped into an update without even a cursory greeting.

"So ballistics came back on the bullet that killed Kevin Scott. It's a match to the three slugs we pulled out of the wall at Grace Memorial. Looks like Scott's partner killed him . . . probably for the drugs."

Penelope stared off into space as Donny paced behind his desk. He continued relating facts: "We came up empty on the interviews at the Franklin Clinic yesterday. Dr. Pamela Bishop was working the day of the robbery at the

Franklin Clinic. Last Friday evening she was called into Grace Memorial to assist with patients from the accident on State Road 20. She pulled an all-nighter. She was there until six o'clock Saturday morning, well outside of our TOD window. Similar story with Nurse Adam Reed. He worked a full shift at Franklin last Friday and then went to dinner and a movie with his girlfriend. Nurse Genevieve Taylor had the day off last Friday and was visiting her brother in Jacksonville. Officer Watson checked the alibis of three other nurses who work at the clinic and they all checked out. I have Officer Meeks following up on Reed and Taylor's alibis, but they seem pretty solid."

When Donny finally looked at Penelope, his expression of alarm confirmed that she was, in fact, losing it.

"Earth to Chance. Hello? Have you been listening to anything I said?"

"Scott was killed by the same gun used in the robbery. Everybody's alibi checks out. Got it," she said on autopilot.

"Chance, what's going on with you?"

You really want to know? Where do I start? "Don, you wouldn't believe me if I told you." A few sobs slipped out before she slapped her hand over her mouth.

Donny gave Penelope a hard look. "Listen, Chance . . . I don't have time for you to go all girly on me here. If you want to sit in on these interviews this afternoon, I need you to be a cop."

Penelope sat silent for a moment, fighting back the tears.

The woman in her wanted to blurt it out and cry on the shoulder of her old friend about how she had followed

Jacob and saw him embrace another woman. She still couldn't wrap her mind around the fact that he might be having an inappropriate relationship with one of his coworkers.

But, instead, she collected herself and said, "I'm good. What's our next step?" She looked at Donny, certain he would remove her from the case after her mini meltdown.

He stared back and then continued. "*We*," Donny said, putting a special emphasis on *we*, "are going to head over to Grace Memorial and interview Sylvia Brown, Tina Shifflett, and Deborah Thompson, and see if they can remember anything new about our vic's partner."

I don't know if I can do that, she wanted to say as Tina's name rang in her head. But she managed to eke out a, "Thanks, Don," unsure if she was thanking him for allowing her to sit in on the interviews, making her act like a cop, or something else.

"I'll buy you a coffee on the way," Donny said, completely ignoring her thanks. "Oh, and your psychologist friend, Dr. Pike, is going to join us."

He is?

CHAPTER **63**

AS PENELOPE FOLLOWED DONNY to Grace Memorial Hospital, the images of Jacob and Tina were blurred by the thought of Gabriel joining for the interviews. Did Donny call Gabriel or did Gabriel call Donny and offer his services? Why would Donny need outside help?

She tried to remain objective, but her cop senses prickled.

Penelope parked her MGB next to Donny's Crown Victoria. They made their way to a back conference room that had been cleared for the interviews. Gabriel greeted them enthusiastically when they arrived.

"Well, Doc," Donny said. "You don't mind if I call you doc, do you?"

"It wouldn't be the first time."

"Well, I appreciate you being willing to help. When Penelope told me you had offered your services, I figured we could use the help. So thanks for jumping right in when I called."

So, Donny called him. He was right. They could use Gabriel's expertise.

"So on the phone, you were telling me about a technique you use to help witnesses remember," Donny said.

"Well," Gabriel began, "it's an experimental forensic trauma interview technique."

"Sounds complicated."

Gabriel smiled broadly, and his eyes danced in his worn face. "It's rather simple. You see, people who endure traumatic experiences . . . like the robbery and the shooting . . . are often unable to accurately recall the details of the experience. They don't record the events in their prefrontal cortex the way they would other events. Instead, that part of the brain shuts down, and they remember only the sensory experiences of the events."

"So directly asking them to remember what the robbers looked like isn't going to work?" Penelope asked.

"Not always. This technique helps us ask how they felt, what they smelled, what they heard, and what they were thinking during their experience. This allows us to help a witness separate the facts from the emotions they experienced during the trauma.

"Well, I hope it works," Donny said.

Nurse Sylvia Brown was the first to be interviewed, followed by Deborah Thompson. Each of the women was able to offer their emotional response and thought process surrounding the events, but little of what they said provided clues as to who the suspect might be.

Penelope could see that Donny was becoming doubtful. Their last interview with Tina Shifflett should prove more fruitful.

Gabriel sat down at the table. Penelope sat next to him, ramrod straight with her hands clasped together on the table, trying to keep her expression blank.

Donny sat to the left of Gabriel and stood and extended his hand as Tina entered. "Thank you for taking the time to speak with us, Ms. Shifflett."

Tina shook Donny's hand and looked from Gabriel to Donny and to Penelope, and then back to Donny.

Donny motioned for her to take a seat. "Ms. Shifflett, I'm Detective Donny Greene. This is Officer Penelope Chance, and that's Dr. Gabriel Pike."

"Penelope and I have met. What's going on? Why am I here?" she asked.

"We have a couple follow-up questions about the robbery that occurred here last Friday."

Tina shifted in her seat and said, "I'm not sure how I can help. I told everything I know to the other detective."

"That's okay, Tina," Gabriel said in a reassuring tone, scooting his seat closer to the table. "Detective Greene and Officer Chance would like me to walk through the experience with you if that's okay?"

"Sure. I'll tell you everything I know."

"Very good. Let's begin by getting comfortable. Are you comfortable, Tina?"

"Yes, I'm fine. Thank you."

"Good. Now let me also tell you that we're all so very sorry for what you went through. Being a witness to such a violent crime had to be upsetting for you."

Tina shifted in her seat again and blinked back tears that formed in her eyes. "It was, very"—she held a hand up to her mouth—"very hard watching Dr. Gordon get shot. It was awful."

"Yes, I'm sure it was." Gabriel continued to speak in a soothing, calming tone. "Now, Tina, I'd like to understand what you are able to remember about your experience. Can you help me with that?"

Tina nodded slowly.

"So what do you remember about the people in the waiting room?"

"It was slow. There were only a half dozen people . . . I think."

Gabriel smiled and nodded. "Okay, that's great. So can you tell me about the people in the waiting room? Did anyone stand out?"

Tina tilted her head from side to side. "There was one guy. He was wearing, um, I think a red shirt?"

Penelope tried not to roll her eyes. She had questions of her own for the medical receptionist. Questions like: What were you doing at the park with my fiancé? Why were you two having a mid-day meeting at a fancy hotel? And . . . are you having an affair with my fiancé?

"Okay, that's good," Gabriel continued. "Now, how did that guy make you feel?"

"Oh, he was dirty. I remember that he was dirty. His hair was messy, and he looked like he hadn't showered or shaved in days."

"That's excellent Tina. That's extremely helpful."

Gabriel prodded Tina gently through several other questions as Donny sat across from them taking notes.

"Tina, what are you able to remember about the sights, smells, tastes, and sounds?"

"Coffee!" Tina said enthusiastically. "I remember smelling coffee. When the guy shot Dr. Gordon, I knocked over Nurse Brown's coffee."

Gabriel nodded to Donny who wrote it down.

"That's good, Tina. Now, what did you feel when the robber fired that first shot? The first one that hit Dr. Gordon in the shoulder."

Tina blinked at the question and then answered. "I was terrified. I froze and I didn't know what to do. I remember feeling . . ." Her voice trailed off as she looked at her lap and fidgeted with her ID badge.

"It's okay, Tina, anything you say will be helpful."

She looked up with wet eyes. "I remember feeling helpless. And I'm a nurse . . . a nurse receptionist, but still a nurse. I'm supposed to help people. But I felt so . . . helpless."

"That's understandable, Tina. Thank you for sharing that. I'm sure that was very difficult. You're doing great, Tina. Now, there's one more thing I'd like you to share with us, if you could."

Tina nodded.

"What is the one thing that you are unable to forget about your experience?"

Tina's eyes welled up again, and the tears spilled over. "Those blue eyes. I'll never forget those bright blue eyes."

Donny leaned closer as he jotted notes.

"Whose eyes, Tina?" asked Gabriel in a soothing tone.

"The guy that shot Dr. Gordon. They were so full of hate, so bright and blue and full of hate. I can't stop seeing them, even when I close my eyes."

Donny and Gabriel looked at each other.

"I'm so thankful for Dr. Gordon and the other doctors. They treat me so well."

Penelope had been silent up until then. But the mention of her fiancé's name prompted her to jump in. "So Dr. Gordon treats you well, does he? In what ways does he do that?" she asked with an innocent expression that belied the underhanded nature of the question.

Gabriel raised an eyebrow and Donny gave Penelope a stern look that almost made her flinch.

"I said *all* of the doctors do," Tina clarified. "They treat all of the employees well."

"And none of the doctors have inappropriate relationships with any of the nurses?" Penelope continued.

"That's enough, Officer Chance!" Donny interrupted. He turned a soft glance to Tina and said, "Thank you for your time, Ms. Shifflett. If you think of anything else, anything at all, please don't hesitate to give us a call."

Penelope watched Donny incredulously as he walked Tina to the door.

CHAPTER 64

"CHANCE!" DONNY SHOUTED. "WHAT was that all about?"

"Why did you cut me off? She's hiding something."

"If she is, it's not relevant to this case."

A whirlwind of emotions threatened to overtake Penelope once again. She tried to focus on the task at hand. "She's lying."

Gabriel shook his head. "That poor woman has been through a traumatic experience, and you were treating her like a suspect."

"I saw her today . . . with Jacob. And I'm pretty sure she was with him at the park yesterday."

"You've been following Jacob?" Donny asked. "Is there something you're not telling me?"

Penelope was silent, and her face began to burn.

"I suggested we follow her fiancé," Gabriel said, coming

to her defense. "I suspected the person that returned her fiancé's belongings might be the person that killed Kevin Scott. Someone with an infatuation who either saw or heard about him getting shot."

"Yeah. Someone like Tina!" Penelope said.

"I don't know, Penelope," Gabriel began. "I don't think she's the one. I think she genuinely cares for your fiancé, but I don't think she's in love with him."

"I know what I saw."

"This is why I didn't want you to continue on this case," Donny said, raising his voice a few decibels. "You're too close to the investigation to be objective."

"That is exactly why you need me on this case . . ." Penelope said, attempting to justify her actions.

Donny cut her off. "You're letting your emotions cloud your judgment. You're a better cop than this, Chance!"

Penelope opened her mouth to speak, and Donny held up a finger as his cell phone rang.

He kept his eyes locked on her as he barked into his phone, "Yeah? Detective Greene here." As Donny listened to the voice on the other end, his eyes never left Penelope's. "You're sure? I understand. Okay. Thank you." Donny hung up and said, "As of this moment, Chance, you're officially off this case."

"Why? Who was that? What happened?"

Donny shook his head slowly. With effort, his tone changed from anger to sympathy. "It was forensics. They found the doc's fingerprints on the prescription pad from Belinda's desk."

Penelope ignored the growing sense of foreboding.

"Only Jacob's? What about Belinda's?"

"Only the doc's."

"Well, that makes sense," Gabriel said. "They're his prescription pads . . . isn't that right? What about the ones you found in the victim's apartment?"

Donny turned to face Gabriel. "Just the vic's. But they also found the doc's prints on the stolen drugs."

Penelope stood and began to pace the room. "No, that can't be. There has to be another explanation."

"I'm sorry, Chance. We're going to have to bring him in for questioning. And I can't have you involved."

Penelope jumped into fight-for-your-man mode. "You can't really believe that Jacob had anything to do with this . . . can you?"

"I don't want to believe he's involved either, Chance. He's a friend, but I can't ignore the facts. I have to go where the evidence leads. You'd do the same thing."

He was right. She would.

Donny placed a hand on her shoulder. "Listen, Chance. I'm sorry about this. Go home. Get some rest."

Penelope stared disbelievingly at Donny. As she stood there, the walls began to close in on her. Her lungs tightened and she could almost taste smoke as she tried to breathe. *This can't be happening.* Visions of her parents, the fire, Jacob, and Tina cluttered her thoughts and darkness pressed down on her.

"Let me give you a ride," Gabriel said from a million miles away.

She waved him off and drifted out of the room, numb and confused.

This raised new questions about Jacob that Penelope couldn't answer. Was he somehow involved?

It can't be true. It can't be.

CHAPTER 65

PENELOPE WALKED OUT OF the cool air-conditioned hospital and into the thick Florida air, unable to focus and in no condition to drive.

Walk it off, Penny. Walk it off.

She walked down West Newberry Road, and ten minutes later she found herself perched on a concrete bench in Cofrin Nature Park. She and Jacob had spent several afternoons having lunch at that very park, watching the children play.

A torrent of emotional pain and anguish stirred at the thought of Jacob. Penelope let her thoughts swirl. What was Jacob's involvement? Why were his fingerprints on the bottles? Did Jacob plant the drugs in Belinda's desk? What was Jacob's relationship with the victim? Who is Kevin Scott's mystery blue-eyed partner? How does Tina fit into all this?

Thirty minutes passed in a flash and then Penelope's cell phone rang, yanking her out of the downward spiral.

She swallowed hard and cleared her throat. She answered on the third ring. "Chief?"

"Chance, what do you think you're doing?" Jackson's voice bellowed.

"Sir . . . ?"

"I just got a call from your friend, Detective Greene. You want to take a guess why he was calling?"

Penelope remained silent.

"It was a courtesy call," Jackson continued, "informing me that you've been removed from the Kevin Scott murder investigation."

"Chief, I can explain . . ."

"Save it, Chance. Imagine my surprise when Detective Greene told me you've been assisting him in the investigation. An investigation I specifically told you to stay away from."

"But, sir . . . Jacob—"

"—is a person of interest," the chief finished. "Yes, I know. Detective Greene told me."

"So, you see why I need to be involved?"

"No, Chance, I don't. I see why you *shouldn't* be involved!"

"Sir, I can't sit by while Jacob is accused of a crime he didn't commit."

"If you want to help Jacob, that's exactly what you need to do. Stay out of it, Chance. Let Gainesville PD do their job. You've already caused enough trouble; working with Detective Greene behind my back, conducting your own investigation, badgering witnesses . . ."

Penelope's stomach turned to stone. "But, Chief . . . I think that woman is having an affair with Jacob."

"Chance, stop! Just stop." Jackson let out an exasperated breath. "Detective Greene may have let you weasel your way into his investigation, but that ends now. I'm still your boss . . . even when you're on vacation."

What could she say? Chief Jackson was right. She let her emotions cloud her judgment and she'd crossed the line. Her head was a mess and her heart was heading in the same direction. There was heavy silence on the line. The tension in Penelope's body grew.

"I'm warning you, Chance. Stay out of this." The chief's voice was hard. "If you don't there *will* be repercussions. I'd hate to see this tarnish your career." He hung up before she could say anything.

Penelope made her way back to her car, the emotional upheaval weighing her down.

CHAPTER 66

WHEN SHE ARRIVED AT home at 8:47 p.m. Penelope barely managed to put on pajamas before she collapsed on her sofa. The strain of the day had caught up with her, and she hadn't even eaten dinner. It was too late to cook, and she didn't care anyway. She didn't care about anything, not after the day she had.

Her phone rang in her purse.

It could be Jacob. They were supposed to meet for dinner. She didn't feel like talking to him but was compelled to check the caller ID. It was Doug.

She didn't feel like talking to him, either, but he was probably worried because she hadn't checked in all day. She let the call go to voice mail and then sent him a text.

Long day. Talk tomorrow.

She set her phone to silent. She needed some time to be disconnected from the world and figure things out. As soon as the screen went dark, an incredibly lonely feeling rushed through her. She didn't want to talk, but she didn't want to be alone. She was used to being alone, and until today, she had enjoyed her private time. Panic like she had never known welled in her throat.

Her life was based on the premise that God had a plan for her. That plan had included making her an orphan at a young age, and she had found solace and fellowship at church. She accepted her lot in life and thrived in spite of her trials and tribulations. God had seen her through the toughest time in her life. It was He who had led her to meet Jacob, her soul mate. Why was He taking all that away?

This line of thinking was new to her.

She was always confident that the Lord would see her down any path, through any obstacles. Why was it so hard for her to trust His plan now when she needed the strength of her faith to see her through this painful time? Waves of self-pity washed over her, and she gave in to the pain, the hurt.

It felt like she cried for hours, or perhaps time stood still and the earth stopped turning altogether. Her future with Jacob meant the world to her. She hadn't realized how desperately she wanted that future until it was being taken away from her.

It wasn't fair.

She sat up and looked around the room. Her furniture, her decorations, they seemed to belong to someone else.

She felt like a trapped animal—a stranger in her home.

She stumbled out the front door and sank to her knees on the porch, taking giant gulps of fresh air.

The stillness and vastness of the night soothed her. She held herself, shivering from cold and exhaustion. Out in the open she felt small, but she didn't feel trapped anymore.

She took a few deep, shaky breaths and saw something glinting out of the corner of her eye.

She turned her head to look.

It was the light of the moon reflecting off the eyes of a panther, not twenty feet from where she crouched on the porch. She was sure it was the one she and Saunders had seen the night before.

The animal sat, motionless as a statue, returning her gaze. It blinked once, then turned around and strode into the darkness.

Somehow the panther acknowledging her existence made her feel real again.

As she gazed up at the stars, she felt God's love all around her, in everything. Surely His plan would become evident to her when the time was right.

If she could only hold things together until then.

PART 4

CHAPTER 67

AT SIX O'CLOCK SATURDAY morning, Penelope awoke on her sofa to the screeching of her cell phone's alarm clock app. She rubbed her hand across her face and through her hair. As she stretched, the events of the previous day came flooding back. A knot twisted in her stomach because Jacob's love was no longer certain, and he was the prime suspect in Donny's case.

For the next hour and a half, she went on autopilot, showering and getting dressed without paying attention to her actions. She made herself a cup of coffee, checked her cell phone, and saw that she had ten voice mails. Eight of them were from Jacob, one was from Doug last night, and one, from a number she didn't recognize, was left a few minutes ago. She listened to that one first.

"Hi Penelope, this is Tina. I'm so sorry about how things went yesterday and I want to meet with you. I have to tell you something important. I don't want there to be any more misunderstandings. Meet me at Spanky's today at twelve thirty? Please!"

Tina? How did Tina get her number? What did she want? Was she going to confess to her?

Penelope tried calling back, but the call went straight to voice mail. Looks like she'd have to wait until noon to find out. She hung up and sent Tina a text message. **Tina, it's Penelope. Got your message. See you at 12:30 at Spanky's.**

Now what was she going to do with herself in the meantime? She dialed Doug's number.

"Hello?" Doug sounded groggy.

"It's me. Why aren't you awake yet? You'll make Trevor late for school."

"Penny? Huh? It's Saturday. No school, no work. Sleeping."

"I'm coming over."

"Huh? Is everything alright?"

"Yes, I'll fill you in when I get there. I'll make pancakes."

"I'll eat them," he said and hung up to catch a few more precious moments of sleep.

Penelope gathered some things from her kitchen and put them into a tote bag. Doug had been a bachelor for a while now, and he had the pantry to prove it.

She pulled her hair into a quick ponytail, grabbed her keys, and headed out the door. Once she was on the porch, she froze. Her eyes drifted over to where she had seen the panther.

Had it been real or a dream? Was it a sign? And if so, of what?

CHAPTER 68

THE DRIVE TO DOUG'S house was quiet and peaceful. She left the radio off and thought of the panther's eyes, shining in the moonlight. The last time she had seen the endangered cat, Saunders had shot at it, and yet it returned to her front yard. It wasn't scared of her. For some reason the thought comforted her—the panther belonged there as much as she did.

As she pulled up Doug's driveway at nine o'clock, Penelope saw two little forms jumping up and down on the porch—Trevor and another boy that looked to be about the same age. As soon as she had parked, Trevor ran down the porch steps, and the other boy followed.

She opened her car door and was the recipient of a hug that was more like a tackle. "Ooof," she gasped as the air left her lungs.

"Trevor!" Doug yelled from the front door. "Don't

tackle your Aunt Penny."

Penelope picked up Trevor and kissed his chubby cheeks until the boy squirmed out of her arms. The other boy stood a safe distance and gave her a quizzical look. "Who's your friend, Trevor?" Penelope asked.

The blond haired boy took a cautious step closer and stuck out his hand. "I'm Hadley Jackson Rye, ma'am."

Penelope smiled and bent down to shake the young gentleman's hand. "Pleased to meet you, Hadley. I'm Penelope, but you can call me Penny if you like."

"Hadley is my friend," Trevor said. "We had a sleepover. What's in the bag, Aunty Penny?"

"I brought coffee for me and your dad," she told him, feigning ignorance.

"Is that all?"

"No, I brought some canned spinach as well." Her mind scrambled to think of other unappetizing things. "And olives. The kind with the red things in the middle."

"Oh," Trevor said, uncertain now.

"And pancakes."

"Yay! You were right, Dad!"

Penelope handed Trevor the canvas bag and followed him to the house. Doug stepped off the porch and greeted her with a warm hug.

"A sleepover, huh?" she asked, giving her brother a squeeze before releasing the embrace. "Sounds like you had your hands full last night."

"They weren't so bad," Doug said with a strained smile.

Penelope watched as the boys rummaged through the bag of groceries. "I thought I knew all of Trevor's friends."

"Yeah, me too. Tracie, Hadley's mom, lived in the same apartment complex as Camille. She used to babysit Trevor."

"Hey! I'm not a baby," Trevor protested.

Doug smiled and ruffled his son's hair. "I know you're not, Trev." He turned back to Penelope and continued, "Anyway, Tracie reached out to me a couple of months back, asking if I needed help and if the boys could have a play day. I think it's been good for Trevor, having someone to play with."

"He sure looks happy," Penelope said.

"Where are the pancakes, Aunty Penny?" Trevor asked.

"We have to make them. Would you and Hadley like to help me?"

"Yes," the boys shouted in unison.

"Okay. Take the bag inside and meet me in the kitchen. I want to talk to your dad for a second."

Trevor and Hadley each grabbed a handle and carried the bag into the house.

When the boys were out of sight, Penelope filled Doug in on the events of the past couple days—about following Jacob and what she saw yesterday.

He was shocked.

"There is no way that Jacob is cheating on you," he said. "There has to be an explanation. He called me twice yesterday looking for you. Said you were supposed to meet for dinner."

"He's called me a few times, too. I let them all go to voice mail."

"Didn't you listen to them?"

Penelope looked away. "I couldn't."

"He's worried, Pen."

"I'm sure he is. Worried about what I've found out."

"You don't know for sure what he's done. You believed in me last year. Can't you do the same for him? At least listen to his messages."

Anger, suspicion, love, and guilt rushed through her. "You're right," she said. "I'll do it now. See you in the kitchen in a few minutes?"

"I'll get the mixer out."

Doug's mixer was an ancient artifact. It had belonged to his grandmother, and the cord was so frayed, Penelope didn't dare plug it in. "Be careful," she warned him.

As soon as he was gone, she listened to Jacob's messages from the night before.

"Hey, Officer Beautiful! When you get a break from fighting crime, give me a call. Are we still on for dinner tonight? Love you."

At the sound of his voice, tears stung her eyes. There couldn't possibly be any tears left to cry, but her body proved that her supply was unlimited. She played the rest of the messages, and Jacob sounded more and more worried as the day wore on.

The last one nearly broke her heart. "Penny, I'm worried. This isn't like you. Please call me." There was a pause, then a heavy sigh before the call disconnected.

The urge to cry hit her hard and fast. She sat on the front step, and after a few shaky breaths, she tapped Jacob's number into her phone. He was probably at work, and it was always busy, so there was a chance he wouldn't answer. Sure enough, she got his voice mail.

"Hello, you've reached Dr. Jacob Gordon. Please leave a message." It was a recording she had heard a million times, but this time, it stole her breath. The thought of never hearing his voice again was something she hadn't considered, until now.

She fought to bury the swell of emotion and said, "Hey, Jacob. It's me. I got wrapped up with some interviews last night and turned my phone off." How much should she say in a voice mail? It didn't seem like a proper way to have a discussion that could lead to a breakup. "We have to talk. I'll try to be available today. I have a lunch meeting, but I'll try to answer if you call." She didn't know how to end the message. It was something that seemed so natural before all of these doubts had crept into her mind. Now it was intimidating. "Bye," she said and disconnected.

Jacob would know that something was off with that message. He already knew that she was avoiding him for some reason, although he didn't seem to know what that reason was. Or he was at least doing a great job of pretending not to know. She allowed herself to feel a tiny flutter of hope that this was all a misunderstanding and that things would go back to the way they were before. She tried to quiet the dissenting voice inside her that said things would never be the same.

"Right. Pancakes," she said aloud and joined Doug, Trevor, and Hadley in the kitchen. She didn't turn her phone off, but kept it on silent and put it in her purse. She needed to do something normal with her family to make her feel like herself again.

The scene that greeted her in the kitchen shouldn't have

been a shock, but to see Trevor, Hadley, and Doug, and the table, and the floor covered in flour genuinely surprised her.

"You couldn't wait for me?" she asked, holding in her laughter.

Trevor's bottom lip trembled. "We were going to surprise you and make you pancakes, Aunty Penny."

"I tried to help them," Doug added, "but I think we're doing something wrong."

"I'll say!" Penelope laughed so hard she could barely stand. She staggered to the kitchen table and fell into a flour-dusted chair.

Trevor saw that she was laughing and decided not to cry. Everyone joined Penelope, and they all laughed until they couldn't speak.

When the giggles died down, Trevor piped up. "You'll still make us pancakes, Aunty Penny?" The concern in Trevor's voice led Doug and Penelope to further peals of laughter.

"Yes, Trevor, I'm still making you pancakes. But you and Hadley are going to be in charge of cleanup."

CHAPTER 69

BY THE TIME THEY had finished breakfast and cleaned up the kitchen, it was a little before noon. Penelope had made Mickey Mouse pancakes and had even convinced Trevor to eat some apple slices.

This was the type of family life that she longed for, and she was relieved to know that even if her relationship with Jacob didn't work out, she could still call Doug and Trevor family. She could take care of them, and they would take care of her.

Even if she never married and had kids of her own, she had these two silly guys to give her life meaning. That would be enough for her.

"You want to go to the park, Aunty Penny?"

"Aw, I'm sorry, buddy. I can't today. I have to leave soon."

"But I want you to stay!" There was a hint of a whine

in his voice.

"I'll take you and Hadley," Doug offered.

"It's not the same."

Penelope picked up Trevor and gave him a hug. "Maybe next time," she said. The fondness and love for his childish view of things warmed her heart. She handed Trevor off to Doug and gathered her purse and keys. "I'm meeting Tina Shifflett for lunch."

"Tina?" he asked.

"The woman I told you about earlier." She lowered her voice and added, "The woman I saw with Jacob. She works over at Grace Memorial, but she wanted to meet with me at Spanky's."

"So, it's about the case or something else?"

"I don't know. Donny and I interviewed her yesterday. She left me a message early this morning. Said she needs to talk."

"Do you want me to go with you?"

"No. I think it'd be better if I go alone. But, thank you."

"Let me know what happens."

"I will." Penelope smiled and gave Trevor a kiss good-bye. "Let your dad take you to the park. Maybe you guys will see an alligator. You should bring the binoculars that I got you for your birthday so you can report back to me on what animals you see."

"Can we go to the alligator park, Dad?"

"Sure, bud. You and Hadley go get ready." Trevor and his friend left the room at lightning speed, and Doug's expression became serious. "Call or text if you need anything, Pen. I mean it. You don't get to be there for me and not let me be there for you."

"I know." It wasn't always easy for him to say what he meant, but she knew what he was saying. "You have no idea how much better I feel after spending time with you and Trevor. You're the only family I've got, and I'm so grateful for it."

Hadley ran back into the kitchen and gave Penelope a hug. "Thank you for pancakes."

"You're welcome, Hadley. It was very nice meeting you."

Doug's eyes looked a little misty and Penelope didn't trust herself to say anything else without getting emotional.

She waved good-bye and left.

CHAPTER 70

ALL OF PENELOPE'S BRAVERY and newly restored courage failed her when she arrived at Spanky's Grill. She was a few minutes early and couldn't decide which was worse—awkwardly meeting her fiancé's possible mistress in the parking lot, or awkwardly waiting for her at a table by herself.

She looked in the rearview mirror and sighed. She looked tired. She ran her hands over her hair and put on some lip balm.

You can do this, Penny.

She walked into the restaurant trying to look as nonchalant as possible. Christene Gamble, the only waitress on duty, greeted her.

"Hey, Officer Penelope. You meeting your honey for lunch?"

"No, not today, Christene." Penelope hoped the stabbing

pain she felt in her heart wasn't showing on her face. She mustered a smile and found an empty booth. Being the first to arrive gave her a slight position of power. Tina was coming to her, not the other way around.

"Anything to drink?"

"Iced tea, please."

Penelope pulled out her cell phone and noticed a new voice mail from Jacob. She pressed play. "Penny, Gainesville Police Department just called and they want me to come into the station for some follow-up questioning. Do you know anything about this? What's going on? I spoke to Doug yesterday and he said you were keeping him in the loop. You think you could pay me the same courtesy?"

Christene set her iced tea on the table, and Penelope jumped.

"You alright, dear?"

Penelope placed her phone face down on the table. "Yeah, I'm fine." It was the truth. She didn't need to tell everyone the details of her life.

"You want to order something, hun?"

"Maybe in a minute, I'm meeting someone."

"Alright, then." Christene buzzed over to the counter to grab a pitcher of iced tea, and then she walked around the restaurant topping off people's drinks.

Penelope stared out the window and watched a hummingbird perched on the stem of a Mamou plant. Had she ever seen a hummingbird land before? She must have, maybe not so close. To see the ruby-throated bird so motionless went against all of her notions about hummingbirds. They were both out of their element.

She picked up her phone and dialed Jacob's number.

"Penelope?" A voice called, startling her again.

She hung up and jerked toward someone calling her name.

Tina Shifflett tentatively moved toward the booth and sat down. She looked distraught, and Penelope's stomach churned as she prepared for the worst.

Christene arrived at this awkward moment to take Tina's drink order. As soon as she walked away, they both started talking at the same time.

"Look, Tina—"

"I'm sorry, Pen—"

Penelope waved her hand benevolently to let Tina know she could go first.

"I'm so sorry, Penelope. I didn't tell the whole truth yesterday."

Penelope took a sip of her iced tea and tried not to choke on it. This didn't sound good at all.

"I wasn't completely honest with you about some things," Tina continued. "I'm getting a divorce."

Black spots swirled in Penelope's vision. They sat in silence as Tina's iced tea arrived at the table.

"I've been spending time with Dr. Gordon ..."

The room began to spin. Penelope willed herself to stay upright. She clutched her iced tea glass so hard she thought it might break.

"It's my husband," Tina said. "He's an alcoholic. I'm divorcing him. Dr. Gordon has been helping me work things out."

"Helping you?" Penelope managed to ask.

"Yeah. He listens mostly. I've seen him work with alcoholic patients and drug overdoses at the hospital. He's so good at talking with the families." Tina took a sip of her iced tea. "He's given me the strength I needed to leave Norm. He even came with me to rent an apartment. I was too scared to go alone."

Penelope's battered heart pounded. Jacob never mentioned helping Tina. Why had he kept it a secret? She tried to keep her voice even as she asked, "Is that what you two were doing at the Hilton yesterday? Talking?"

A blush rose in Tina's cheeks. "You know about that?"

"I do," Penelope said, her voice hardening. "I saw the twirl, the tango. I saw the kiss. I saw the whole thing."

"He's doing it for you."

"Really? Doing it for me?" *That's a new one.*

"Yes. He's learning to dance."

"Dance? Wait, what are you talking about?" Penelope's cop instincts were waking up. Did she overlook something?

"He wanted to surprise you for your wedding dance. There's a ballroom dance class at the Hilton every Friday. I've been helping him practice . . ." Tina's big brown eyes filled with tears. "It was supposed to be a surprise. I think I just ruined it."

Christene sidled up to the edge of the table, took one look at Tina, then turned to Penelope and said, "I'll just come back for y'all's orders."

"Penelope, say something. Please say you forgive me." Tina burst into tears, sobbing uncontrollably.

What was she supposed to say? This was the last thing she expected to hear. It all made sense now, the mysterious meeting at the park, the hotel, the twirl, and the kiss. The memory of the kiss on the cheek had changed—now it seemed perfectly innocent.

"I don't know what to say," she told Tina. She reached into her purse to find a tissue for Tina, but she had used them all. She grabbed some of the rough, brown napkins from the dispenser on the table and handed a wad of them to Tina.

Tina pressed the entire wad into her face, smearing her makeup and choking a little on her sobs. Penelope reached out for her hand. If someone had told her yesterday that she would be comforting a crying Tina Shifflett today, she would have thought they were crazy. The absurdity and the relief of the moment flooded her emotions, and she started to laugh.

That only served to intensify Tina's sobs. "I'm so, so sorry! I'm such a fool!"

Penelope squeezed her hand. "You're not a fool," she assured her. *I was the fool.*

"But I ruined your wedding . . ." Tina's mournful, makeup-smeared eyes met Penelope's.

"You did nothing of the sort," Penelope said.

She had jumped to conclusions based on inadequate evidence, let her emotions take over, and judged her suspect guilty without due diligence. That was bad police work and even worse fiancée behavior. How could she have ever thought Jacob was capable of having an affair? If she had just been open with him from the get-go, she would have saved herself so much heartache.

Tears began to well up, but Penelope stifled them. She

waved a hand at Christene, summoning her to the table. "We'll have an order of the sweet potato hush puppies and two chocolate chip cookies."

Penelope moved to Tina's side of the table and waited for her tears to ebb.

Several long minutes later, Tina blew her nose loudly into the damp wad of napkins and turned her red swollen eyes to meet Penelope's.

"You didn't do anything wrong," Penelope assured Tina. "I understand why you didn't want to say anything."

"I didn't wa—" Tina took a deep breath and started over. "I didn't want to ruin the surprise."

"I know. Is there anything else you were holding back?"

"No, just that." Tina blew her nose one more time.

The food arrived at the table, and Tina went straight for her cookie. She ate it with the innocence and vigor of youth, getting a smear of melted chocolate on her lip and leaving crumbs on her brightly printed scrubs.

Tina finished her cookie and glanced at her watch. "I have to get to work."

Penelope stood to let Tina out. "Of course. And Tina, I'm sorry to hear about your divorce. Thanks for being honest with me."

Tina put a five-dollar bill on the table, hesitated, and then gave Penelope a hug before leaving.

Penelope ate her hush puppies in silence and planned her next move. She'd always trusted her faith and she trusted God now to help her put the pieces together. He wouldn't let a man like Jacob into her life only to rip him away. The sooner she could sort out this whole mess the better. She dialed Jacob's number and it went straight to voice mail. "Jacob, call me when you get this. There are some things I need to tell you. I love you."

Penelope knew what she had to do. She had to start from the beginning—reexamine the evidence. She'd be disobeying a direct order and putting her career on the line, but it was a chance she had to take. She took a deep breath and blew it out again. "Lord, I trust You to help me through this and show me where all the clues lead. By Your strength alone. In the name of Jesus Christ, Amen."

CHAPTER 71

FORTY-FIVE MINUTES LATER, PENELOPE parked her MGB in one of the few empty spaces at Grace Memorial Hospital. She pulled out her cell phone and found Gabriel's number. "Gabriel, it's Penelope. Can you meet me in the lobby?"

Gabriel was already waiting in the lobby when Penelope walked through the front entrance. "What's going on, Penelope? Is everything okay?"

"No. Everything is not okay. I want to run over a couple of things again."

Gabriel looked at her with concerned eyes. "Penelope, you're not supposed to be investigating this case. Detective Greene and I got an earful from your chief yesterday."

"I can't just sit by while they build a case against Jacob."

"You can look at the same thing a million times, but it's never going to change. The police have been over the evidence."

"I'm sorry, I shouldn't have asked for your help. It was selfish of me. You've done more than enough already. I can do this on my own." She turned to walk away.

"Now wait a minute . . . I said I'd help and I'll help. Jackson is *your* boss . . . not mine." Gabriel placed a hand on her shoulder. "But don't get your hopes up. Just because you want something to be there, doesn't mean it will be. You have to face the fact that your fiancé may be guilty."

She nodded, but her gut told her things weren't going to play out that way.

"So where do we start?" Gabriel asked.

"With the surveillance footage," Penelope said, pointing toward Dave Sayre, the security guard from the night of the robbery.

Dave watched people walk past as he stood at his post in front of the glass double doors that led to the hospital clinic. Some walked by quickly, like they had somewhere to be, and others sauntered along like they had hours to spare. Dave's eyes followed the people until he saw Penelope and Gabriel.

"Hi Dave," Penelope said, approaching the security guard.

Dave tipped his hat. "How are you, Officer Chance? What brings you here?"

"Dave, I was hoping you could help us. Any chance we can have one more look at those surveillance tapes from last Friday?"

"Well, sure. I don't see what harm it can do." He turned and beckoned for them to follow.

Gabriel glanced at Penelope, but she looked straight ahead. They followed Dave down the hall to the security surveillance room where he pulled in a couple of extra chairs and cued the tape from the Friday before. "Coffee?" he asked.

Penelope nodded, and Gabriel shook his head no.

Dave picked up a receiver and asked someone to bring them coffee. Penelope didn't notice who brought her coffee, and as she took a drink, she realized she probably hadn't thanked them. Her hand froze with the coffee in front of her mouth.

"Um, Penelope, you okay?" Dave looked mildly concerned.

"Yeah, I'm just tired," she said and took a drink of coffee to illustrate her point.

"So I'll show you the clinic video," Dave said. "I'm sure you've already seen it, but it's a good place to start."

He played the video Penelope had seen the night of the robbery. When Jacob entered the frame, her heart shuddered, but she managed not to make a sound. After the attack, the video played a little longer, but she could see nothing that she hadn't noticed the first time she watched it. "What about the lobby?" That's what she needed to see.

"What are you thinking, Penelope?" Gabriel asked.

"I want to see Kevin Scott and the other suspect exit."

Dave closed the clinic video. "This isn't as high quality, and there are four angles shown on one screen." He opened another file, hit the play button, and she saw what he meant. The screen was divided into four small screens, and even though the monitor was large, it was hard to tell what was going on in the video. "We're watching it at ten times the speed of the action."

Penelope leaned in and put her elbows on the desk. The whole scene lasted about thirty seconds. She watched one quadrant of video for one full loop, and then she randomly focused on the bottom left video for another full loop. This video showed five people in the lobby at the time of the robbery—one male and three female figures. During the last ten seconds of the loop, the fifth person enters the screen. She paused the video. "Is this you, Dave?"

"Yes, that was right after I got the call about the robbery. As you can see, they got the jump on me. Not my proudest moment."

Penelope pressed play. As Scott and his partner ran past, Scott stuck his arm out and clotheslined Dave to the ground. "Look at this," she said to Gabriel.

"I'm looking," he said. "What am I looking at?"

"There," she said pointing to the screen. "Where did she go?"

"Where did who go?"

Penelope played the video again. After Dave gets knocked to the ground, the video jumped to one less person in the lobby. "Donny has statements from four people in the lobby. Dave, Donald Hernandez, an orderly, Betty Jo Tillman, a nurse, and Ruth Clark, the main lobby receptionist. Who is our fifth person?"

Dave saw it, too. "I'll get someone to confirm the staff on duty at that time," he said. "See if we can identify that fifth person." He picked up the receiver and relayed his request.

The loop had started again, and Penelope noticed something strange. One of the individuals looked familiar. She couldn't see their face, but she didn't need to. This person was identifiable by shape alone. She watched to see if the shape disappeared after Scott and his partner ran by. Sure enough, it did. "Gabriel, I think that's Genny."

"Who?"

"Nurse Genny Taylor."

Gabriel leaned in closer. "Nurse Taylor?"

"She works at the Franklin Clinic."

"What makes you think that's her?"

"Her shoulders, the way she is standing. Her shape. The way she moves."

Nurse Genevieve Taylor was unforgettable, in a way. She moved with military purpose. It had to be her.

The loop started over, and Gabriel leaned in to watch. "That could be anybody."

"Watch," Penelope said, as they neared the part of the video when Kevin and his partner ran through. "Now you see her. . . Now you don't. Dave, any footage from the exit?"

"We only have one angle outside at the front entrance. Let me pull it up." He clicked the play button and sat back in his chair. An older model car sped into the frame and then disappeared. Dave paused the video. "We couldn't capture a license plate, but that's definitely Kevin Scott's Oldsmobile."

"Could you press play, Dave?"

"You want me to rewind it?"

"No, just let it play."

"What are you thinking, Penelope?" Gabriel asked.

Penelope held her breath and sat silent. After a few seconds, a small, mid-size car drives past. A few moments later a dark sedan passes. Then she saw it. "There! Pause the video." The video frame flickered with the image of a light colored, Toyota 4Runner. "That's Taylor's SUV. I'm sure of it."

"Are you positive? Could be coincidence," Gabriel mused.

"I don't think so. Dave do you recall seeing Nurse Taylor from the Franklin Clinic here Friday?"

"I don't think I've met Nurse Taylor."

"If you saw her again would you be able to identify her?"

"Sorry, Penelope. Everything happened so fast. I don't remember that other person being there."

"It's probably nothing, Penelope," Gabriel said. "It's a common vehicle."

Penelope leaned forward again, narrowing her eyes at the screen. It was hard to tell the figures apart because of the quality and size of the images, but she was sure it was Taylor. She'd seen enough of the woman to recognize her from a mile away.

"I get what you're saying, Gabriel," Penelope said. "But I think I'm going to call Donny. What harm can it do to double-check our facts?"

"I think you're grasping at straws here, Penelope."

"Well, it's not grasping if I'm right. Besides, if I'm wrong we're just back where we are now."

Gabriel breathed in deeply and turned his eyes back to

the screen. "Which is supposed to be off the case . . . isn't that right?" He looked annoyed as he drummed his fingers on the table. "Didn't Detective Greene already speak to her?"

"He did. But I want to follow up with him." Penelope turned to Dave and asked, "Dave can you burn me a DVD of the lobby video and the footage from outside?"

Dave nodded and searched for a blank DVD.

Gabriel stood. "If we're going to do this we should be looking for someone else, someone the police overlooked."

"You taught me to go where the evidence takes you . . . and that's what I'm doing."

CHAPTER 72

PENELOPE COLLECTED HER THOUGHTS and then dialed Donny. She stepped out of the small security room just as the detective picked up. "Donny, it's Chance. You got a minute?"

"Not really, Chance. I'm in the middle of something."

"I think I've found something."

"You are not supposed to be—"

"I know, I know," Penelope interrupted. "I'm sorry about yesterday. And I know you don't want me anywhere near this case . . . but humor me, Don. For old time's sake?"

She heard a sigh on the other end of the line, followed by, "You have thirty seconds."

"I'm at Grace Memorial reviewing the surveillance footage, and I noticed there were five people in the lobby during the robbery. Not four."

She could hear Donny rustle papers on the other

end, checking his notes. "We have statements from four witnesses."

"I know. The fifth person leaves right after the perps exited the lobby. I think you need to get her statement."

"Her?"

"I think it's a female," Penelope said, walking back into the security office.

Gabriel sat next to Dave, fidgeting and looking as if he needed to be somewhere else.

"Are you fishing for something that isn't really there?" Donny asked. "Detective Ballard is questioning Jacob now."

"I know, Donny," Penelope said, feeling unbalanced. She took a deep breath. "Just check this out."

Donny remained silent.

"Donny, Please."

"Okay, Chance. I'll give you an hour."

"Great! I'll be there in ten." Penelope ended the call and took a deep breath. This was the break in the case she had been waiting for.

"And?" Gabriel prompted.

"And Donny wants to have a look. Let's go." She thanked Dave and Gabriel followed her out of the office. "When we get there—"

"Actually, Penelope," Gabriel interrupted. "I'm going to have to sit this one out."

"What?"

"I have a patient." He looked at his watch and nodded as if confirming. "I need to run or I will be late."

"Oh . . ."

"You will let me know how it goes, won't you?" he

asked, trotting off in a half run, half walk.

Is that why he'd looked so uncomfortable earlier? She'd known Gabriel for a long time, and he often forgot things, and did things that seemed a little odd—another one of his many idiosyncrasies.

"I'll text you later," she said, calling after him.

CHAPTER 73

WHEN PENELOPE ARRIVED AT the Gainesville Police Station, Donny's office door was closed, but she could hear the low rumble of conversation coming from inside. She sat in the only chair outside his office. The chair was uncomfortable and reminded her of elementary school when the bad kids were sent to the principal's office. The image made her want to laugh, but she knew that if she started, she might not be able to stop, and now was not the time for humor.

Her phone chimed in her purse, and she pulled it out without thinking. It was a text from Gabriel. How's it going?

For a man that was seeing a patient, Gabriel's mind was very much on this case. He was back to his usual mentoring self, trying to stop her from being too disappointed when things didn't go the way she wanted them to go. *That* was the Gabriel she knew.

Before she could answer, her phone buzzed. This time, it was a text from Doug. **Are you okay?**

There were at least two people in the world who cared about her. Her eyes welled up as a feeling of demented happiness flooded through her. She had family and friends on her side after all.

GPD, waiting for Donny, she wrote back to Doug and waited for the *delivered* message to appear. When the message delivered, another surge of emotion flooded her body. She had never felt this . . . unhinged before.

Her phone buzzed again. Another message from Gabriel. **Everything ok?**

She knew that God would give her the strength to handle everything that was happening today. She was waiting on that strength to arrive and make itself known.

All good. Waiting for Donny. She replied to Gabriel.

Another message popped up from Doug. **Trevor says hello.**

And there it was. A spark, something she could hold on to—something good in her life that required her to be strong. Thinking about Trevor would get her through the day. She let out a breath she hadn't realize she was holding. Her rapidly changing mood was confusing, and she wasn't going to question the sudden clarity she felt.

Thank you, she mouthed heavenward.

Tell him hi. Call you later. She wrote back to Doug. She was pleased with how normal it sounded.

No Die Hard! Doug wrote, a moment later.

Penelope laughed. Doug always compared her to the cop from *Die Hard*. She hadn't seen the movie, but she knew he was asking her not to be a cowboy cop.

A familiar voice at the far end of the squad room caught Penelope's attention. She slipped her phone into her purse and looked up. Detective Ballard was escorting Jacob toward the exit. She tried to read their faces. Both were serious, but there were no cuffs on Jacob, so that was a good sign. She was walking toward them when Donny's door opened.

"You don't give up, do you?" she heard Donny's voice behind her.

She glanced at Donny, held up a finger, and looked back toward Jacob . . . but he was already gone.

CHAPTER 74

"DOES JACKSON KNOW YOU'RE here?" Donny asked Penelope.

She lowered her gaze. "No."

"You got me into a whole heap of trouble yesterday. I thought you got the okay from Jackson to shadow me on this case. I thought you were keeping him in the loop, which is why I called him."

"I'm sorry I didn't tell you, Donny. I thought I was giving you plausible deniability."

"A plausible ulcer is what you're giving me." Donny shook his head. "This better be good. I'm putting my neck on the line letting you in the building."

"It is. I promise."

"Let's have a look then."

Penelope followed Donny down the hall. "Just before you came out, I saw Detective Ballard walking Jacob out.

That's a good sign, isn't it?"

Donny gave a non-committal grunt as they reached the evidence room. He opened the door and ushered her in. Once they were seated next to each other at the table, he motioned for her to take the controls. Penelope inserted the DVD and double-clicked the lobby video file. "Here," she said when the five people appeared on the screen.

"I see . . ."

"And then . . . there! She's gone." She minimized the first video and opened a second. "This one is from the parking lot." She pressed play and waited. "Okay, here's Kevin Scott and his accomplice driving by."

"I've seen this a dozen times before, Chance."

Penelope brought up the lobby video again and pressed play. "Okay, now wait for it . . . there. That person right there," she said pausing the video and pointing to the screen. "She followed Kevin Scott and his partner out of the hospital."

"You keep saying *she*."

Penelope explained how she recognized Nurse Taylor. Donny listened, nodding as they viewed the footage several times.

"All right . . . what else?" he asked.

Penelope played the footage from the entrance that showed the parking lot and said, "Here, Taylor's truck drives past. Twenty seconds later."

Donny rubbed his chin and looked skeptical. "I don't know . . ."

Penelope bit her cheek and watched Donny's face as he went through the video another time.

"Wait a minute," he said, watching Kevin and his partner exit the hospital. He started the video from the beginning. "Penelope, I think you were right about something being off about the second perp."

"The second perp? What do you mean?"

"That first night when you first viewed the footage. You said you felt like something was off about this perp. The way they moved, I think you said."

Penelope nodded. "Yeah, I remember."

"The way they moved. That's it. I know who Kevin Scott's accomplice is."

"Who?"

Donny stared at the screen. He was in his own world for a moment, one where Penelope wasn't sitting right next to him, bursting with curiosity. "Why didn't I see this before?"

"Who, Donny? Tell me!"

Donny snapped back to the here and now. He replayed the parking lot footage and paused on a single frame—a frame where the perps could be seen exiting the hospital.

"We were under the assumption the accomplice was male," Donny said, flipping through his notes. "White or Hispanic male about five feet seven inches tall with light blue or gray eyes. That's what was off."

Penelope moved to get a closer look at the screen.

Right before the perps disappeared from view—for a split second—Scott's accomplice glanced back toward the hospital. And she had removed her bandana.

"It wasn't a guy . . ." Penelope voiced what they were both seeing.

"It was his girlfriend . . . Denise Wilson,"

"Donny, that means—"

"I know," Donny said as he left the room. "I need to print a screen grab and get an arrest warrant for Denise Wilson."

Penelope sank back into her chair and let out a deep breath. If Kevin Scott's girlfriend was his accomplice, did that mean she shot him? It was her gun that killed him. But if she shot him, why did she report him missing? And why dump his body in Franklin?

At least with the focus on apprehending Ms. Wilson, less focus will be on Jacob.

"Thank you, God."

"What's that?" Donny asked, walking back into the room fifteen minutes later.

"Just talking to myself. Do you think Wilson killed her boyfriend? What's her motive?"

"I don't know. Money? Greed? When she came in the other day, she seemed genuinely shocked that he was dead."

"You think it could have been an act?"

Donny rubbed his hands across his eyes. "I think we need to figure out what this is all about."

"Which part?"

"Taylor. How does she fit into all of this?"

"If I'm right . . . and that is her in the video, I think she may have witnessed the murder."

"But why not come forward, and why lie about not being there?"

"Maybe she was scared?"

"Maybe," Donny replied, giving Penelope one of his

patented, meaningful looks. "But she doesn't strike me as the type that scares easily. No, I think there's something else going on here."

Donny turned his attention back to the video monitor, and for the next forty-five minutes he reviewed the lobby and parking lot footage.

"Hmm . . ." he finally said.

"What is it, Don? You see something else?"

He pointed at the monitor. "You tell me."

She squinted at the screen and shook her head.

"The brake light," Donny said.

"Brake light?"

"Yeah. I didn't notice it before, but the truck's left brake light is out. Watch when they brake going over the speed bump."

Penelope noticed it too. "You're right." Donny had a keen eye for detail, and this proved it. He was a great detective. "If Taylor's truck has a burnt out driver side brake light, we might be able to place her at the scene."

"Exactly," Donny said, already picking up the phone. "Get me Genevieve Taylor from the Franklin Clinic for questioning." He paused and listened. "I know I already interviewed her. I want to see her again. Make it happen." He hung up only to have his cell phone ring. When he finished that call he turned to Penelope and said, "I have to run."

"Where you going?"

"To arrest Denise Wilson. That was Ballard. The warrant just came through."

"What about me?" she asked.

"You stay put. You're not even supposed to be here, remember?" Donny said, already half way down the hall.

CHAPTER 75

PENELOPE WENT OVER THIS new puzzle in her mind. Things were becoming clearer now that they had at least one suspect, but the picture was still out of focus.

While she waited for Donny to return, she typed a message to Gabriel. **Donny is picking up Kevin Scott's girlfriend. She was his partner in the robbery.**

Less than a minute later Gabriel replied, **So that wasn't Taylor after all? That's great news!**

No. Bringing Taylor in for questioning as well, Penelope replied and set her phone on silent.

Two hours and three cups of coffee later, Donny and Detective Ballard returned with Denise Wilson in custody. While Ballard questioned Wilson, Donny and Officer Caleb Meeks prepared Interrogation Room 2 in anticipation of Genevieve Taylor's arrival. Penelope sat in the observation room, sipping her fourth cup of coffee, watching Officer

Meeks set up a second camera. He fumbled with the camera and earned a warning glare from Donny.

Ten minutes later, Donny joined Penelope in the observation room, bringing her up to speed on the Wilson arrest and reviewing his strategy for questioning Taylor.

"So you're going to let Meeks interview Taylor?" Penelope asked with a sarcastic smile, pointing at the officer through the two-way mirror.

Donny let out a loud laugh, and Meeks jumped in the next room. The rookie officer turned toward the mirror, smiled, and then finished setting up the camera.

"Yeah, right. Glad to see you haven't lost your sense of humor, Chance," Donny replied. "No. I think I'll do this one by myself." The phone in the observation room lit up but made no sound. Donny stood and picked up the receiver, mumbled something, and hung up. "Our guest has arrived. They're bringing her in now. I'll send Meeks in to keep you company." His eyes twinkled. "You can watch the master at work together. Maybe you'll both learn something."

Penelope gave Officer Meeks a broad smile as he entered the observation room.

He closed the door, sat down, and turned on the recording equipment. "Ma'am," he greeted her, making a strange face.

Worried that her emotions were showing, Penelope pulled out her small notebook and remained silent.

Two minutes later the door to the observation room burst open, and the awkward silence broke as Dr. Gabriel Pike hurried into the room looking more disheveled and less dignified than Penelope had ever seen him.

Meeks said nothing but raised an eyebrow at the eccentric doctor's unusual entrance.

"You all right?" Penelope asked Gabriel.

"Oh yes, I'm fine." Gabriel crouched next to Penelope and stared into the interrogation room.

"Do you want a chair?"

"Oh . . . no, that's okay," he said, eyes already glued to the scene unfolding on the other side of the two-way mirror.

"Officer Meeks, this is Dr. Gabriel Pike," Penelope said. "Gabriel, this is Officer Caleb Meeks."

The two men gave each other a nod and turned their attention to Nurse Genevieve Taylor as she entered Interrogation Room 2 followed by Detective Donny Green. Seeing Taylor up close reaffirmed Penelope's suspicion that she had been at Grace Memorial Hospital the day of the robbery. Her large shoulders and peculiar gait were as evident in the footage as they were in real life.

"Have a seat," Donny said to Taylor. "Would you like some water?"

"No, thank you." Taylor looked unflappable as usual. It was part of her job every day to stay calm in any situation.

"She didn't ask for a lawyer?" Gabriel asked Penelope.

"She's not under arrest. She's just here for a follow-up interview. We want to find out why she lied about being at Grace Memorial that day."

"You mean, if that was her in the video?"

"Right," Penelope said. "We arrested Denise Wilson on robbery and murder charges an hour ago. It also looks like Wilson was counterfeiting prescriptions. And get this . . . she was also a patient at the Franklin Clinic."

"So Wilson could have planted the drugs in Belinda's desk?"

"Easily. She had an appointment at the clinic last Monday."

"A day before Belinda was arrested?"

"Yep . . . and three days after the robbery. Detective Edward Ballard is questioning her now. If that is Taylor in the video, and she did witness something, it could really help the case against Wilson."

Gabriel nodded and turned his attention to the interrogation room.

"Well, Ms. Taylor," Donny began, "I want to thank you for coming in. I have a few questions about last Friday."

"I've already told you where I was," Taylor said.

Donny shuffled through the papers in front of him. "Right. You had that day off . . . Correct?"

"That's correct."

"Remind me again . . . what did you say you did that day?"

The stoic nurse cast her level gaze across the table directly at Donny. "I drove to my brother's house that Friday morning. I spent the night, and then I drove back Saturday morning. On my way back I got a call from Dr. Gordon asking for a ride. I picked him up at Doug Foster's house, and we rode into work together."

"So you didn't go to Gainesville at all that Friday? Before going to see your brother, perhaps?" Donny kept his voice friendly, but Taylor was starting to show signs of irritation. She leaned back in her chair and crossed her arms. She appeared to be affecting a look of boredom, but this was a defense posture.

Penelope leaned in and absorbed the interview. Out of the corner of her eye, she caught a glimpse of Gabriel fumbling with his cell phone. He seemed to be checking his email or texting someone.

"No," Taylor said. "I didn't go to Gainesville that day."

"Well, Ms. Taylor, are you sure you're not mistaken about that?" Donny was giving her an out. Letting her own up to the truth before bringing up the surveillance footage.

"No," Taylor insisted. "I was in Jacksonville."

"Did you take 301 or I-17?" Donny asked.

"I took I-17."

"And what type of car do you drive, Ms. Taylor?"

"A Toyota 4Runner. Why?"

"What do you think your brother would say if I asked him where you were last Friday?"

"He'd say I was at his house!" Taylor snapped, her brow starting to glisten under the harsh florescent lights.

Penelope glanced at Gabriel. "You know she's lying, right?"

"I don't know . . ." he said, meeting her gaze. "She seems to be telling the truth."

Penelope shook her head and turned her attention back to the interrogation room.

"Now, Ms. Taylor, do you understand that in the state of Florida it's a crime to lie to a detective in a criminal investigation?"

"Yes, but I'm not on trial here."

"No, you're not on trial." Donny stopped speaking and stared across the table at Taylor.

"And I was not in Gainesville on Friday. If anyone said I was, they are mistaken," Taylor said, filling the silence. She spoke with a confidence she clearly did not feel.

"Well, Ms. Taylor, we have evidence that says otherwise."

"That's impossible. What are you talking about?"

"Evidence that proves you weren't in Jacksonville that day. At least, not at the time of the robbery."

Penelope watched as Taylor sat silent. She appeared to be processing the information before speaking again.

Gabriel learned over to Penelope. "What evidence is Detective Greene talking about?"

"The surveillance video."

"Ah . . ." Gabriel nodded.

"Did you drive your truck here today, Ms. Taylor?" Donny asked, breaking the momentary silence.

"Of course."

"You don't mind if I have an officer take a look at it, do you?"

"Yes, I mind." A bead of sweat trickled down the side of Taylor's face. "Why would you do that?"

"To check for damage." Donny removed his cell phone from his suit jacket pocket and placed it on the table in front of him. "If I call my officer right now, what's he going to tell me?"

Taylor opened her mouth to speak and then closed it again. She appeared to be crumbling.

Donny picked up the phone. "What's he going to tell me, Ms. Taylor? This is your one chance to come clean."

Donny waited and when Taylor didn't speak, he tapped

a few numbers into his phone.

"Wait," Taylor said, uncrossing her arms and leaning forward. "Okay, okay . . . I admit it."

"You admit what?"

Taylor shifted in her seat. "I think I caused an accident last Friday."

CHAPTER 76

PENELOPE SAT BACK IN her chair and exchanged a glance with Gabriel.

"What is she talking about?" Gabriel wondered out loud.

Penelope's heart dropped to her stomach. Flashes of the accident she'd passed last Friday night rippled through her mind.

The red and blue lights pulsing . . .

The little girl's lifeless body prone on the wet asphalt . . .

The two vehicles twisted in a heap of mangled metal . . .

Could that be the accident Taylor was talking about?

Gabriel's question went unanswered as Donny, recovering from his own surprise, continued questioning Nurse Taylor.

"Why don't you walk me through it, Ms. Taylor? Tell me what happened," he said smoothly, giving the outward indication that he already knew all about it.

"I didn't mean for it to happen." Taylor paused and wiped the sweat from her brow with the back of her hand. "I'm not even sure if I caused it. I heard about it the next day."

"Start from the beginning, Ms. Taylor," Donny said. "What accident and where?"

"On State Road 20."

"And when did this accident occur?"

"Last Friday night."

Donny turned toward the mirrored glass and made a circling motion in the air with his index finger. Officer Meeks apparently recognized the gesture, leaped to his feet, and swiftly exited the observation room.

"Last Friday night?" Donny echoed.

"Yes," Taylor confirmed.

"And what makes you think you caused the accident?"

"It happened about the same time I passed a car a few miles before County Road."

"And what time was that?" Donny asked.

"About six thirty," Taylor said.

"And which direction were you traveling?"

"East . . . back toward Franklin."

"From?"

"My brother's house."

"So you took I-17 to your brother's house and I-301 back?"

"Yes,"

"Okay, so tell me what happened on State Road 20," Donny said.

Taylor paused and took a breath. "There was one car ahead of me. They were going thirty miles an hour in the fifty-five. I know it's a no-passing zone, but I was in a hurry."

"So you passed anyway?"

"Yes, and as I did a truck came over the hill in the opposite direction."

"Then what happened?" Donny asked.

"The truck flashed its high beams, and I got back into my lane. I did it kind of fast," Taylor said, and then added, "But I didn't hit anybody."

"You didn't hit the truck or the car you passed?"

"No. I checked my truck the next day, after I heard there was an accident. No dents or —"

A quick knock on the interrogation room door cut Taylor off midsentence.

Officer Caleb Meeks entered the room, handed Donny a couple sheets of paper, and exited as quickly as he had entered. Seconds later the rookie officer rejoined Penelope and Gabriel in the observation room.

Donny scanned the papers. "So, I'll ask again, Ms. Taylor. . . . What makes you think you caused the accident?"

"I think I may have cut that car off. Because, I remember looking in my rearview mirror. After I passed the—" Taylor took a ragged breath. "I never saw the car come over the hill."

"Why didn't you stop?"

"I-I was in a rush . . ."

"Well you may very well be at fault, Ms. Taylor," Donny said, reading from one of the sheets of paper. "According to this accident report filed by the Florida Highway Patrol, the driver of a silver Honda Accord said a light colored SUV passed her on the left and then swerved back into the eastbound lane. The driver of the Honda Accord was temporarily blinded by the high beams of a blue Chevy Tahoe traveling westbound and coming over the grade. The driver of the Honda Accord drifted into the westbound lane, sideswiping the oncoming Chevy Tahoe."

"It also says here, the driver of the Honda Accord remembered the SUV having a driver's side taillight out."

Taylor clutched her hands together in her lap and stared at the floor, slowly shaking her head. "I've been meaning to get that fixed. I just haven't had enough time . . ."

"The bad taillight isn't really the issue here. A five-year-old girl was seriously injured in that accident, Ms. Taylor. Luckily her injuries were not life threatening."

"I know," Taylor said, wringing her hands. "I called Grace Memorial Hospital Saturday when I heard about the accident. I feel awful about not stopping."

Penelope watched Taylor intently. The woman seemed genuinely remorseful, but any feelings of pity Penelope might have had were tempered by the fact that the SUV in the surveillance video also had the driver's taillight out.

Taylor was at the hospital at the time of the shooting.

"At this time Ms. Taylor, I'd like to advise you of your rights . . ."

"Why? Am I under arrest?"

"You did just admit to fleeing the scene of an accident."

Taylor nodded and slumped in her chair.

As Donny read Taylor her Miranda rights in the interrogation room, a faint digital rendition of The Beatles song, *Help!* sounded in the observation room.

Penelope glanced over her shoulder at Officer Meeks.

"It's not mine," Meeks said, raising his hands in mock surrender.

"Sorry, it's mine," Gabriel said, pulling the offending cell phone out of his pants pocket. He glanced at the caller ID and said, "I have to take this."

Penelope nodded.

"It's pretty cool that an old guy knows about novelty ringtones," Meeks said to Penelope after Gabriel left the room.

"It's not a novelty," she told him. "It's a song."

Meeks gave her a blank stare.

"By The Beatles."

Meeks shook his head, and Penelope spared a moment to mourn the new generation's lack of musical taste before turning her attention back to the spectacle unfolding in the interrogation room.

After Taylor acknowledged that she understood her rights and did not wish to have a lawyer present, she asked, "What happens now?"

"Well, Ms. Taylor, we can start with you being honest."

"I told you everything, Detective."

"No, you haven't, Ms. Taylor. You claimed to be in Jacksonville Friday night, yet you just admitted to causing an accident near Franklin that same night."

Taylor looked like she was on the verge of tears. Her makeup was smudged, and her hair was coming out of its tight up-do. "But isn't that why I'm here? Because of the accident? Isn't that why you wanted to look at my truck?"

"No, Ms. Taylor . . . it isn't."

"I don't understand."

"Ms. Taylor, what were you doing at Grace Memorial Hospital last Friday, about one o'clock?"

CHAPTER 77

DONNY'S STRAIGHTFORWARD APPROACH WAS a surprise. Penelope had expected him to dance around the subject for a while, but he was cutting to the chase.

"I told you. I wasn't at Grace Memorial Hospital last Friday," Taylor said.

"You don't go and chat with the nurses from time to time?"

"I do. Sometimes. I know a few of the nurses."

"But you're saying you weren't at Grace Memorial Hospital on Friday, March twenty-second? For a doctor's appointment perhaps? Or to catch up on who's dating whom? Or to discuss the latest offerings in comfortable white shoes?"

Penelope couldn't see Donny's face, but she knew that he was pulling his confused-cop routine. He used it when he had solid evidence against someone, and they were lying to his face.

"No, I told you. I had the day off and drove to Jacksonville."

"To visit your brother . . ."

"That's right."

"And what did you do while you were visiting your brother?"

"What did I do?"

"It's a simple question, Ms. Taylor. What did you do while you were visiting your brother?"

"Nothing, I just visited. I told you."

"I think you're lying to me."

"I'm not lying."

"What were you really doing that day, Ms. Taylor?"

"How many times do I have to tell you? I was—"

"Visiting your brother," Donny finished. "Yeah, I got that. But you've already lied about spending Friday night at your brother's . . . Why should I believe you now?"

"Because it's the truth."

"That's not what the evidence is telling me."

"What evidence? What are you talking about? I already told you about the accident, and there isn't any evidence because I didn't hit anyone."

Donny turned toward the mirrored glass and motioned to Officer Meeks again.

"This oughta be good," Meeks said as he left the observation room.

A minute later he emerged in the interrogation room carrying a large laptop. Taylor became agitated when she saw the computer, and her powerful shoulders tensed as she gripped the sides of her chair.

Gabriel came back into the room and usurped Meeks' seat behind Penelope.

Penelope turned and asked, "Is everything okay?"

"Yes, yes," he said in a dismissive tone. "It's just a patient who's been calling me all day. Marital troubles."

"Do you need to leave? It's okay, I think Donny's about to get a confession."

"You think so?" Gabriel mumbled.

Penelope looked at him strangely. Taylor's been lying this whole time. Why couldn't Gabriel see that? Was she missing something?

"Play the video," Donny said in the interrogation room, nodding at Officer Meeks.

The rookie officer angled the laptop screen toward Taylor and pressed play on the video player. For some reason, Donny was showing Taylor the footage of the robbery from inside the pharmacy.

Why would he show her that footage first? Why not start with the incriminating lobby and parking lot footage?

Taylor watched the video silently, her lips pursed. She hardly moved. Only the rise and fall of her breathing kept her from looking like a statue.

Penelope braced herself as the video showed Denise Wilson shooting Jacob.

That same moment, Taylor twitched in her chair. Her head lowered and her eyes darkened. She appeared to be growing more agitated and seemed particularly upset about the attack on Jacob.

"Why are you showing me this?" she said. "They're

hurting Jacob. I don't want to see this."

"Oh, I'm sorry. Officer Meeks must have played you the wrong video." Donny continued his confused-cop routine to gauge Taylor's reaction to the footage of the actual crime.

Smart move. Taylor was visibly shaken.

Donny nodded to Meeks, who clicked a couple of buttons with the mouse, and the four camera angles appeared on the screen.

Taylor squinted at the video. Her demeanor relaxed when she saw the grainy footage. "What am I supposed to be looking at?" she asked with a shaky laugh.

Penelope repressed the urge to giggle as she watched the nurse squinting at the computer screen, looking as if she were trying to read the last line of an eye chart.

Donny pointed at the relevant square on the screen. Despite the poor quality of the video, it was obvious that the woman standing in the reception area at Grace Memorial Hospital that day was Genevieve Taylor. Meeks clicked another button and isolated the video feed that showed Taylor's distinctive silhouette. Another click and the screen split. The parking lot footage appeared on the opposite side of the screen. Now the computer was showing Taylor in the lobby on one side, and her truck following the suspects on the other side.

Donny leaned in close, just like Taylor, and he pointed at the screen. "Isn't that you, Ms. Taylor?"

"Certainly not," she replied.

"It sure does look like you."

"You can't see that woman's face. It could be anyone."

"But not you?" asked Donny. "Okay. But that is your

silver Toyota 4Runner . . . is it not? With the same burnt out taillight."

Taylor opened her mouth as if to speak but then closed it firmly.

What could she possibly say? There she was in grainy, black and white, at the time of the robbery. And that was her truck with the burnt-out taillight driving by just afterward. There was no denying it. Why wasn't Donny pushing it?

Donny pulled up the footage of the robbery from inside the pharmacy, paused the video, and pointed to the computer screen. "How do you know Kevin Scott and Denise Wilson?"

"I don't know them."

"They were patients at the Franklin Clinic."

"A lot of people are patients at the Franklin Clinic," Taylor said, trying to maintain an even, natural voice.

"What about from Grace Memorial Hospital?"

"I don't work at Grace Memorial Hospital."

"I'm aware of that, Ms. Taylor. But we already established that you do go to Grace Memorial Hospital on occasion . . . to talk about shoes."

"Yes. But I'm not there on a regular basis."

"But you were there that day."

Taylor sat silent, her jaw clenched.

"Here's what I think, Ms. Taylor . . . I think you, Mr. Scott, and Ms. Wilson were all partners. You would have been valuable. You had the inside knowledge."

Gabriel wheeled his chair next to Penelope's. "Detective Greene thinks Taylor was a partner in the robbery?"

Penelope leaned forward in her chair. She was shocked. "He never discussed this theory with me."

Was Donny keeping her out of the loop on purpose, or was he playing a hunch?

"That's not true!" Taylor said, denying her involvement.

"You were their lookout, weren't you? It was your job to keep an eye on the lobby while they robbed the pharmacy."

"No!" said Taylor, losing her battle to remain calm. "I've never seen those two before."

"What happened? Did they cut you out of your share?"

Taylor gripped the ends of the table so tightly that her knuckles turned white. "I said—"

"What was your cut anyway?" Donny interrupted. "How much did they pay you?"

Penelope watched as Taylor's whole body began to shake.

Donny leaned forward in his chair, his voice becoming casually conspiratorial. "Was it your usual fee? What they paid you for the other robberies?"

"I wasn't involved in this or any other robberies . . ." Taylor said between clenched teeth.

"Was shooting Dr. Gordon part of the plan?" Donny asked, probably hoping to get a reaction.

Penelope's stomach clenched at the thought.

"No!" Taylor shouted across the table and with a quick push of her leg, she flung her chair backward, crashing it into the cinderblock wall. She stood upright and slammed her balled fists against the metal table. "That's not how it happened!"

Gabriel wheeled back from the two-way mirror and

Penelope was on her feet in a ready stance at the same instant—fully prepared to charge into the interrogation room, if needed. Her hand instinctively went to her waist for her gun that wasn't there.

Officer Meeks moved to restrain Taylor, but Donny waved him off as he stood to meet Taylor's glare. "Why don't you have a seat and tell me how it did happen, Ms. Taylor?" Donny said calmly. "The truth this time . . ."

CHAPTER 78

HELPLESS WITHOUT HER WEAPON, Penelope stood and watched Genevieve Taylor pace the interrogation room, while Donny gave the impression of being cool and calm as he sat on the edge of the table. How could Penelope have misjudged Taylor all these years? Jacob even longer. This was a truly frightening woman. Not only had she lied about being at Grace Memorial Hospital that day, now she looked like she was preparing to take on the entire Gainesville police force.

Detective Donny Greene continued to press the nurse on her involvement. "Tell me what happened, Ms. Taylor. We know you were at Grace Memorial Hospital. You were involved in the robbery. It's right there on video. Did you kill Kevin Scott?"

Taylor continued pacing, mumbling to herself. "He said this would prove my love . . . I had to prove my love . . ." She seemed to be in her own world.

"He? He who?" Penelope asked aloud.

"Ms. Taylor! Did you kill Kevin Scott?"

"It wasn't like that . . ."

"What was your involvement in the robbery?"

Gabriel rose from his chair, clenching his phone in his fist, and Penelope shot him a quizzical look.

"It's the office," he mumbled, walking toward the door.

"You're leaving now?"

"It's an emergency. Stop by my office when you wrap up here. That's where I'll be," he said and abruptly left the room.

Penelope was torn between following Gabriel to make sure he was okay and watching the rest of the interrogation. She made a mental note to stop by his office later that evening and then she turned her attention back to Taylor. *Who was telling her to prove her love and to whom?*

"Ask her who 'he' is . . ." Penelope said to the empty observation room. "Ask her who she did this for."

It took all of her willpower not to rush into the interrogation room shouting, "Who is he? Who do you love?"

"Ms. Taylor! Answer the question!" Donny barked. "What was your involvement in the robbery?"

"None. I had none. It wasn't like that . . ."

Donny changed tactics. He sighed audibly, and said, "Tell me what it was like then." He walked around the table, righted the chair that Taylor had thrown, and then he took a seat on the other side. Speaking in a calm, conversational voice, he said, "Have a seat, Ms. Taylor. You know, I'm trying to help you here. I can only do that if you talk to me.

Tell me the truth."

Taylor gave Donny a confused look, stared at the chair for a moment, and then sat, clutching the sides of the metal chair with both hands.

"Maybe it wasn't your fault. Maybe you're protecting someone. Am I right?"

Taylor didn't say a word.

"I think I'm right," Donny continued. "Was Dr. Gordon involved? Is that who you're protecting, Ms. Taylor?"

"No. Jacob is a good man. He isn't involved in this."

"The suspects were both patients at the Franklin Clinic. That means he knew them."

"A lot of people are patients at the clinic. We treat them and they go. We don't know them."

"Yeah, but they are there and you talk to them. Alone in a little room . . . nice and private. Any kind of conversation could happen. Any kind of plans could be made. Ms. Wilson had an appointment last Monday."

"I told you, I treat them and they leave."

"Maybe you do. Maybe someone else goes a little deeper. Did Dr. Gordon plant the drugs in Belinda's desk?"

"No! He would never do something like that."

"We have his fingerprints on the bottle."

"No. I don't believe you!"

"We sure do. You don't have to believe it, Ms. Taylor, but it's not going to make it any less true. Jacob Gordon is a person of interest in this case. We even brought him in for questioning."

"Jacob isn't involved. He didn't put those drugs there."

"If he didn't, then who?"

"I don't know," Taylor said softly.

"You and I both know who did," Donny said.

"Do you? Because I don't," Penelope said to herself. "And you still haven't asked her who *he* is."

Donny continued to press Taylor. "Do you want to tell me what you were doing at Grace Memorial?"

After a few tense moments, Taylor paused, looked Donny in the eyes, and said, "I had an appointment."

"And is there a doctor I can call to verify that?"

"He wasn't in."

"You had an appointment, but the doctor wasn't in? You expect me to believe that?"

"I had an appointment," Taylor insisted.

"I don't know, Ms. Taylor . . . sounds to me like you're making stuff up. What was your involvement with Mr. Scott and Ms. Wilson?"

"I wasn't involved with those low-life criminals."

"Then why do we have you on tape following them out of the hospital?"

Taylor's eyes blazed. "Because I wanted to catch them."

Penelope's heart caught in her throat. It was possible that Taylor was crazy and spouting nonsense, but it sounded like she was admitting some involvement.

"It doesn't look to me like you're trying to catch them. It looks more like you were following your partners to make sure they got away safely."

"I wanted them to pay for what they did."

"For cutting you out of your share?"

"For hurting Jacob!" Taylor growled.

"Did you make them pay?" Donny asked. "Did you kill

Kevin Scott?"

"It wasn't like that." Taylor stood and turned away from him.

"Sit down, Ms. Taylor," Donny demanded.

Taylor ignored Donny's demand and Officer Meeks took a step toward her. Donny waved him off.

"I didn't want him dead," Taylor said.

"So you admit following Kevin Scott?"

"Yes," Taylor finally admitted, "I followed him. Him and his partner. But I didn't want him dead. I wanted him in jail where he belonged."

"But you followed him, waited for the right moment, and then killed him instead." "No!" Taylor shouted. "It was an accident."

"An accident, Ms. Taylor?"

"He came at me . . . in the parking lot. Must have seen me following him. He had a gun . . . I was defending myself. The gun went off . . . it was an accident. I tried to help, I really did."

"How is dumping the body in the Franklin River helping, Ms. Taylor?"

"I was taking him to the Franklin Clinic. 9-1-1 would have taken too long. He was losing a lot of blood. I tried . . ." Taylor paused and looked off into space, her eyes becoming glassy. "No. This isn't right," Taylor mumbled to herself, sounding confused. "It's not supposed to be happening like this. He said if I really loved him, I had to find a way to prove it. I did that. He said to show him how much I cared, and then we could be together."

Penelope's heart went cold. Could she be talking about

Jacob? Did Jacob ask for proof of her love? The room began to spin, but she was snapped back into reality at the sound of Donny's voice.

"Ms. Taylor, I'm not going to ask you again. Sit down!"

Taylor turned around quickly and shouted, "Jacob is supposed to be with me!"

Penelope watched the scene. The next few seconds seem to happen in slow motion.

With one quick swipe of her right arm, Taylor sent the laptop flying toward Officer Meeks. He jumped out of the way and the computer crashed into the door, leaving a nice-sized dent. Another swipe and Donny's papers littered the room.

Donny stood, and before he could restrain Taylor, she clocked him with a right hook. Donny fell backward, crumpling to the floor in front of the two-way mirror.

Before Officer Meeks could react, Taylor was barreling toward him. Meeks drew his gun, and in one quick motion the former combat nurse disarmed the rookie officer. Meeks tried to retrieve his weapon and bumped Taylor's arm. The gun discharged into the mirrored glass.

Penelope instinctively ducked and protected her face with her arm. She was showered with broken glass as the bullet lodged in the back wall of the observation room.

From her crouching position Penelope saw Taylor catch Meeks with an left upper cut, his body landing against the door with a loud thump. The officer posted outside tried to push the door open, but Meeks' motionless body blocked his entry.

Ever fiber of Penelope's being was telling her to stay

down. Taylor could come rushing through the broken glass at any second. Instead, she took a deep breath and tried to remain calm as she stood. Penelope brushed the glass from her clothing and stared at Taylor through the jagged hole left by the broken glass. "Genny . . . put down the gun."

Startled, Taylor swung the gun toward Penelope. "You! What are *you* doing here? This is all your fault!"

"Chance!" Donny shouted from the ground. He had landed badly and was attempting to recover. "Stay down!"

Penelope held up her hands. "Genny, please . . . put down the gun. You don't want to do this."

Taylor took two steps toward the broken window. "Don't tell me what to do!" she shouted.

Penelope stood her ground.

"You aren't worthy of Jacob," Taylor said. "All that time we spent together, saving lives together. That means something! Something real! Jacob belongs with me . . . not you!"

While Penelope kept Taylor distracted, Donny repositioned himself to take another run at her from behind.

"Who told you to prove your love?" Penelope asked. "Was it Jacob? Did Jacob tell you to prove your love for him?"

Taylor's face twisted. "Jacob had nothing to do with this," she said. "The fact that you think that shows you aren't worthy of him. You think you're so much better than me. Officer Penelope Chance . . . so perfect . . . so chaste. You're not good enough for someone like Jacob."

That was it. She couldn't take anymore.

CHAPTER 79

DETERMINED TO TAKE TAYLOR down, Penelope launched herself toward the deranged nurse. But before she could get through the broken window, Officer Gail Watson tackled Penelope in mid-air, and both crashed to the floor of the observation room.

"Let me go! Get off me!" Penelope shouted.

"Stay down, ma'am!" Watson demanded as half a dozen officers stormed the observation room, responding to the commotion.

Three of the officers went through the broken window, disarmed Taylor and pinned her to the floor. Only then did Officer Watson release Penelope.

"What's going on here?" a booming voice called from the doorway of the observation room.

Penelope and the officers turned in unison to see who had spoken.

The newcomer looked to be in his early fifties and wore a dark blue suit, designer glasses, and shoes that were polished to a high shine. A lawyer—an expensive one at that.

"I'm looking for Ms. Genevieve Taylor," the man said.

Donny, Officer Meeks, and the other officers appeared in the window of Interrogation Room 2, and together they stood Taylor up and placed her in handcuffs. Donny was breathing heavily, and Meeks was red in the face.

The blood in Penelope's face rose as she stared at Taylor.

"Can I help you?" Donny asked, trying to regain some dignity.

The lawyer ignored him and took a couple of steps closer. "Are you Genevieve Taylor?"

"Who are you?" Taylor snapped at the man.

"I am Derek Conrad, attorney-at-law," he said to Taylor, and then turned to Donny. "Detective, can you please tell me why my client is in handcuffs? It is my understanding that she was called in for questioning regarding an incident at a hospital at which she is not employed."

If Donny Greene was surprised at the lawyer's arrival, he didn't show it. He nodded at the broken glass. "See this mess? Your client caused it by assaulting two police officers." He caught the hurt look on Penelope's face. "Make that three. She's going to jail."

"Not so fast. I'd like to consult with my—"

"You can consult with her all you want," Donny interrupted, "at the county lockup."

Donny looked at the officers standing around, and they all leaped into action. Two officers grabbed Taylor by the shoulders and leaded her outside to transfer her to lockup.

Derek Conrad stood motionless in the bright white hallway and watched the crowd disperse as his client was led away. "Detective, I demand to know what happened here," he said imperiously.

"Call my secretary and make an appointment like everyone else." At that, Donny turned and stormed back to his office. At the end of the hall, he looked back. "Chance!" he hollered. "My office. Now."

CHAPTER 80

DONNY CLOSED THE DOOR to his office and sat on the edge of his desk. Penelope took a seat across from him. She opened her mouth to get the first word in, but was silenced by a knock on the door.

"Come in," Donny called.

Detective Edward Ballard poked his head into the room. "I heard the gun shot . . . is everybody okay?"

"Ballard. Yes. Come in," Donny said. "Everyone is fine. A few bumps and bruises. And you missed Chance here trying to break her academy obstacle course record . . ."

Penelope glared at Donny. Ballard walked into the room and closed the door behind him. "What happened?" he asked.

"I was caught off guard," Donny explained, flexing his jaw and massaging his chin. "And Officer Meeks got a little over anxious. The suspect became agitated and Meeks pulled his service weapon. The suspect disarmed him, and as Meeks went to grab the gun, it discharged."

"A nurse disarmed one of our officers?"

"She's a big nurse . . ." Donny said.

"And she's former military," Penelope added.

Detective Ballard turned toward Donny. "This is the same nurse you brought in for follow-up questioning?"

"She is . . ."

"And she's a suspect now? Related to one of our cases?"

"She's our killer."

"Our killer?" Ballard asked, taking a seat next to Penelope. "Whoa . . . that escalated quickly. I was questioning the vic's partner, Denise Wilson, when I heard the gun fire. I thought for sure Wilson was our killer. Kevin Scott was killed with her gun—the same gun used in the robbery."

"You gotta love surprises. I sure didn't see this one coming . . ." Donny said.

"So, how does the nurse fit into all this?"

"Turns out Nurse Taylor was at Grace Memorial the day of the robbery," Donny explained, "and she witnessed the whole thing. I'm guessing she took it personal when they shot her friend, Dr. Gordon. She followed the suspects and the vic confronted her in the parking lot of his apartment complex. She said he pulled a gun. There was a struggle and she said the gun went off . . . claims it was an accident. Said she even tried to save him."

"Tried to save him?" Ballard asked.

"Yeah. Loaded him into her truck and drove him to the Franklin Clinic, but it was too late."

"And she caused a pretty serious accident on State Road 20 in the process," Penelope said.

Ballard whistled through his teeth. "Well, how about that. We've got Wilson on the robbery and prescriptions forgery and Taylor on murder. Wilson insisted she didn't shoot her partner. Guess she was telling the truth."

"And we have Officer Chance to thank for it," Donny said, motioning toward Penelope.

"How so?" Ballard asked.

"Chance recognized Taylor in the lobby surveillance footage. I must have watched that tape a hundred times, but I never noticed Taylor, and I wouldn't have spotted Wilson if Chance hadn't insisted I review it one more time."

"Sounds like some fine detective work," Ballard said, smiling and nodding at Penelope.

"She is persistent," said Donny.

"Thank you," Penelope said and exhaled a breath of relief. She thought for sure Donny or Ballard would lay into her. She was prepared to defend her actions . . . but a compliment? She wasn't prepared for that. She managed a weak smile and took a couple of deep breaths as Donny kept talking.

"Taylor's on her way over to booking and then to lockup. I'm going to get a search warrant for her truck and residence."

"Well, good job you two," Ballard said, standing and moving toward the door.

"How did it go with Jacob, sir?" Penelope asked Ballard.

The detective paused, his hand on the doorknob. "I don't think your fiancé has anything to worry about."

"What about his fingerprints on the stolen drugs?" Donny asked.

"The doctor claimed that he assists the pharmacist with stocking inventory from time to time. They keep detailed records of that type of stuff, so we called Grace Memorial and they confirmed Jacob Gordon assisted with stocking that batch."

"So Jacob is no longer a suspect?" Penelope asked.

"As far as I'm concerned, your fiancé is a victim in all of this."

"Thank you. That's a relief."

"Thank you for your help on this case, Officer Chance." Ballard said as he walked out the door, closing it behind him.

Penelope turned to face Donny. "It all makes sense now, Donny. Taylor must have planted the drugs to frame Belinda. If she had the drugs in her truck, all she had to do was grab a couple bottles while you were searching for Jacob's missing prescription pad. She knew you'd check Belinda's desk eventually."

"Yeah, but why frame Belinda? Why plant the drugs?"

"Because of something Taylor said when I arrived that morning. She seemed to be in her own world and she said, 'I told him not to hire her.' Said she knew it was a mistake."

"So you think Taylor was jealous of Belinda Crowe?" Donny asked.

"That would be my guess."

"We'll know more once we search Taylor's truck and home."

Penelope nodded slowly, unable to shake the feeling

that a few pieces of the puzzle were still missing.

"I've seen that look before. Chance, we have our killer. It's done. Genevieve Taylor shot Kevin Smith. She was in love with Jacob and the gunshot may have put her right back into a combat situation . . . who knows?"

"I guess."

"There will always be questions in cases like this. You know that, Chance. This isn't like TV where everything is wrapped up with a nice little bow in sixty minutes. But this one is close. Once we search Taylor's truck and her home, I'm confident we'll have more than enough to take to the State's Attorney's Office. And more than enough to get a conviction."

Penelope didn't reply. Her eyes were focused on the wall behind Donny's desk.

"What?" Donny asked.

"We still need to find out who 'he' is before we eliminate any suspects."

"He who?"

"The 'he' who told Taylor she had to prove her love to Jacob."

"You don't think she was talking about Jacob, do you?"

"I don't know," she admitted. "There's something missing in the details."

"I'll take another run at Taylor tomorrow, but I doubt I'll get much more out of her with that fancy lawyer present."

"Who called a lawyer for her, do you know?" Penelope asked.

"I don't know. You were there. She never requested one. Look, Chance. It's late. We've solved a case. It's all down to the paperwork now, so if you don't want to get recruited into that, you'd better get out of here. Go home. Kiss that presumed innocent fiancé of yours goodnight and get some rest."

Penelope smiled weakly and walked out of the office.

CHAPTER 81

FIFTEEN MINUTES LATER, PENELOPE pulled into the parking lot of Grace Memorial Hospital. Things were becoming clearer, but the picture was still out of focus. Perhaps Gabriel could help shed some light on the case.

She gathered her things before heading inside. Her car was in a sorry state. It smelled like cold coffee and dirt. It wasn't like her to leave empty coffee cups and old receipts in her car, but she had been so busy with wedding planning and her unofficial investigation that she hadn't had time for basic maintenance.

As she grabbed her purse, her phone slid out onto the seat. Her heart skipped a beat when she saw she had a text from Jacob.

Got an emergency call at the clinic. I'll talk to you later. xoxo.

Penelope smiled and put the phone in her purse. It wasn't unusual for Jacob to get shanghaied on an emergency case. She wanted to talk to him, but she knew that he would have called her if it were possible. She would have to wait to talk to him.

A wave of remorse flooded her body. How could she have thought that he would be unfaithful to her? It all seemed so preposterous now. She squelched the thoughts and focused. Slinging her purse over her shoulder, she headed into the building.

In the lobby the front desk was quiet. A woman's typing on a keyboard was the only sound in the usually busy hospital.

A whisper of unease stirred in Penelope's stomach as she walked past the reception area. She paused and glanced to her right. The clinic was equally quiet. Through the double glass doors, she saw a few patients seated on the soft, green cloth chairs and reading outdated magazines. She didn't recognize the person behind the desk. As if she heard the thoughts about her, the desk nurse looked up and smiled kindly.

Penelope smiled back and headed to the staircase. She played Taylor's words over in her mind. She had said Penelope was "not good enough for Jacob." How long had Genevieve Taylor been harboring a crush on Jacob? Was killing Kevin Scott really an accident? She had disarmed Officer Meeks with ease . . . couldn't she have done the same with Scott?

Anger and hurt could drive a person to do terrible things. If someone had hurt Jacob—had killed Jacob—what would she have done? If Taylor thought Jacob was dead, perhaps she killed Scott to exact revenge for the murder of the man she secretly loved?

Penelope shuddered at the thought of Genny being in love with her fiancé for who knew how long. Jacob had known Genny for a long time. If the feelings were mutual he would have acted on them by now.

Penelope froze mid-step.

Maybe that was the missing piece.

Could Jacob be this mysterious *he* that Taylor was talking about? Could he have encouraged her to prove herself worthy? Taylor obviously hated Penelope and had hidden it quite well for some time. Was Taylor planning to murder Penelope so she could have Jacob to herself?

Penelope jogged up the remaining stairs and burst into the fourth-floor hallway to find it as empty and silent as the staircase.

Where is everyone?

A door burst open, and Penelope jumped back. She relaxed when she saw a custodian pushing a linen cart out the door.

Pull it together, Penny!

She gave the older man a polite nod and didn't encounter anyone else on the way to Gabriel's office. The door to his waiting area was slightly ajar and the light was on.

"Hello?" she called softly as she pushed the door open.

No answer.

She walked inside and called, "Hello?" a little louder.

Still no answer.

She strode across the tiny waiting room to Gabriel's office and tapped a knuckle on the door.

"Gabriel?"

There was no answer, but the gentle pressure of her knocking pushed the door open slightly.

She peeked inside. Pale moonlight illuminated the dark room.

"Gabriel? You in there?"

He wasn't.

She stepped back into the waiting room, pulled out her cell phone, and dialed Gabriel's number. As soon as she pressed send, she heard his distinctive Beatles ringtone from inside his office.

"Gabriel?" she called out, pushing his office door open.

This was alarming. He always had his cell phone with him. What if he had fallen and was trapped underneath mountains of paperwork and binders?

She walked toward the sound of the ringtone and spotted his blinking cell phone atop a stack of files on his desk. She searched the cluttered desk for a piece of paper to leave him a note since he obviously didn't have his phone with him.

She reached for the desk lamp and accidentally knocked the small stack of files and Gabriel's phone onto the floor.

Way to go, Penny . . .

She would make a terrible spy.

She turned the lamp on and could see how messy Gabriel's office was. If she didn't know better, she would have thought the place had been ransacked, but that was the way he always kept it. His office at the college was the same way. She glanced down at the files scattered on the floor. Loose papers were everywhere.

This kept getting worse and worse. How was she going to explain this? All she meant to do was write a simple note. Gabriel would certainly understand if he caught her red-handed.

She laughed at the absurdity of the situation. She'd straighten the files, replace the papers as best she could, and leave a note.

She picked up Gabriel's phone and gathered the files, putting the loose papers on top. Hopefully, the papers would have names or something to indicate the file where they belonged.

Gabriel's handwriting was impossible to read.

One of the papers was a prescription for something, but the name was illegible. The rest were similarly unhelpful so she set them aside.

The files, however, had typewritten names, made on a typewriter, not a computer. Most likely they were typed on the ancient relic of a typewriter the professor had wedged into his piles of papers and binders.

She smiled at his idiosyncrasies, but the smile disappeared as she flipped through the files, reading the names.

One of the files was labeled *Taylor, Genevieve.*

CHAPTER 82

GENEVIEVE TAYLOR WAS A patient of Dr. Gabriel Pike's? He had never mentioned knowing Taylor.

There had to be a logical explanation.

Was Gabriel bound by doctor-patient confidentiality? He probably couldn't confirm or deny knowing Taylor, even if Penelope asked.

One question nagged at the back of her mind . . . Did Gabriel know about the shooting of Kevin Scott?

Penelope replaced the stack of folders on the edge of the desk and took a seat. She had a tough decision to make. Medical records were confidential, and she was probably already breaking a handful of laws by entering Gabriel's office and touching his files, but she was in too deep, and curiosity got the best of her . . .

She flipped Taylor's folder open.

She saw a few pages of notes from a legal notepad.

Gabriel's writing was sloppy and hard to read, but she could make out a few words here and there. *PTSD* was one. Then the words *left undiagnosed* were followed by a word Penelope couldn't decipher.

A flood of guilt welled up inside like molten lava. Snooping through someone's medical file without his or her permission was not only wrong, it was highly illegal. Penelope closed the file and something that had been attached with a paperclip slipped out.

She watched it flutter to the floor.

It looked familiar—too familiar.

She reached for the small piece of paper and held it under the light.

It was a Chinese fortune—the missing fortune from Jacob's wallet—affixed with Scotch tape to the back of a business card-sized piece of paper. Penelope gently touched the fortune with her forefinger and read the words aloud. "The love you seek is closer than you think." Tears sprung to her eyes.

Why did Gabriel have Jacob's fortune? Did Taylor give it to him? Did she tell Gabriel about the robbery and the "accidental" shooting of Kevin Scott? Was Gabriel also bound by confidentiality if Taylor confessed to a past crime?

The puzzle in Penelope's mind became a little clearer as a few more pieces fell into place. Taylor must have kept the fortune as a memento when she returned Jacob's belongings. She returned the items anonymously because she killed the suspect. She must have told Dr. Pike during one of their sessions, and she gave him the fortune.

Penelope flipped the paper over and horror rose inside her.

The fortune was attached to the back of the black-and-white photo booth picture of her and Jacob. She wiped the tears from her eyes. Jacob's face had been crossed out with a ballpoint pen.

This was not good.

Her head spun with new questions . . . like why was Jacob's face crossed out? If Taylor was in love with Jacob, shouldn't Penelope's face be crossed out?

What was Gabriel's role in all of this?

He had inserted himself into the middle of the investigation. How long had he known about Taylor's involvement? Was Gabriel's offer to assist in Penelope's unofficial investigation his way of leading her to Taylor or was he trying to throw her off the scent?

She scanned her memories. He had acted professionally—except when they were watching the surveillance footage earlier. When she spotted Taylor, he kept trying to divert attention from the new clue. She had chalked it up to another one of his idiosyncrasies, but had there been a more sinister reason for Gabriel's behavior?

A knotted ball of fear coiled in the pit of her stomach. Was Jacob in danger?

Penelope bolted out of the office without turning off the light or closing the door—the overwhelming urge to get to Jacob drove her every step.

She hurried to the stairs, pulled her phone out of her purse, and dialed her fiancé's number. "Pick up, pick up," she chanted.

There was a clicking sound by the time she reached the second-floor landing, and her heart soared . . . but it was just his voicemail. She waited for the beep and then practically shouted into the phone. "Jacob! I need you to call me right away." She searched her brain, trying to think of what else to say. "I need to see you!"

Penelope ended the call, and burst out of the stairwell into the lobby. Everything seemed to be business as usual, with the exception of a few strange glances directed her way.

She headed toward the parking lot.

In the safety of her own vehicle, Penelope fished her headphones out of her purse and called Donny.

It went straight to voice mail.

"Donny, call me as soon as you get this! Taylor was a patient of Dr. Pike's." She took a breath. Then another. Finally she added, "I think there's something else going on here. Something we're missing. I think Jacob may be in danger. Call me back!"

CHAPTER 83

IT WAS ONLY A twenty-minute drive to the Franklin Clinic from Grace Memorial Hospital, but when you fear someone you love may be in danger—twenty-minutes can feel like an eternity.

Halfway between Gainesville and Franklin, Jacob's caller ID flashed on Penelope's phone.

"Jacob!" she answered. "Thank God, you're okay."

"Why wouldn't he be okay, Penelope?" a familiar voice asked.

"Gabriel? What are you doing with Jacob's phone? Where's Jacob?"

"Your fiancé is fine, but he has something he wants to tell you," Gabriel said, his voice sending a shiver up her spine.

"Gabriel, put Jacob on the phone!" Penelope demanded.

"Sorry, Penelope, he can't come to the phone right now.

And you need to hear this in person. Come to the Franklin Clinic."

"Don't do it, Pen—" she heard Jacob's voice say right before the line went dead.

Tears blurred Penelope's vision, and she swiped her eyes with the sleeve of her sweater.

She dialed Jacob's number, and it went straight to voicemail.

Seconds later her phone rang to life.

"What did you do to—"

"Chance, it's Donny."

Penelope had never been so relieved to hear her friend's voice. "Donny! I think I know who *HE* is."

"Slow down, Chance."

"I know who he is, Donny. The person Taylor referred to during the interrogation. The person behind all of this. It's Dr. Pike. It's been him all along."

"Pike?"

"Yes! I don't know why, but he's somehow behind all this."

"Chance, it's been a long day. You're probably just—"

"No Donny . . . it's him. I was in his office. I saw his files. Taylor was his patient."

"Without a court order? Chance, you know—"

"Yes, I know, Donny! Get the court order! Get a warrant! For his files . . . for his office . . . for his house. He has Jacob . . ."

As soon as her fiancé's name left her lips, Penelope lost her ability to speak.

What did Gabriel want with Jacob? What was he planning? Did Taylor reveal something about Jacob in one of her sessions that Gabriel wanted her to hear?

"Chance, are you still there?" Donny sounded panicked, and she could hear him gathering his things and covering the mouthpiece of the phone as he shouted directions to his officers. "Chance? Where are you?"

This was all wrong.

"D-D-Don—" She tried to speak but she choked. She cleared her throat and tried again. "Donny, you have to get to the Franklin Clinic. Gabriel is holding Jacob hostage."

"Hostage? Chance, tell me where you are."

Penelope came to a skidding stop in the Franklin Clinic parking lot. Gabriel's Hummer was parked next to Jacob's Mustang. *Lord, please let Jacob be okay.* The dark tinted windows of the SUV made it impossible to tell if Gabriel was inside.

"I'm here, Donny. I'm at the Franklin Clinic and so is Gabriel."

"Chance, I'm radioing Franklin PD now for backup and I'll be there as soon as I can. Stay where you are!" Donny yelled through her earpiece.

Penelope removed her backup Sigma from the lock box in her trunk. "I'm going in, Donny!"

"Chance, no! Wait for backup."

She clicked off the safety and kept her pistol at a low ready position as she made her way toward the entrance.

"Chance, do you hear me? Don't go in there alone," Donny pleaded. "I'll have backup there in five minutes."

"Jacob might not have five minutes . . ."

With Donny still on the line, Penelope cautiously

entered the Franklin Clinic.

The door was open and it was dark inside.

She tried the light switch in the waiting area.

Nothing.

She took cover in front of the reception desk. "Donny?" Penelope whispered through shallow breaths. "I'm inside. The lobby is empty. He cut the power."

"Chance, pull back now! Jackson is already en route. Someone called 9-1-1."

A muffled whimpering sound came from the other side of the desk.

"Who's there?" Penelope whispered.

"Penelope?" Another whimper. "Is that you?"

It was Belinda.

Penelope squat-walked around to the receptionist's side of the desk. The frightened office manager was wedged underneath and clutching her cell phone to her chest.

"Oh, thank God!" she said, starting to crawl out.

"Stay put," Penelope said and Belinda froze. "Who else is in the building? Any patients? Staff?"

"No patients. Dr. Gordon is in his office . . . and I think there's a man back there with him."

"Did you get a look at him?"

"No. I was in the break room when I heard a truck pull into the parking lot. I walked to my desk to have a look, and that's when all the lights went out. I saw a man coming toward the door, and I panicked. It looked like he had a weapon, so I hid and called 9-1-1."

"Was it a gun?"

"I think so. It was dark."

"Donny, are you getting this?" Penelope whispered into her microphone.

"I am," Donny confirmed. "Chance, get Belinda out of there. Jackson should be on site now."

Headlights swept across the windows, temporarily lighting up the room.

"Which way did the man go, Belinda? Did you see?"

Belinda pointed toward the administrative area.

"How long has he been back there?"

"About ten minutes."

"Were there gun shots?"

Belinda shook her head. "No . . . just a lot of shouting. I was afraid to move."

"Listen, Belinda. Chief Jackson from the Franklin Police Department is outside. You know Chief Jackson, right?"

Belinda nodded.

"I need you to go out there and tell him everything you told me. More, if you can think of it."

"I'm scared," Belinda sobbed.

Penelope held out her hand. "It's going to be okay."

Belinda took Penelope's hand and slid out from under the desk.

"Donny, radio Jackson and let him know that Belinda is coming out."

"You too, Chance," Donny said. "Get out of there. We don't know what we're dealing with."

Penelope hung up and switched her phone to silent. Once Belinda was safely out the front door and in Jackson's care, she made her way back to the receptionist's desk.

Her blood pounded in her ears, and she tried to remain calm.

She had to get to Gabriel before he hurt anyone. She had to talk him out of whatever he was planning to do.

CHAPTER 84

WITH HER EYES FULLY adjusted to the darkness, Penelope moved from the desk to the double swinging doors that led to the administrative area. She paused, peeked inside, and pushed one of the doors open with the barrel of her gun. Her eyes darted back and forth, looking for signs of life. At the end of the hallway, she saw that Jacob's office door was ajar.

She took a shaky breath and considered her next move.

Her phone vibrated in her front pocket. She glanced at the caller ID, and with her headphones still on, she pressed *answer*.

"Chance, Chance, are you there?" Chief Jackson's voice came through her earpiece.

"I'm here, Chief," Penelope whispered back, holding the microphone to her mouth.

"I have a team waiting outside. What can you tell us?"

"I'm not positive, but I'm assuming one subject, Dr. Gabriel Pike, is isolated in the left wing of the building . . . in Jacob's office. The subject may also be armed and holding Jacob hostage."

"We've confirmed with Belinda that the rest of the building is clear. We have the exits covered," the chief said. "If this is a hostage situation, we'll wait for your signal. You got that, Chance?"

She mouthed a quiet, "Got it, Chief," into her microphone.

Penelope pushed through the swinging double doors and ducked into the first office on her left to maintain a barrier between herself and Gabriel.

Jacob's face flashed through her mind. She had to keep him safe. That was her main priority. And to do that, she needed to establish communication.

She steadied herself, took a deep breath, and called out into the darkness. "Jacob? Are you back there?" Her voice sounded alien. She hardly recognized it as her own.

There was a shuffle and the door to Jacob's office opened a little wider.

"Penny? Is that you?" It was Jacob.

She resisted the urge to run to his office and embrace him.

"You alone?" he asked in a strange tone of voice.

"The police are outside. But it's just me inside . . . for now."

Silence.

"Jacob? Are you okay? Can I come back there?"

"Not yet, Penelope," she heard Gabriel say from somewhere inside Jacob's office.

She still didn't have a good visual. She moved one office closer.

"Gabriel, you've got me here . . . now let's talk. I'm sure you have a good explanation for what's going on, and I'd like to hear it . . . but what do you say we let Jacob go first?"

"Good, Penelope. Take charge of the situation. Assure me that you don't suspect me of any wrongdoing and that you just want to talk."

Busted!

He knew the protocol as well as she did.

"I think Jacob is fine where he is . . . for now," Gabriel continued.

"I need to hear that from him."

"I'm fine," came Jacob's voice a moment later.

"See, just like I told you. Isn't that right? Now, let's have a chat," Gabriel said.

"What do you want to chat about, Gabriel?"

"Let's start with what you learned from Genny. What else did she tell you?"

His voice was scratchy, but his words were clear. His intentions were another matter.

"Not much. A lawyer arrived before we could ask her more questions. Was that you, Gabriel? Did you call a lawyer for Genny?"

"Why would I do that? I barely know the woman."

"That's not true," Penelope said. "She was a patient of yours."

"Did she tell you that?"

"I went to your office. I saw a file with her name on it."

Gabriel was silent for a moment. "Did you open it?"

"I didn't have a court order."

"That's not what I asked!" He sounded angry now.

"I didn't open it. A stack of files fell on the floor and I noticed her name when I picked them up . . . but I didn't read any of it. I couldn't read your handwriting," she said, trying to sound lighthearted.

"Why were you looking for me?"

"You told me to meet you at your office, remember? I was worried about you."

"Worried?" he asked.

"Yes. I was in your waiting room and I tried calling. I heard your ringtone coming from your office. It was dark. I was worried. I thought something might have happened."

Gabriel was silent.

"How's Jacob? Can I check on him?" Penelope tried.

"He's fine! If you want him to stay that way, you will continue chatting with me."

"Sure." Penelope said, squinting down the dark hallway, trying to see any movement in the office.

Nothing.

"Chief, are you still there?" she said into her microphone.

"I'm here, Chance. What do you need?"

"Lights. I can't get a visual on the subject or Jacob. Maybe the lights will flush him out of the office."

"Give me a few minutes to find the breakers."

CHAPTER 85

PENELOPE HEARD JACKSON BARKING orders, and a couple of minutes later the lights flickered on, one at a time, and then the rest came on all at once.

"Who else is here?" Gabriel shouted. "Who turned the lights back on?"

Penelope unplugged her headphones. From this point forward, Jackson would be able to hear her, but she wouldn't be able to hear him. She was on her own. "It's just me inside."

"I don't believe you," Gabriel snarled.

"It's just me for now," Penelope said, stepping into the hallway. "But the entire Franklin police force can come swarming in at any second. You need to show me that Jacob is okay. You said Jacob had something to tell me?" She took a few steps down the brightly lit corridor and caught a glimpse of Gabriel picking up a gun from Jacob's desk.

She took several steps back as Gabriel led Jacob into the hallway.

He appeared unhurt.

Her eyes trailed downward and saw Gabriel's gun pressed firmly into Jacob's ribs. She lifted her eyes to meet Jacob's and tried to take strength in the love she saw there.

"Tell her," Gabriel said, nudging the barrel of his gun deeper into Jacob's side. "Tell her how you're not worthy of her love. Tell her how you made Genevieve Taylor fall in love with you. Go on . . . tell her!"

Jacob looked at Penelope affectionately and said, "I love you, Penny. I'd never dream of cheating on you."

A swift shadow of anger swept across Gabriel face, and he dealt Jacob a vicious blow to the temple with the butt of his gun.

Penelope winced as Jacob dropped to the floor. She fought the urge to lash out or to run to her fiancé. She needed to stay focused on Gabriel. "I guess we're finally alone," she said, advancing a step closer.

"Don't move." He slowly lifted the gun from his side and leveled it at her chest. "I know how to use this."

She believed him.

"Detective Greene and Chief Jackson will be wondering what's going on, and they will come in any second now. There's not much time. You've got a choice to make: Talk to me or talk to them. I'm your friend. I can take care of this. Just let Jacob go and—"

"You're not my friend!" he snapped at her. The hand that held the gun was shaking. "We are not friends!"

What had upset him so much? She had thought they

were friends, but this tactic wasn't working the way she planned.

"Fine, we're not friends. Just tell me what I need to do to end this."

Gabriel's eyes widened, and Penelope caught a glimpse of the torment he was trying so desperately to hide.

"It was almost done. You had to poke your nose into it. You wouldn't stop digging . . ."

"You were right there digging with me, Gabriel."

"You had Belinda. You could have left it at that."

"She's an innocent woman."

"Who among us is truly innocent?" Gabriel snapped. "Certainly not him!" He gave Jacob a slight kick. "But she wanted him. And if she played it right, she could have had him."

It was becoming clear. "You mean Genny? She could've had Jacob?"

"Of course! I told her what to do. But I never told her to kill anyone . . . that just shows how badly she wanted to prove herself to him. And he was still too stupid to see it!" Gabriel gave the unconscious Jacob another kick in the ribs.

"He's not good enough for you. He's barely good enough for her." He cast his eyes scornfully down at Jacob's prone form. "He doesn't love you the way I love you. He doesn't know you the way I know you."

His words were shocking, and his kicks at her defenseless fiancé tore at her heart, but Penelope refused to show it. "So all of this . . . with Taylor . . . with helping me with the case . . . everything . . . was because you thought you and I belong together?"

"I never meant to fall in love . . . it just happened. He can't protect you like I can protect you."

"Protect me from what, Gabriel?"

"He's not who you think he is. No one in your life is."

No one is who I think they are? What's that supposed to mean?

While Penelope struggled to gather her thoughts, Gabriel continued. "I remember when I met you. I saw the flames, and the flames were reflected in your eyes. I knew it then." Gabriel's eyes went out of focus and looked as if he were reliving an old memory.

Was he thinking of when they met during her freshman year of college?

"You were my professor, Gabriel . . . my advisor . . . my mentor." She tried to keep the disappointment out of her voice. "I trusted you."

Penelope took a step toward Gabriel, and he pointed his gun at Jacob's head as she did. "I'm sorry, Penelope. This is how it has to be."

Penelope raised her gun and Gabriel's eyes went wide.

A shot rang out and echoed down the long hallway.

Gabriel jerked and then doubled over—a swatch of blood spread across his stomach turning his white shirt deep crimson. "I was just trying to—" Was the last thing he said before he dropped his gun and sank to his knees, his mouth gaping like a fish, his jaw refusing to function.

"Nooo!" Penelope screamed, looking down at her gun.

Had she shot him?

Impossible.

There had been no jolt, no smoke, and the sound had come from behind.

She turned and saw Chief Jackson at the other end of the hall.

His service pistol still smoking.

EPILOGUE

ONE

The following day . . .
Sunday, March 31, 2013, 11:05 a.m.

THAT SUNDAY MORNING, THE choir sang jubilantly as Penelope sat in the middle of the church on the velvet covered pew.

She looked to her left and smiled at Doug and Trevor.

Doug claimed he was just going to church for Trevor. Whatever his excuse, she was glad that he was there.

Penelope turned to her right and, instead of the empty seat that greeted her in the courthouse just two weeks before, this seat was taken by the man she loved.

A wave of gratitude overcame her as she sat amidst her family in God's house.

She gave Jacob's hand a gentle squeeze.

He looked at her and squeezed back. The blow Gabriel gave him to the head opened up the old wound and created a new one, requiring additional stitches.

After last night's confrontation at the Franklin Clinic,

Jacob was rushed to Grace Memorial Hospital. After a few tests the staff had him stitched up, bandaged up, and released.

Jacob agreed to spend the night at Doug's house so Penelope could keep an eye on him. They ended up talking on the couch into the early hours of the morning.

Penelope told Jacob everything . . .

How she suspected he might be involved somehow.

How she had jealous thoughts when she saw Nurse "Bunny" and Nurse Taylor taking care of him.

How she spied on him without his knowledge.

How she thought he might be cheating on her when she saw him with Tina in the park, and then again when she saw them leaving the Hilton Hotel.

And how, even in the end, she had doubts when she learned Taylor was in love with him.

She told him everything, leaving out nothing.

When she was finished she took a deep breath and asked if he could ever find it in his heart to forgive her.

She was prepared for the worse.

Instead, Jacob took her hand and said, "Of course I forgive you. You have one of the toughest jobs in the world, and twice now you've had people you loved caught up in it. I never doubted you, but I understand how you have to look at things objectively, and I admit I must have looked pretty suspicious."

Tears came to her eyes. "I should never have doubted you," she told him.

"You're a cop, Penny. You have to look at things objectively. I'd expect nothing less from you. If I'd had a little more of your objectivity I would have seen that Genny needed help. She was dealing with PTSD right under my nose and I didn't see it. And I promise you I didn't see that she had feelings for me either."

"Well, that is to be expected," she told him with a grin. "You are a handsome doctor . . ."

Jacob sat up straight and feigned being offended. "A handsome, *engaged* doctor."

"You can't blame yourself for Genny. She did seek help . . . unfortunately from the wrong person. She was vulnerable and Gabriel took advantage of her vulnerability. The robbery may have been the trigger that set her off, but Gabriel was pulling the strings. And I had no idea he had feelings for me."

"It seems that you and I are more sought after than either of us thought . . ."

"It does seem that way."

"Well, as your soon-to-be-husband, I want my soon-to-be-wife to talk to me the next time she thinks I may be led astray. We are going to figure out a way to better communicate with each other while it's just us . . . before there are little Pennys and Jacobs running around. We'll need to present a united front."

"With God's guidance, we'll do it," she told him.

The pastor's sermon about second chances pulled Penelope out of her reverie and back to the present. Her heart swelled with love for Jacob, for their future, and for God seeing her and Jacob through this safely.

After the service, Penelope stood in the parking lot visiting with some of her church friends. Chief Curtis

Jackson pulled up and parked his cruiser next to Penelope's car. He strode over and shook hands with Doug, Jacob, and Trevor.

"You missed a wonderful service, Chief," Penelope said.

"Maybe next time, Chance. I'm here to see how you and Jacob are doing."

"We're good," she said, really meaning it.

"We are," echoed Jacob. "The only thing troubling me now is whether to grow my hair longer to cover this scar on my forehead—or get it cut shorter and embrace the tough-guy biker look."

Jackson smiled. "You'll need a few accessories to pull that one off. Like a leather jacket, a few tattoos . . . and a bike."

"Not happening," Penelope said. "Don't you give him any ideas, Chief."

"Well, I'm glad to see you're recovering nicely." The chief nodded to Jacob and then turned his attention to Penelope. "Chance, may I have a word in private?"

"Sure, Chief." Penelope followed Jackson as he walked a short distance away.

"Sorry to show up unannounced," he said, pausing at his cruiser and turning toward Penelope. "But I wanted to catch you before you came into work tomorrow."

"No problem, Chief. What's up?"

"I'm not the type to sugarcoat things, so I'll jump right into it. I'm sure you were planning to return tomorrow, but I'm putting you on a seven-day suspension without pay."

"Suspension? But we closed the case . . ."

"It wasn't your case. Everything worked out this time, but next time you might not be so lucky. I warned you that your actions would have consequences. You disobeyed a direct order—several orders, in fact. I can't have that type of behavior in my department. You're my senior officer . . . you need to set a better example. You're lucky to still have a job, Chance."

"But they overlooked several—"

"And you brought Pike into it."

"He was already involved."

"I'm not arguing with you on this, Chance," Jackson said. "You put yourself and more than one civilian in danger. This isn't something I want to do. But it is something I have to do. Seven days. No discussion."

Penelope opened her mouth, and then closed it. "Alright. Seven days. I understand, Chief. I'm sorry, and it won't happen again."

"Well . . . alright then," Jackson said, "I'll let you get back to your family." As Penelope turned to walk back to the group, Jackson called out. "Oh, and Chance?"

"Yes, Chief?" she said, turning to face him.

"Next time you decide to take a vacation, do me a favor . . . take it!"

"Yes, Chief." Penelope forced a smile and walked back to Jacob.

"What was all that about?" he asked.

"Well, let's just say I'm going to be free next week to do some *actual* wedding planning."

"Is Jackson giving you another week off?"

"Something like that . . ." Penelope said, giving Jacob a

hug. "Shall we head over to Spanky's?"

"Yes, I'm starving," Jacob said.

Then, she heard Trevor say, "Me too!" He bounced up and down, and Doug picked him up and carried him as they made their way to their cars.

Penelope's phone rang and everyone stopped and looked at her.

She looked at her phone and then at Jacob. "It's Donny."

"It's okay. Take it. It might be important."

She silenced the phone and tossed it into her purse. "It can wait. Family is more important."

Jacob leaned down and gave Penelope a kiss. "I love you, Penny."

"I love you back!"

TWO

DETECTIVE DONNY GREENE HUNG up without leaving a message for Penelope.

"No answer?" Detective Edward Ballard asked.

"Nope," Donny confirmed. "Got her voice mail."

The detectives stood in the den of Dr. Gabriel Pike's home and looked around, trying to take it all in. Every square inch of the room was covered in newspaper clippings, pictures, articles, and notes about Penelope.

Pike had been following her every move from the death of her parents in the fire, to her college graduation, to her enrollment in the police academy, to her joining the Franklin Police Department, right up to her involvement in the Michael Findley case.

"Probably just as well," Ballard said. "In all my years on the job, I've seen plenty of nut jobs, including that guy who kept all the human ears in his freezer. But I've never seen anything like this."

Donny scratched his head and looked at Ballard. "What are we looking at here? Some sort of shrine?"

"Definitely belongs in the *Stalking for Dummies* book," Ballard said. "It might be best not to tell Chance about this."

"Agreed," Donny said. "At least for now . . ."

But he knew she'd find out soon enough.

THE MYSTERIES CONTINUE WITH...

MISSED CHANCE

COMING NEXT!

JOIN PENELOPE ON HER FIRST BIG CASE...

ONE
CHANCE

AVAILABLE NOW!

AUTHOR'S NOTE

Another Chance is a work of fiction. Anyone familiar with the city of Gainesville, Florida (Go Gators!) will recognize many of the street names and some of the landmarks. They will also recognize the literary liberties I've taken with the surrounding geography. Please do not use this novel as a road map, you will get lost! The town of Franklin is invented and the fictional Franklin River is not the imaginary line that separated the two cities. Certain long-standing institutions, agencies, and public offices are mentioned, but they are used fictitiously.

One of the challenges with writing a story is coming up with names for the secondary and supporting characters. Each one needs to be unique (of course) and it needs to fit the character. With Another Chance I wanted to do something different. I didn't want to use random names. I wanted it to be personal, and I wanted involve the readers.

Although the characters themselves are figments of my imagination and have no real life counterparts and any resemblance to real people is purely coincidental, twenty-two of my readers graciously allowed me to use their names. You may recognize many of them from the story . . .

Cast of Supporting Characters
(In Order of Appearance)

Kevin Scott . . . . Robber
Pam Gonsalves . . . . Superior Court Judge
Teresa Behrmann . . . . Psychologist
Sandy Scott . . . . Grace Memorial ER Nurse
Dave Sayre . . . . Grace Memorial Security Guard
JR Bray . . . . Grace Memorial Doctor
Edward Ballard . . . . Gainesville Detective
Sylvia Brown . . . . Grace Memorial Nurse
Tina Shifflett . . . . Grace Memorial Medical Receptionist
Deborah Thompson . . . . Grace Memorial Pharmacist
Belinda Crowe . . . . Franklin Clinic Office Manager
LeeAnna Coffey . . . . The Coffey Shop Co-Owner
Travis Coffey . . . . The Coffey Shop Co-Owner
Catherine McPhie . . . . Gainesville Police Officer
Judy Preston . . . . Franklin Police Dispatcher
Tony Egland . . . . Franklin Volunteer Firefighter
Tammy Harris . . . . Gainesville Chief Medical Examiner
Caleb Meeks . . . . Gainesville Police Officer
Gail Watson . . . . Gainesville Police Officer
Hadley Jackson Rye . . . . Trevor Foster's Friend
Tracie Rye . . . . Hadley Jackson Rye's Mother
Christene Gamble . . . . Spanky's Grill Waitress

Let me state, for the record, that nothing in this story is intended to reflect reality. The characters physical description, age, occupation, beliefs, and actions (good guy/gal or bad guy/gal), etc. are purely fictional and not based on the reader for which they are named.

A great big thank you to the supporting cast of Another Chance for allowing me to have some fun naming my characters.

HELP PENELOPE SOLVE THE CRIME...

CRIMES OF CHANCE

INTERACTIVE SHORT STORIES!

ACKNOWLEDGEMENTS

First and foremost, I am so thankful for you, dear reader. I know there are a hundred and one other books you could have bought, and I sincerely hope you enjoy reading Penelope's story as much as I enjoyed writing it.

I'd like to take this opportunity to thank my behind-the-scenes heroes, who worked tirelessly to make sure Another Chance was the best that it could be.

To my brainstorming/plotting partner, inconsistency finder, proofreader, cheerleader, and dear friend, Dina, thank you for supporting me at every stage of the process. I owe you a debt of gratitude. Without your help and endless encouragement, this book never would have reached fruition. P.S. Penelope thanks you for assisting with the wedding planning parts.

To the talented, Crystal McLaren, thank you for helping me tell Penelope's story. I still miss our monthly coffee sessions.

To veteran police investigator Lee Lofland, former NYPD Detective Sergeant Joseph Giacalone, and D.P. Lyle, M.D. Your combined experience and knowledge of police procedure, criminal investigation, and forensic science helped me add a layer of authenticity and believability, and I thank you. Any process or procedures I didn't get right fall on my shoulders.

To my extraordinary developmental editor, Linda Hull, who has worked with me on all my books, thank you for ripping the story apart and helping me put the pieces back together, for adding your unique sense of humor, for your last minute additions, and for providing the polish to my sometimes rough prose.

To my amazing "Team Chance" beta readers, Laurie Cook, Barbara Carter, JR Bray, Jackie Whipple, Sylvia Brown, Pam Gonsalves, Becky Kossa, Mary Ann Schreck, Susan Wachtel, Bev Smith, Judy Harrell Umphress, Tina Shifflett, Tanya Abbott Cloer, Jill Jones, and Shelley Makohon, thank you for your invaluable contributions. Large chunks of the story were reworked based on your feedback and suggestions, (part four was completely rewritten) and it made all the difference. I am genuinely grateful.

To my delightful copyeditor, Quata Merit, thank you for making the editing process a pleasure.

To my meticulous proofreader, Belinda Crowe and my eagle-eyed "Oops Detectives," Kathy Hernandez, Lisa Dill, and Suzanne Mathewson, thank you for finding those pesky gremlins that slipped through the cracks. Your hard work is the icing on the cake!

To my mother, father, and sister, thank you for supporting and believing in me. I love you so much and couldn't do it without you.

To Meeghn and Michael, thank you for your love, support, and friendship. Words cannot express how grateful I am (but I'll try) . . . the 75,699 words of Another Chance are dedicated to you.

To my good friend David, thank you for listening to me moan and groan during our weekly lunches (and then telling me to get back to work).

A special shout out to Matt, Gary, and Shannon. Thank you for your friendship and support over the years.

Of course, I can't go without acknowledging my posse of friends that meet with me for coffee, lunch, and dinner: Sue, Ziad, Naomi, Peter, and Allan. Thank you for keeping me on track.

And most of all to my Heavenly Father, thank you for bringing these amazing people into my life and for choosing me for this incredible journey.

Also by Daniel Patterson

ABOUT THE AUTHOR

Daniel Patterson is the bestselling author of One Chance. Before turning his attention to writing, Daniel spent his days working as an executive in the Internet industry. A San Francisco native, Daniel currently resides in Southern California where he is busy working on the next book in the Penelope Chance Mystery series.

To learn more about Daniel Patterson, his current projects and upcoming releases, visit him on his Facebook page at: facebook.com/DanielPattersonAuthor